I0552984

Fading Shadows

CLIFTON LABREE

© 2003 by Author, Clifton LaBree

Published by
Fading Shadows Imprint
New Boston, New Hampshire

ISBN: 978-0-9746450-1-8

Cover Design by Vivian LaBree

No parts of this book may be used or reproduced without written permission from the publisher except brief quotations of critical articles and reviews.

This book is a work of fiction. The characters and incidents are fictional. Any resemblance to actual events or persons is entirely coincidental.

Fading Shadows is a story of love, sacrifice, and commitment to the virtues of courage, loyalty, and selflessness which defined the World War II generation. It is an emotional and heartfelt story that will warm the reader's heart.

Dedicated to my wife Pauline, and my family, with thanks for all their support and encouragement

Chapter One

Glenn Hastings stood above the cliffs watching the churning waves relentlessly hurl themselves against the rocky shore, and then slowly return, defeated, out to the sea in fragmented streams. He knew that this rhythmic assault upon the jagged coast of Maine would continue indefinitely, until the granite shore was reduced to minute sand particles. Glenn stared intently as the wind whipped the top fringe of the waves into plumes of mist hoping to find in the boiling cauldron before him a part of himself that had been absent for a long, long time.

Glenn was a tall gray-haired man with broad shoulders and an erect posture. His piercing dark eyes reflected his inner anguish. A visible scar ran across his left cheek and down his neck, one of the several wounds that had brought his military career to an end. He wiped a film of salt spray from his eyes and continued to stare, not sure what he expected to discover, yet, he felt compelled to return to this place. His searching soul found a kindred spirit in the restless sea. Right now, the future was less important to him than that part of yesterday which still gripped his heart.

The sea never changed. It looked the same as when he had stood on this same rock many years ago. The Nubble Lighthouse in the distance still stood on the cliffs above the grinding water below, warning wary sailors of the dangers of its rocky shore. He had carried this same image of the lighthouse in his memory for years, and now, he had reached the end of his journey.

1

It had all started a few weeks ago when he went to Europe with some of his old buddies from their Army regiment on a military tour of the Normandy beaches in France, where he had been severely wounded. It was the twenty-fifth anniversary of the battle that forever changed the face of Europe and his life.

He had spent two weeks touring the battlefields, renewing friendships, and sharing wartime experiences that he had never related to his family. They could never understand what it was really like and he chose not to tell them. His veteran friends knew... For years he thought very little about the war except for occasional nightmares. He had placed it on the back burner of his consciousness while he had feverishly set about trying to rebuild his life. Though it was not easy to put the horror out of his mind, the demands of a family and career had soon dominated his existence. Glenn was needed and his awareness of that fact had fueled his determination to work harder, even though his family life had become drastically altered by circumstances beyond his control.

His carefully constructed life all started to change a month ago when he received a phone call from a familiar voice from the past. He remembered it well.

"Is this Glenn Hastings, Captain Glenn Hastings?" the caller had asked.

"Yes, who's calling?"

"It's me, Johnny Bowman. Is that really you, Captain?"

"Yes it's me," answered Glenn, astonished to hear this name from so long ago. Master Sergeant Johnny Bowman had been his company clerk. "How are you, Johnny? It's great to hear your voice. How long has it been?"

"It's been over twenty years since I last saw you in the hospital. Listen Captain, I don't have much time, but I wanted to let you know that a lot of our old buddies from the regiment are getting together for a twenty-five- year anniversary trip to Normandy and Belgium. We had a hard time tracking you

2

down; it was almost as if you never existed," Sergeant Bowman commented triumphantly.

"Well, it's been difficult, Johnny," was Glenn's only reply.

"You don't owe me any explanations, sir. I just wanted to determine if you could make the trip. I'm sure it won't be easy for any of us, but it's one we've got to make at some time or another. What do you say? It would be great to see you again, and I speak for the old gang when I say that."

Glenn hesitated, "I'm not sure, Johnny…"

"Listen, if you're worrying about money, you should know that you've got friends who won't accept that as an excuse."

"I appreciate that Johnny, but that's not it, I was only thinking about the trip itself. I'm a far cry from the energetic company commander I used to be."

Johnny laughed. "Hell, Captain, that's true of all of us. I'm not trying to push you into something you don't want to do, but the trip could be important in helping all of us put that episode in our lives to rest. I really hope you can join us, it just wouldn't be the same without you, sir."

Glenn smiled grimly. "If you put it that way, Johnny, I can't gracefully refuse. You're right, the trip may help," he added, reflecting on what the trip could mean for him and his men.

"That's the spirit, Captain. I'll send the information out to you by mail. We'll assemble in Boston for the flight to France. It'll be terrific to have what's left of the old gang together again. I don't know about you, but my hair hasn't gotten any more gray, but it has definitely gotten more scarce," laughed Johnny.

The two weeks Glenn spent in France and Belgium reminiscing with those members of the regiment who had gone on the guided battlefield tour had dredged up feelings and emotions he had successfully suppressed for a long time. Those wartime years had been the most inspiring and frightening period of his life. It was impossible to ever be the person he had once been. The war changed everything, forever. The battlefield tour had cultivated a renewed sense of direction that Glenn had been lacking since the war, and he was thankful to have arrived at such a pivotal point.

As soon as Glenn said good-bye to Johnny and the others in Boston he had an uncontrollable desire to return to York on the coast of Maine, where he had been stationed for several months guarding the coastal regions against possible attack or insertion of enemy saboteurs from the sea. Acting decisively on his yearning to revisit a part of his past, Glenn immediately drove the automobile he had left in Boston up the scenic coast to York.

The coastal resorts were almost deserted when Glenn arrived. The summer tourist season had not yet started and only a few scattered automobiles lined the roadway. Dark clouds hung low overhead, blocking the sun, and the brisk May wind sent a chill down his spine. He had not been to York since his tour of duty ended, and wasn't sure if it was the dampness of the day or the familiar coastal area, but long suppressed memories flooded his mind. They were so strong it was almost as if he had returned to 1942, twenty-seven years ago.

Glenn had spent those few months in York conducting coastal security patrols in conjunction with the Coast Guard. At a point in the middle of Long Sands Beach, across from the large Anchorage Hotel, a 155 mm coastal cannon had been assigned to his platoon. It became the control center of his beach sentry posts. Now, many years later, Glenn drove his car along the road until he arrived at the former gun emplacement site. There was no evidence that any such installation had ever existed. His sentry posts had been positioned on either side of the gun emplacement at one thousand foot intervals along the entire beach. Glenn sadly scanned the beach, remembering how it was.

The children from the families living near the shore used to flock around the men on sentry duty, he recalled. They were impressed with the soldiers' rifles and sub-machine guns and grateful for their handouts of Hershey chocolate bars. It was impossible for civilians to buy any type of chocolate bar during the war. The children, especially the boys, seemed to know when the army command cars would be making their rounds to distribute meals to the soldiers at their posts. While the kids never refused any of the foodstuff from the soldiers, they were disappointed when it did not include gum or chocolate bars. Tootsie rolls were also a popular treat.

Thoughts of the local children brought a smile to Glenn's lips. Back then, the war had dominated everyone's thoughts and actions. There was compassion and generosity and support among neighbors as they labored in common cause to help bring the war to an end. It was a time of shared sacrifice. Dreams and aspirations for a better tomorrow were placed on hold until the war could be terminated. People were determined to make it through the difficult period and they collectively locked arms in unity to complete the job.

Children lived in an atmosphere of anxiety and uncertainty, even despair, when their families were recipients of telegrams notifying them of the death or injury of a loved one. Yet, the children found the period exciting. Great things that they did not completely understand, were taking place, and in their innocence, they shared the intensity of the nationwide movement to defeat the enemies of their country. The presence of armed soldiers and coast guardsmen walking the beaches, and the sight of army truck convoys filled with men and equipment and sometimes armored cars coming and going in their civilian world filled the kids with awe and respect. The world around them was erupting in chaos and violence. The children sensed the solemnity and severity of the times, as they played soldiers' games and worshipped the young protectors who stood at the lonely sentry stations between their homes and the evil enemy.

Families that had members in the military services were quick to brag about their fathers, brothers, and uncles proudly embellishing their accomplishments to their friends and neighbors. On those occasions when the family received word of an injury or death to their loved ones, the tragedy permanently shattered the family's dreams for the future, and the entire community mourned their loss.

The children's heroes were featured in the numerous magazines and comic books so popular at that time. To be a soldier was the dream and hope of most young boys, the personification of the nation's strength, reflecting the prevailing attitudes of their parents. The American citizen-soldier was the most respected person in the country regardless of social or economic position.

Glenn drove by the location where his platoon had been encamped in temporary quarters near the water's edge. At that time, he was an inexperienced young second lieutenant fresh out of Reserve Officers Training Corps at the University of Pennsylvania where he had majored in civil and mining engineering. York was his first posting as an Army officer. Though the temporary quarters were supplied by the Army camps in the region, the soldiers still ended up purchasing many things from area merchants which had boosted the local economy. There was a great deal of contact with the local population who took an interest in the needs of the young soldiers, frequently inviting them into their homes after duty hours. Dances were often sponsored by the United Service Organization (USO) volunteers and the Red Cross also helped to make the soldiers feel at home.

Glenn's memories of this period were locked away in his heart. He never spoke to anyone about them. He had often asked himself just why things happened the way they did; he never found an adequate answer.

Glenn turned the aging Studebaker Hawk onto the road leading from the beach to York Village. The last time he had traveled it was in a Jeep in 1942. Now there were more houses and fewer trees, but the old village gaol on the hill across from the Post Office remained the same as when it was first built in the 1600's. Glenn also noted that the original one-room schoolhouse nearby had been refurbished. It had been just an empty shell during the war. A short distance west of the village common, Glenn approached the elementary school on his right. He slowed down and pulled into a parking space in front of the two-story red brick building, turning off the ignition key with a shaking hand.

A lump filled Glenn's throat. He was almost afraid to look at the building. When he did glance up, a flood of sadness enveloped him. He had so many unanswered questions about what might have been.

Suddenly, he was transformed back to 1942, when he was a young officer climbing the driveway beside the school building in a Jeep and turning into the parking area at the rear. He had been asked to speak to the children about the duties of his platoon at the coast. He had enjoyed public relations work with children.

The minute he stepped out of the Jeep, he was swamped by kids of all ages thrilled to see a soldier at their school. It was hero worship of the highest form. He remembered how the children had looked up to him as if he were ten feet tall. One student had asked him if he brought any guns, Glenn had smilingly explained that a school was not the place for firearms. Glenn stood out in the crowd. He was six feet tall with broad shoulders, looking every inch the soldier. He projected decisiveness and confidence without a trace of arrogance. His intense dark eyes softened as he acknowledged the children, who idolized him without even knowing him. The United States Army uniform guaranteed immediate acceptance for anyone who wore it.

"Children, children," exclaimed a woman's voice behind Glenn. "Let the soldier have some breathing room. Welcome, Lieutenant, I'm Kathleen Cohen."

"How do you do, Miss Cohen," he answered politely. "I'm Glenn Hastings. It was nice of you to ask for a speaker from the detachment. Looks like you're stuck with me."

Kathleen returned his smile. "We appreciate your taking the time to visit us. Why don't you come inside and meet the other teachers. We'll let the children play outside a little longer."

"That will be fine," responded Glenn, waving to the kids as he entered the school house. "They look as if they need to work off some energy."

"Most of the time they're great," she told him earnestly. "Just about every one of them has some family member in the military. A few have relatives that were killed or injured in the war. That's been difficult for all of us to handle."

"I can understand that, Miss Cohen."

Shortly after Kathleen Cohen introduced him around the school, the elementary classes, one through six, assembled on the first floor of the school house and on the four sets of stairs at the four corners of the building. The large amphitheater was filled with wide-eyed children who listened with rapt attention to Glenn's every word. He spoke about the war and why the United States had chosen to become involved, and ended with some suggestions as to how the students themselves could contribute to the war effort. His recommendations included helping out at home in order to maintain as normal an environment as possible while the children's fathers, brothers, and uncles were away doing the actual fighting. He also suggested that they could band together to collect scrap papers, scrap metal, and milkweed seed pods for the manufacture of parachutes. At the close of Glenn's speech, the students gave him an enthusiastic standing ovation that touched him deeply.

Afterwards, several of the children lingered, hoping to shake his hand. The boys were more assertive than the girls, who generally approached him tentatively with giggles and admiring eyes. He never forgot the admiration and unqualified acceptance they had shown him, a stranger in their midst.

That had been a long time ago, and Glenn's eyes misted as he looked longingly at the school and remembered Kathleen Cohen.

From the moment he met her on the children's playground, he knew there was something special about her. She was attractive and vivacious with her shiny long black hair that fell to just below her shoulders. There was a warmth and approachability about her that made people feel comfortable in her presence. She was also a good listener, and perhaps that was her most endearing quality, for it made people feel that what they had to say was truly important to her. It was an honest character trait that helped define her. The students warmed to her, yet at the same time, they treated her with great respect. Kathleen was clearly a strict disciplinarian when the occasion warranted.

After the school rally, Kathleen walked Glenn out the door to his Jeep. They chatted a few minutes before saying good-bye.

"Are you from around here?" Kathleen asked.

"No, I'm from the coal mining regions of Pennsylvania," he told her. "This is the first time I've ever been to Maine. It's a beautiful state, and I'm pleased to be posted near the coast. If there weren't a war going on it would be ideal, but now is not the time to be thinking of anything except doing our duty."

"If you would like to stop by and visit my parents and me, Lieutenant, we would be happy to share our table with you for a good home-cooked meal." She had offered what numerous families had been doing on a regular basis for the servicemen in the area.

"It would be my pleasure, Miss Cohen. Tell your parents that I'll call after I check my schedule," he replied enthusiastically. "Sometimes army chow leaves a little to be desired."

"So I've heard," Kathleen grinned.

"Thanks for inviting me to speak to the kids. They were great. After all is said and done they're the main reason we're fighting this war. I'll always remember this visit and I appreciate your offer of hospitality. May I have your telephone number so I can let you know about my schedule?"

"Okay, yes," she responded. "Our number is 288J. You may call anytime, my parents are real homebodies."

"Well, Miss Cohen, thanks again. I'll be in touch. Good-bye," Glenn assured her as he climbed into the Jeep.

"Good-bye, Lieutenant," Kathleen Cohen called from the school door.

Glenn remembered that it was four days later when he called the Cohen residence and showed up that evening for a home-cooked meal. Mr. and Mrs. Cohen were second generation New Englanders and they welcomed Glenn into their home with grace and sincerity. Kathleen's father, Ernest, was a big man with large gnarled fingers that gripped Glenn's hand like a vice. His face was lined and weather-beaten from a lifetime of grueling work as a lobsterman on the rugged Maine coast. He had a deep booming voice that could be heard a long way off. However, Glenn soon discovered that the sturdy Ernest Cohen possessed a very gentle and calm disposition, and the two men took an immediate liking to each other.

Mrs. Gladys Cohen was a fitting compliment to her husband, thin and petite with a sparkle in her eye. She gave the impression of being frail. In reality, she was a bundle of energy and a tower of strength for the family. She ruled over the Cohen domain with love and compassion tempered with a natural zeal for orderliness. The house was spotlessly clean. Kathleen most

10

resembled her mother. They shared the same smiling eyes. Glenn felt welcome and enjoyed his visit.

Kathleen's brother, Philip, was in the Coast Guard. Glenn noticed the picture of him in his uniform prominently displayed on the piano in the living room. He too resembled his mother. "Phil is aboard the Coast Guard cutter *Acushnet*," Ernest Cohen added. "We never know exactly when he's at sea but the ship is stationed at Portland and we get to see him occasionally. He never talks about it, but I expect his ship is on submarine patrol when they're not doing convoy escort to England or Murmansk, Russia."

"Phil went out to sea as often as Dad allowed on the lobster boat, so it was natural for him to pick the Navy or the Coast Guard," Kathleen told Glenn.

"I've got a soft spot for the Coast Guard," Mr. Cohen remarked. "They never falter when they're needed. They've helped me out countless times, and the other fishermen have nothing but respect and affection for the work they do."

"I understand that duty at sea in the North Atlantic is a challenge," Glenn replied. "You have every right to be proud of your son."

"And what about you, Lieutenant?" asked Kathleen curiously. "What did you do before the war started?"

"I was a student at the University of Pennsylvania studying engineering. I graduated in June of 1941 and joined the Army immediately after graduation. I received a commission through the Reserve Officers Training Corps and had just completed the basic infantry course when Pearl Harbor was bombed," answered Glenn. "A short time ago I was assigned to the platoon I now command in York, but I don't believe it will be a permanent posting."

"You must miss your family, Lieutenant Hastings," Mrs. Cohen commented with concern.

11

Glenn hesitated, unsure of how to answer, but the warmth of Mrs. Cohen's voice convinced him to explain. "Both of my parents died in an automobile accident when I was very young, so I lived with my grandparents. They ran a small dairy farm. Yes, I do miss them. My grandfather passed away two years ago while I was in school and my grandmother moved in with my aunt. Grandma's a gentle soul and I love her dearly. My world with them was filled with love and respect. They were two of the hardest working people I've ever known," Glenn paused, remembering his grandparents fondly. "Incidentally, I'd appreciate it if you would call me Glenn. I get enough of that 'Lieutenant stuff' at the camp."

Mrs. Cohen smiled graciously. "Then Glenn it is," she announced with finality.

That evening was the beginning of a special attraction between Glenn and Kathleen. It developed naturally after the first dinner he had shared with the Cohens. When he was with Kathleen it was easy for him to forget about the war. The attraction was mutual and they eagerly anticipated the moments they shared. They didn't spend long periods of time together, because his command demanded most of his time and energy. The platoon was spread thin trying to maintain sentry posts and Jeep patrols in those inaccessible rocky areas along the coast. Glenn frequently conducted joint patrols with the Coast Guard which ran an armed patrol boat up the York River as far as they could navigate, about eight miles from the coast at high tide. Glenn maintained a mobile Jeep patrol on either side of the river at the same time.

Glenn tried to take the river patrol whenever possible. The patrol route took him past a small general store on the bank of the river run by Kate Marshall, an elderly lady who also ran a coal and wood fuel business. He frequently stopped there for an orange soft drink and to visit a few minutes. She was a lovable eccentric who wore a hearing aid and listened to those things she was interested in and ignored everything else. She seemed to be pleased when Glenn stopped by, always refusing to take his money for the drink. He took advantage of the visit to find out if she had heard of anything suspicious or out of the ordinary. She was an information broker and made a point of knowing everything going on in the neighborhood.

Across from the Marshall store, next to the Sewall Bridge, was the York Country Club, an exclusive golf course and club for the local aristocrats and socially conscious families of the York area. Glenn remembered that he and Kathleen attended a dance at the club. All military personnel were welcome. Kathleen told him that, normally, she would never attend such an occasion if he had not been in uniform. Her family did not have the right bloodlines required to become a member. She was pleased to accompany him. It was her way of defying conventional tradition and the haughtiness of the "blue bloods" that rigidly maintained their positions. Kathleen occasionally displayed an impish kind of humor that came naturally to her, like the time when she mocked some of the sophisticated upper crust mothers of her students. They had laughed a lot together.

Glenn drove the Studebaker past the familiar country school house and Mrs. Marshall's general store. It had been vacant for years, but was still standing and in need of paint and repairs. The faded sign above the well-worn entrance door was still visible. Nothing lasted forever, he sighed, hoping to find it as he remembered it in 1942.

As he passed over the river, the pounding of the wooden timbers of Sewall Bridge rattled beneath his car. He found himself perspiring and not completely in control of himself. Driving up the hill toward Kathleen's house he entertained a sickening feeling that he was making a mistake. His better judgment was overruled as he crested the hill above the bridge where he pulled over to the side of the road. There before him, just as he remembered it, was the cedar-shingled cape cod cottage that had belonged to Kathleen's parents. He unconsciously turned off the ignition key.

13

A choking sob passed his lips and his heart pounded so forcefully that he was certain this trip was a mistake. He should never have come back! Then, he caught a glimpse of a solitary figure walk around the corner of the house across the lawn and disappear. Glenn stared in amazement. His vision was blurred by tears, but regardless of all the years that had passed, he recognized Kathleen Cohen.

Chapter Two

Tears flowed freely down Glenn's cheeks, accompanied by pain so acute he had trouble catching his breath. He watched the small cape house apprehensively for several minutes, gripping the steering wheel so tightly his knuckles turned white. He struggled to overcome a powerful urge to rush to the house and announce himself. Only his iron discipline restrained his natural instincts. Too many years had passed and too many things had happened during those trying times for him to now introduce himself. Time, as well as choices he had made over the years had changed everything, including himself, and the world around him. Glenn knew that the mere fact that he was seeking consolation and refuge in a particular time of his life, did not mean that he was going to find it.

With a heavy heart, he turned the Studebaker around in the middle of the road and slowly drove back across the bridge toward York Harbor, where he had reserved a room with an ocean view at a small inn.

Later that night, in the sanctity of his room, Glenn attempted to honestly evaluate his present circumstances. He had hoped that this trip to Maine would offer him the strength and direction he was so desperately seeking. But instead of providing him with a fresh perspective for the future, it was creating emotional chaos and confusion within him. He was troubled, and had to admit that if things continued in the same way, he had reason to fear for his sanity.

That night, Glenn prayed to a God he had not always acknowledged. His prayers were fervently offered as a last resort in the face of his inner turmoil. Sitting in a rocking chair, gazing out the window overlooking the ocean, Glenn opened up his heart, and asked forgiveness for his past sins and begged his Lord for help and guidance. He had lost his way, and now he found himself frightened, confused, and alone. He also prayed for the courage and strength he would need to walk the path to which he was directed.

Afterward, exhausted, and emotionally drained, Glenn lay down on the bed and closed his eyes. Soft rays of moonlight slashed across his upper body as he fell into a deep and peaceful sleep. In the middle of the night he awoke suddenly and sat up rubbing the muscles on his left leg where the brace that he wore irritated the skin. It was a miracle that he still had his legs, he reflected, and another miracle that he could walk. The severe wounds he had received in France during the breakout from the Normandy beaches had been the genesis of his long days of torment.

Unable to doze off again, Glenn moved to the chair by the window, gazing out into the night, and relived the chain of events that had begun when he was stationed at York.

Glenn had always known that his time commanding the security platoon on the York seacoast was temporary. Though he was an inexperienced officer, his training had made him more prepared to command troops in combat than most of the raw men then graduating from the army's officer candidate schools or the colleges. Therefore, Glenn speculated that he would most likely be picked for overseas duty at the first opportunity. His predictions had proved all too accurate.

The fact was, after several months of guard duty, Glenn was tiring of the post. While it was wonderful to see Kathleen as often as he could, and he enjoyed socializing with her circle of friends around town, there was a war raging beyond their shores and he wanted to play a more decisive role in its execution.

Glenn had showed up at school one day about the time Kathleen had just herded the last of the children out of the building and into a waiting bus. She was in a good mood and full of smiles.

"Well, Lieutenant Hastings," she remarked coyly. "You look as if you're having a good day."

"Seeing you just made it better," he answered, giving her a quick kiss on the cheek. "I've got a surprise and a request for you. Close your eyes and hold out your hands."

"No tricks now."

"Of course not."

"Okay," she agreed, holding out her hands with palms up. Glenn placed a small card with two silver first lieutenant bars in them.

"You can open them now," he told her happily.

Kathleen instantly recognized the bars. "Oh Glenn," she exclaimed, clasping her arms around his neck. "I'm so proud of you. You've worked so hard and truly deserve the promotion."

Glenn embraced her tightly. "It would mean a lot if you would pin them on me," he said, choked with emotion.

"If I'm going to do that, you'll have to kneel down."

"I'll kneel for you anytime," he responded lightly.

"Now don't be flippant," she laughed. Glenn liked her playful impulsive ways. He had fallen in love with her so completely that it frightened him when he thought of the war still ahead of them. It could last a long time and he knew that war did not permit meaningful relationships to blossom with certainty.

Glenn dutifully sat on the bumper of his Jeep while she quietly removed the gold second lieutenant bars and replaced them with the silver ones. She was reflective at first, then asked tentatively, "Does this mean that you'll be given a new duty station?"

He sighed and replied honestly, "I haven't been notified yet, but we should prepare ourselves for that eventuality. The Army is building new divisions as rapidly as the training centers can turn out the men. The units will need officers and I'm quite certain they'll rotate me out of security duty."

Kathleen stared back at him. "How soon will it happen?" she asked quickly. Glenn could feel her body tense.

"I don't know for sure, Kathleen. But we should not take anything for granted. The future is full of uncertainties and I believe that we should treasure what we have now and take one day at a time until the war is over."

"What are you trying to say, Glenn?" Kathleen asked, dissatisfied with vague generalities.

Glenn smiled at her. "I'm trying to say that I love you, Kathleen. I don't want to be ordered away from here without telling you how much more meaningful my life has been since you came into it."

Kathleen's eyes filled with tears. "I feel the same way, Glenn. In fact, I fell in love with you the first time you visited the school. I'm so proud of you. You've even won over my parents and they share my pride. I'm a little frightened of the future," she confessed. "What would I ever do without you?"

"Would it embarrass you if I kissed you here in the school parking lot?" he asked.

"No," she replied, stepping into his outstretched arms. Regardless of the uncertain future, she felt secure and safe in his strong embrace.

"Whatever happens," Glenn whispered in her ear. "I'll be able to face an uncertain tomorrow a lot easier knowing that you'll be here waiting for me after the war is over."

Kathleen drew back from his embrace and looked into his eyes. "Are you proposing, Glenn?" she questioned.

"Yes, I am, Kathleen," he said, catching his breath. "But, we have to wait until the war is over. Really we hardly know each other. It's only been a few months."

"I know you're right," Kathleen replied. "My answer is yes, once this ugly war is over. This horrible war," she repeated nervously. "It interferes with everyone's lives."

"That's what makes it so difficult," said Glenn, releasing her and holding her at arms' length. "We can take some comfort in the fact that we're not alone. The whole country is carrying a heavy burden and we're obligated to do our part."

"I understand," Kathleen nodded, not trusting herself to speak.

"Listen," said Glenn, intentionally changing the subject. "I also stopped by to ask you to tell your father that I'll be free to go out with him on the boat this Saturday. I'm looking forward to it and will be ready first thing in the morning."

"That will be nice," said Kathleen. "He said that you two had talked about it. Be sure to dress warm because it gets pretty chilly out there, especially if there's no sun."

"I will," answered Glenn, kissing her one last time before climbing into the Jeep. "I'll see you later, teacher."

"Good-bye, Glenn," Kathleen called as he drove away.

The following Saturday at dawn Glenn showed up at Ernest Cohen's fish house and boat landing on the York River. He was eager to observe how lobsters are harvested for market. The lobster boat was christened *Santa Marie* and was so marked on both sides and the rear. It was piled high with lobster traps made out of oak lumber. Glenn parked his Jeep beside the shed, and was immediately greeted by an exuberant Ernest Cohen.

"Welcome aboard, young man. You're just in time for some hot tea," he exclaimed. "You do drink tea, don't you?"

"Yes, I like tea," answered Glenn.

"We're creatures of habit and tradition," the muscular lobsterman declared as he led Glenn into the small shed. It contained various pieces of boating equipment and supplies, and on a large shelf next to the door was a steaming tea pot on a hot plate. On the wall behind the shelf was a peg board filled with white porcelain mugs similar to the one Glenn was holding. He noted with curiosity that each mug was inscribed with the names of family members and friends. Glenn gladly accepted a white porcelain mug. There was a chill in the damp air and the warm cup felt good in his hands.

Ernest Cohen explained, "We drink a lot of tea. Some fishermen prefer coffee, but our family has always been tea drinkers. Each mug on the wall is for the exclusive use of the owner. We have extras for guests."

Glenn smiled and said, "I like the idea of upholding traditions. They give you something permanent to cling to. I'm glad to have a chance to go lobstering with you, sir. I sure hope I can be of some help instead of being just an observer."

Ernest Cohen grinned broadly. "I welcome any help you care to offer, young man. Listen, why don't we agree to call each other by our first names? It'll be easier for both of us."

"That suits me fine, Ernest," Glenn agreed.

"Come on, let's climb aboard. The tide is on its way out and it's a good time to take advantage and save fuel." Ernest motioned for Glenn to follow him to the control cowl where he started the engine. "This boat has a rebuilt Chevrolet six cylinder engine. It's a popular engine for lobster boats, dependable and economical. If you want, Glenn, you can pull in our mooring lines."

Glenn didn't hesitate and quickly lifted the two looped ropes up and over the pilings on the dock. The swift river current immediately pulled the boat away from the landing toward the center of the channel.

"You'll find that the wind and cold is more tolerable the closer you stand to the windshield, Glenn," Ernest advised him.

"It's also easier to hang on and steady yourself. Sometimes an unwary passenger can be thrown off balance during a quick maneuver and be swept overboard."

For a while the boat moved smoothly down the placid waters of the river channel, but this changed abruptly as they approached the turbulent Atlantic. At the point where the channel entered the ocean they met a patrol boat from the Coast Guard Auxiliary heading up the river channel in the opposite direction. Glenn recognized the crewman at the helm of the patrol boat and waved to him. The patrol boat pulled closer.

"Hail *Santa Marie*. Good luck trying to convert that soldier-boy to a sailor," laughed the coastie good-naturedly, speaking through a megaphone.

"We'll let him try out his sea legs on this trip," Ernest hollered back with a wave of his hand.

"If I get seasick and the coasties hear about it, my name will be mud," remarked Glenn, shaking his head. Ernest turned the boat to a northerly course a thousand feet off shore.

Mount Agamenticus rose out of the relatively flat coastal plain standing alone. It served as a common landmark for mariners in the area. Ernest told Glenn that they were going to drop off some of the lobster traps, which were already loaded with bait fish. The balance of the traps would be used to replace those that were damaged or broken when they hauled them out of the water. About ten percent of the traps needed to be replaced every trip. Ernest's lobster buoys were painted white with a red stripe running diagonally across the top and sides. Each fisherman had his own distinct color scheme that was known and honored by all others. It was an unwritten custom for traps to be placed a reasonable distance from other buoys. Severe fines could be imposed upon anyone found guilty of raiding someone else's traps. It was a sacred trust that was rarely violated.

For the next five hours, Glenn assisted Ernest pulling in the traps attached to the surrounding buoys. It was hard work and now Glenn understood how Ernest got his muscular arms. Drawing the buoy and rope toward the boat was not too difficult, but the water-soaked trap and net were a heavy lift from the water to the deck of the boat. Once onboard, they flipped open the access door to grab the lobsters. Those that were too small for market they threw overboard, the larger ones they plugged with small spear-shaped wooden pegs that held the claws closed. Marketable lobsters were collected in large steel wire baskets positioned in the center of the deck. Then they would replenish the trap with fish bait, secure the access door, and drop it overboard again. They pulled a hundred traps that day with an average of two marketable lobsters per trap.

When they reached the end of Ernest's trap line he turned the boat southward and cruised at three-quarter throttle toward the river. The Chevrolet engine effortlessly pulled the wooden craft through the small swells. Glenn was ready to call it quits. Daily workouts with his men had put him in good physical condition, yet, his arms and back ached from lifting the heavy traps. He was not in as good a shape as he had expected.

Nevertheless, Ernest glanced at him approvingly. "You did well, Glenn. It takes a while to build up to this job. You helped make my day an easier one."

"My respect for lobstermen has increased a hundred fold," Glenn replied. "I can only imagine what it must be like out here when the seas are rough or during a storm."

Ernest nodded. "The prudent fisherman tries not to take chances, but sometimes it's necessary to empty the traps even when it's stormy, otherwise the lobsters eat each other. Yes, it can be dangerous, especially when you're alone. A wise fisherman will take precautions such as wearing a life belt and informing someone when you expect to return. That way if you don't return on schedule, the Coast Guard can be notified."

"Is this a normal catch for you?" asked Glenn, admiring the six baskets overflowing with lobsters.

"It's sort of typical for this time of year," Ernest replied.

"Do you retail them or wholesale to a broker?"

"If someone comes around when I'm available, I'll sell a lobster or two retail, but it's easier to just wholesale the catch. When we get back to the landing we'll empty the catch into my holding crates."

They were silent as they neared the landing dock. Ernest shut down the engine and turned to Glenn. "I don't know about you, Glenn, but I'm hungry."

Glenn grinned. "You must have read my mind. The sea air and the strenuous work has made me ravenous."

"Sometimes I bring a lunch on the boat with me, but I much prefer to have a more leisurely one when I return to the landing where we can boil up a fresh pot of tea."

"I'm with you, sir," replied Glenn with a satisfied smile. "It had been a good day," he reflected. Working alongside the powerful, yet gentle, fisherman was something he wouldn't have missed for anything. He could lift the wet traps out of the water with two fingers, while Glenn, twenty-five years his junior, struggled. Even though Ernest was a large man he was as gentle as a child and as sure-footed on the boat's rolling deck as a ballet dancer.

Back at the landing the two men opened a lunch basket Kathleen's mother had prepared for them. Ernest turned on the hot plate for tea. As soon as it was ready, he poured a cup for each of them. Then, Ernest told Glenn that the tradition was to make a toast in thanksgiving for their safe return to harbor and a bountiful catch. They clicked their mugs in toast and ate heartily of the sandwiches and apple pie and drank countless cups of scalding hot tea. Ernest used the mug marked with his name. Glenn used one for guests.

That day, Kathleen's father, Ernest Cohen, proved to be good-natured and easy-going. He had earned Glenn's respect as a man worthy of admiration.

Chapter Three

The world was bursting back to life after a long dormant winter. The buds on the maple trees outside Glenn's window at the inn were swollen, impatient to blossom. Those buds that had already developed into tender green leaves rustled softly in the sea breeze, a whispering promise of life's renewal.

Glenn had fallen asleep in the chair beside the window. When he awoke, the sun was warm and bright. A light rain in the morning had freshened the landscape. Shadowy plumes of mist reached for the warmth of the sun and slowly disappeared. He stretched in his chair, feeling in better spirits than he had for a long time. Last night he had made a pact with his God and felt a serenity that was very, very welcome.

After showering and dressing, Glenn left his room with a new spring in his steps and went in search of the small dining room the inn operated for its guests. He found it to be light, cheerful, and well-appointed with Colonial period furniture, including a large tavern table positioned against an interior wall and piled high with breads, muffins, and a large coffee urn. The walls were covered with seascapes and paintings of large sailing ships. Glenn took a seat by a window with an ocean view, and ordered a breakfast of toast, eggs, and bacon with baked beans. It felt good to be hungry.

* * *

The waves pounding against the rocky shore below reminded Glenn of his last days in York during the summer of 1942. Less than two weeks after receiving his first lieutenant commission, Glenn had received warning orders notifying him that formal orders would follow shortly, and that he should be prepared to turn over his platoon and camp as soon as his replacement reported at York. The notification wasn't unexpected.

Though Glenn preferred being with troops in combat, he was reluctant to leave his relationship with Kathleen. They had spent a lot of time together that month, especially when school was closed for the summer and she was not teaching full time. In fact, that August Glenn saw her almost every day and was a frequent guest at the Cohen residence for supper. The evening that he received the warning order, he had stopped by the house to tell her. She was alone in the kitchen eating a sandwich when he rang the doorbell.

"Come in, Glenn," she had said, noticing him through the window. "Mother and Father have gone to a movie at the hall. They wanted to see Sergeant York. I didn't expect to see you tonight. Is anything wrong?"

"That depends on your definition of 'wrong'," Glenn held out his arms to her.

Stepping into his embrace, she whispered, "Your orders came through..."

"Yes," Glenn replied, holding her tightly. "I'm not certain how much longer I'll be here, and I won't be able to tell you when I'm leaving, but I wanted to let you know that it's imminent."

"Oh, Glenn," she cried out, clinging to him. Suddenly the future was filled with uncertainties. Images of violence and catastrophe flashed through her mind making her feel sick to her stomach. She murmured softly, "It has been swell, hasn't it?"

"These have been the happiest days of my life," he uttered simply. "Tell me that you'll be here when I return, Kathleen. I have no other place to go and I'd like to dream that when this war is over, we can be together for a lifetime."

"Yes, I promise you I'll be here, and my heart will be counting the days until you're back. I do love you, Glenn. No matter what happens, that's never going to change."

The news of Glenn's transfer shook Kathleen even more than she had expected. She had been hoping for more time to accustom herself to the idea of Glenn's leaving, but time was a precious commodity ever since the war started. She had been thinking about his potential departure for days. Now that it was upon them, she felt shattered and frightened. The love they shared was so special and now it was threatened by an unknown future. How could she ever let him go? They clung passionately to each other wishing tomorrow would never come. That evening they gave themselves to each other in body as well as soul. The fact that it might be the last time, perhaps the only time, that they would be together was a distinct possibility neither of them could deny.

Afterward, they clung passionately to each other as if, together, they could prevent tomorrow. Finally, reluctantly, Glenn spoke. "I hate to mention it, but I've got a guard detail to mount out, so I really have to go. I'll try to see you tomorrow. This has been a beautiful evening, Kathleen and I..." His eyes filled with tears at having to leave so quickly.

"Shh, Glenn," whispered Kathleen, holding a finger to his lips. "This was something we both wanted, and I don't want to hear you apologize or feel sorry for what happened. It's been a beautiful evening for me too. I'll never forget it."

Glenn gathered his things and added, "If I'm not able to see you and your parents again before I ship out, please give my best to your mother and father. I've appreciated the way they've made me feel welcome and will always remember their kindness."

"I'll tell them, Glenn," Kathleen assured him. "Oh, how I hate to see you go. It just doesn't seem right for it to end this way."

"It's not ending, Kathleen. I'll carry your memory in my heart and I'll always be with you in spirit." Glenn took her into his arms one last time. "Good-bye, my love. Be brave and have faith that our dreams will come true."

"I'll try, but right now, it's difficult," she had answered truthfully. "My prayers will always be with you, Glenn."

"I'll write as soon as I can to let you know my address. I'm so glad I was sent to Maine where I found you. Until next time."

"Until next time," she cried softly. He opened the door and left. She stepped out onto the porch and waved to him as he drove down the hill in his Jeep and disappeared from sight. The last precious memory Glenn had of Kathleen was of her standing on the porch waving bravely while tears ran down her cheeks.

* * *

"Are you all-right, sir," interrupted a waitress. The question startled Glenn, who was reliving a precious moment from the past.

Not wishing to share his feelings with anyone, he nodded and replied, "I'm fine, ma'am."

"Can I get you anything else?"

"No, thank you, the breakfast was great," he replied absently and, finally, she left him to himself.

Glenn walked from the inn in search of a path leading to a walkway along the top of the cliffs overlooking the shore. He wanted to stretch his legs and enjoy the warmth of a sunny day in May. His injured left leg would always need some type of support. Years ago he had accepted his condition and adjusted to walking with the brace. He still had a slight limp, but he was grateful simply to be able to move about without assistance. While he could not run or jump like he had before the war, compared to what might have been, he considered himself most fortunate.

As he walked along the shore, Glenn reflected that his tour of duty at York was the happiest time of his life. He never deceived himself that the thing he wanted more than anything in the world was to see Kathleen Cohen, or what ever her name might be now, before he got any older. He held back out of fear of rejection again. While he was lying in an Army hospital a bloodied mass of flesh and bones, with the doctors predicting the worst, all of a sudden Kathleen's letters had stopped coming. For the ensuing months, as he straddled that thin line between life and death, he had been unable to write her or even to have anyone write for him. The mortar round that almost killed him had destroyed part of the left side of his jaw and mangled his legs. He was unable to speak or walk, and the prognosis for a normal life was not encouraging. Sometimes he didn't care whether he lived or died. The pain was excruciating. When life continued to be a struggle of endless days and anguished nights, he regularly questioned the logic of continuing the fight.

His worst fears during that time in the hospital were that he would become an object of pity and a burden to Kathleen. He loved her too much to allow that to happen. Glenn could still recall the day that he made up his mind not to contact Kathleen or inform her of his injuries. It had been the longest and saddest day of his life. He had wept for hours, tortured in the belief that a beautiful part of his life had slipped away... gone forever.

* * *

Glenn continued along the pathway at the top of the cliffs, stopping occasionally to enjoy the ocean below. It had always been a source of comfort to him. He had grown up in the interior of Pennsylvania near the coal fields, and the first time he saw the ocean was when he began classes at the University of Pennsylvania near Philadelphia on the Delaware River. As a student, he had frequently walked along the riverfront, awed by the large ships tied up at the miles and miles of docks. His first duty station at York had only renewed his fascination with the ocean's infinite moods.

At last, Glenn reached the end of the walkway, and sat down on a rock and rested as he gazed at the water. He could hear the gentle lapping of the waves against the rocks. He sat motionless for a while, lost in his thoughts of Kathleen and the past. Stirred by old memories, Glenn decided to take a ride out to Long Sands Beach. Retracing his steps along the pathway he walked with a purpose to his Studebaker, looking forward to another trip down memory lane.

Decatuer's store at the junction of the village road with the beach was no longer in operation. He had often stopped there for a bottle of tonic and cigarettes. The temporary Army camp had been located almost directly behind the store in an open field. He stopped for a few seconds to see that now, the open space was filled with small cottages. He could still hear the sounds of his men griping about the weather, food, and anything else they could think of. They had been homesick and lonely despite the hospitality of the civilian population. The young men had often been cold and frightened on night beach patrol, but they had done their duty, and he had always been proud of them.

Turning north along the beach boulevard, Glenn soon came to the Anchorage Hotel where his platoon had served a coastal battery installation. Now, a drive-in restaurant stood where the gun had been positioned, he shook his head in amazement at all the changes. Glenn had made the trip on the spur of the moment without bringing additional clothing. He was still dressed in his business clothes, which were inadequate as well as uncomfortable, so he decided to drive to Portsmouth, New Hampshire, about ten miles away, to buy more comfortable and appropriate clothing. Portsmouth was large enough to contain an assortment of different stores to choose from.

Cruising south on U.S. Route 1 in Kittery, Maine, Glenn, noticed a Ford station wagon approaching in the opposite lane being driven erratically, weaving in and out of his lane. Alarmed, Glenn pulled to the right just as the Ford came abreast of him. Then, the Ford altered course and collided with Glenn's Studebaker at the front left quarter of the car, crushing the fender and passenger compartment. The blow pushed Glenn's Studebaker sideways into a ditch where it came to a stop against a bank that prevented it from rolling over.

Glenn had predicted the maneuver and had turned as far to the right as the road allowed. It was almost as if the Ford had zeroed in on him and intentionally hit him. The impact smashed his body against the windshield and steering wheel. When the Studebaker came to a stop Glenn was stretched to the limit of the seat belt, slouched on the floor between the seat and dashboard, unconscious, and covered with blood. Jagged shards of glass from the windshield and side windows had cut his hands, head, and face.

The driver of the Ford was shaken but unhurt. Climbing out of his vehicle he had the presence of mind to turn off the Studebaker's ignition key. Within minutes, several passing motorists had stopped to render assistance. A young sailor from the Portsmouth Naval Yard was the first to arrive. He calmly and efficiently checked Glenn's pulse and evaluated his condition, telling those present that Glenn should not be moved until the ambulance arrived and the medical technicians could examine him.

The Maine State Police arrived on the scene several minutes after the accident, and shortly thereafter an ambulance from Portsmouth showed up. Glenn was still unconscious when the medical technicians examined him. The technicians and the policeman transferred Glenn from the wrecked automobile to the ambulance. Within minutes Glenn was being wheeled into the emergency room of the Portsmouth Hospital.

Attendants cut away the outer clothing so that the resident physicians could examine every inch of Glenn's battered body. X-rays revealed that he had two broken ribs and two fingers on his left hand were broken. His upper torso was bruised and black and blue.

Pieces of glass were removed from Glenn's face and neck, and his entire body had to be wiped clean and sterilized. He regained consciousness temporarily and fell back into blackness several times during the process. During those moments of consciousness, he was aware that every portion of his body hurt, but the most excruciating pain was down his legs. He could hear the people talking around him. Glenn was no stranger to hospitals. They all sounded and smelled the same.

It was almost as if he were back in the field hospital in France during the war. His presence in the Portsmouth Hospital served to intensify the still-vivid memories from that fateful time twenty-five years before.

* * *

The tenaciously contested hedgerows surrounding the fields of southern France were the scene of some of the most bitter fighting of the war. Glenn's company had just relieved another company in the line and had suffered serious casualties effecting that relief. The perimeter of every field was surrounded with a living fence of brush and lower vegetation so thick a man had trouble crawling through it. The access tracks leading to them had been zeroed in by the German machine gunners and mortar teams, extracting a heavy price for the advance of the American divisions.

Options for maneuver warfare were limited. Glenn had ordered a flanking attack by his company that resulted in quick and shattering losses before he could recall his troops. Desperately gathering two squads of riflemen around him, Glenn instructed them to maintain a steady volley of fire so that he could move closer to the German's machine gun stronghold and use a rocket launcher to knock it out. On the count of three, the supporting squads fired everything they had as rapidly as possible while Glenn sprinted across the open ground with his bazooka and a satchel of grenades.

He safely made it to an exposed knoll in the center of the field, where he fired three rounds from the bazooka, thereby destroying the gun emplacements. Seconds later, another German machine gun had opened fire on Glenn. He was hit by the volley but had managed to throw a couple of grenades, one with each hand, at the enemy positions. The chattering machine gun was silenced. Then, a mortar round had exploded right next to him, lifting him into the air and dropping him back on the ground. The men rushed to his inert body and set up a defensive perimeter around him while two medics loaded him on a stretcher and carried his bleeding body from the battlefield.

* * *

Glenn was brought back to the present when a Maine State Trooper from the scene of the accident suddenly entered his private room in the Portsmouth Hospital to assess his condition. It was not uncommon for Maine officers to use the New Hampshire facility. It was the closest and best equipped hospital for twenty-five miles and the Maine border towns used it regularly. Glenn asked the nurse standing beside the officer where he was.

"You're in the Portsmouth Hospital, sir" the nurse replied. "We're going to take care of you. You've had an automobile accident. Are you comfortable enough to answer a few questions for the policeman?"

By that time, sedatives had kicked in and the pain had subsided. "Yes," Glenn told her.

The officer pulled up a chair next to the bed so that Glenn could see him without moving his head. "I'm Corporal Rand of the Maine State Police, Mr. Hastings. You've had some bad luck, but it could have been worse. I know that you're uncomfortable and in pain, so I'll try to be brief."

"Go ahead, Corporal," Glenn said weakly.

"I called in your license plate numbers and have your name and address. I'll leave it with the hospital officials if you don't mind."

"It's fine with me."

"Can you tell me what happened?" Corporal Rand asked.

"There isn't much to tell," explained Glenn. "I noticed the car that hit me was swerving in and out of both lanes. I started to slow down and pulled to the right hand side of the road as far as I could when he struck me. I'm afraid I don't remember anything after that, Corporal."

"That's all right," the policeman assured him, writing in his notebook.

"Where's my car, officer?"

"I had it towed to a safe compound in Kittery. If there is anything from the car that you need I'd be glad to get it for you. The automobile is in pretty bad shape. I suspect that the frame is bent. The other driver was drunk out of his noggin. He's on his way to Alfred where he'll face a judge in the morning. Do you want to file any charges against him, Mister Hastings?"

Glenn considered the question a moment before replying. "No, I expect the judge will deal fairly with him without my adding to his problems."

"Very well," replied Corporal Rand. "I hope you recover quickly. I wish you well. Your records list you as an army veteran of the Second World War. I served in Korea and it's always a privilege to shake another veteran's hand."

"Thank you, Corporal," said Glenn, offering his right hand to the officer.

"I almost forgot, sir," Corporal Rand added. "I found this case in your automobile glove compartment." Corporal Rand placed a velvet case in Glenn's hand. "I took the liberty of opening it. Does it belong to you?"

"Yes, it's mine," answered Glenn. "It was awarded for actions in the hedgerows of Normandy."

"You've earned my respect, sir, and I salute you."

"Thanks again, Corporal Rand," Glenn said, fingering the soft velvet. He opened the case to make certain nothing had been disturbed. It was still there, his Medal of Honor!

Chapter Four

Doctors at the Portsmouth Hospital told Glenn they would like to keep him under observation for two or three days, in case something unforeseen developed. The broken ribs would most likely heal on their own without any assistance from them, provided he didn't twist or move his body excessively. They concluded that a plaster-of-Paris cast was unnecessary for his chest and instead, bound it securely with several layers of heavy bandages. The doctors insisted on placing Glenn's two fingers in a plaster cast. His body still hurt all over, but he requested that the staff refrain from giving him heavy doses of pain killers. He hated the way sedatives made him feel and preferred to endure the pain rather than take the strong drugs to reduce it. Over the years Glenn had developed a high tolerance to pain and was certain he could handle it with simple aspirin administered on a regular basis. The doctor agreed.

Even though the accident had been an ordeal, Glenn knew that he had been lucky to come through it without incurring more serious injuries. However, his faithful 1956 Studebaker Hawk would certainly be missed. He had purchased it in celebration of the first steps he had taken after the war without crutches or a cane. He had fallen in love with the automobile the first time he had seen it in a dealer's showroom. The car was coal black with a red interior, a supercharged 289 V/8 engine and an automatic transmission. Few cars on the road could keep up with it. It was a purchase in which he had indulged himself, and never regretted the decision.

How vividly Glenn recalled those times. His engineering company was growing steadily by then, and he had been working day and night for years building it into a successful consulting firm with a reputation for competence and integrity. He had built a railroad in Peru and Canada, and before he left Canada, his company had contracted for the design and construction of a plant to produce aluminum from the rich fields of bauxite ore in northern Canada. The company also undertook a project to design and construct new dockside facilities in Philadelphia capable of handling containerized goods packed in large steel boxes the size of trailer truck bodies. The system was revolutionizing the transportation and shipping industry and Glenn's firm was a pioneer in the growing field.

Success wasn't guaranteed, but Glenn was resolved to stick to a narrow area of specialties and worked hard to maintain a high level of excellence. The premise worked, and his company became a leader in design and engineering for the transportation and shipping industry on the eastern seaboard. Glenn had worked tirelessly to keep up with the new technology flooding the engineering world during those postwar years, and he aimed to develop the company to a point where he could manage it with a small staff. He took a personal interest in every project and remained intimately involved in day-to-day operations, enjoying a great sense of achievement as part of a team effort when each job was completed on budget and on time.

Whether he had realized it or not, at the time, Glenn now acknowledged that he had used the business as an escape from the tragedies of his personal life. His many accomplishments and financial successes had really meant very little to him. The thing he had wanted the most, and still yearned for, was a simple life filled with harmony and contentment. For a short time, he had found that ideal with Kathleen and her family. Their warmth and sincerity had left an impression that still moved him. But why had Kathleen stopped writing to him when he needed her the most? Why didn't she try to contact him by phone or some other means? Those two questions were still at the root of his inner torment, but Glenn knew, he could not blame Kathleen for everything. He, too, had contributed to the break between them, a distance that had grown like a cancer, until he could stand it no longer.

Glenn's condition had made it impossible for him to write or call anyone for several months. Later, after his condition had improved, he could and should have called or written to let Kathleen know what had happened to him. Instead, he had remained silent, and his regret over that choice still haunts him. It had been a difficult time and it was still hurtful to think about.

The injury to Glenn's jaw had required intense speech therapy. It was exhausting, and he had felt like a fool trying to sound out simple one-syllable words like "dog" and "cat." Underlying his weariness had been the terror that he might never be able to talk again. The shrapnel that had pierced his throat and splintered his jaw, had also destroyed some important vocal muscles. In addition, one metal fragment had lodged against his jugular vein, a thousandth of an inch deeper; and he would have died quickly on the battlefield from loss of blood before the medics found him.

He had been severely wounded, and was lucky to be alive. The Army surgeons had operated so many times that he had lost count. Reconstruction of his jaw had required the work of some of the finest surgeons in the Army. His only visible scar ran from his left cheek down his neck. Since the scar was more noticeable when he let his beard grow, Glenn had made a habit of keeping himself closely shaved and used ample amounts of shaving powder to help mask the darker color of the scarred skin. It did not bother him at first, but when he noticed people staring at it, he became self-conscious and was determined to keep awkward encounters to a minimum. He had developed the habit of turning that side of his face away from people he was talking to.

Any success he had had in learning to speak and walk normally, when all the experts had doubted it was possible, Glenn owed to a disciplined and indomitable physical therapist, Jessica Holt. He could still picture her clearly. She was a small-framed strawberry blonde with delicate facial features and an outgoing personality with more energy per pound than most people. She had never accepted excuses such as, "I can't," "It's too hard," or "It's impossible." In fact, Glenn doubted he would have walked again if it had not been for her. Jessica had taunted and coaxed him to supreme levels of effort and determination. She had a sharp tongue that frequently got under her patients' skin and made them mad. He could hear her now: "C'mon, Glenn, you can do better than that. If you want to be a cripple all your life go ahead and sit down, but if you've got the guts I thought you had, you'll give it more effort. It's up to you, it's no skin off my rear…"

Oh, how he had hated her then, Glenn remembered with a smile. Occasionally she had insulted him so much that he felt like striking her, just to shut her mouth. He had found her infuriating, but that had changed over time. Eventually, as he had come to know a softer, more caring person beneath the tough front Jessica presented to strangers, he had fallen deeply in love with her. Her vivacious and positive outlook had been contagious and Glenn's helpless physical state had made him vulnerable. He had looked upon her as his only hope for salvation and reached out to her in desperation, and she returned his affection.

By 1945, one year after being wounded, Glenn was able to talk again. At first it was awkward. As a result of constant practice and determination, he had actually been able to carry on a conversation without anyone detecting that he had been injured. Only Glenn himself, after hearing a recording of his speech, noted that he sounded his words a little more distinctly than he had before. As a younger man he had had a tendency to talk too fast and slur some of his words.

At that point, Glenn's doctors had undertaken a serious effort to determine the limitations of his legs. Jessica had been an important part of that team of evaluating experts. He had learned to get around in a wheelchair by then, but had begun experiencing difficulties holding down food and passing body waste. It took another year for the Army internal medicine specialists to get his body functions back on track. They had been baffled because Glenn never had any invasive wounds to the stomach or chest areas; eventually they attributed the digestive difficulties to emotional stress.

It didn't take long for Jessica to become an obsession with Glenn. Most of his improvements he had associated with her, and she had proudly flaunted him to others as her prize patient. In retrospect, Glenn saw that love had probably not been a factor in their relationship, but at that time, he had equated his gratitude and affection with love. They were married in 1946, a few days after he had taken his first step with his right leg without the aid of the workout bars. It felt like the greatest achievement of his life, and he would continue to build upon it.

After a simple wedding ceremony before a Justice of the Peace, Glenn and Jessica had moved to a small apartment near the therapy center, with easy access for Glenn in his wheelchair. He visited the center every day and worked himself to exhaustion. He and Jessica seemed happy together. Staff members and other patients had seen a softer, more patient Jessica who smiled more often. It wasn't long after their wedding that Jessica announced to Glenn that she was pregnant. She was not as happy about the news as Glenn, who was thrilled at the prospect of becoming a father.

A baby would bring stability to their lives and give them someone else to be concerned about. It had given Glenn an incentive to increase his efforts to walk so that he could get on with the important part of his life that had been missing since the war started — getting back to his engineering work. He had started developing designs and computing engineering criteria for a small number of projects passed on to him by some of his engineering professors at the university.

Jessica had never embraced the reality that she was going to have a baby. She continued to work at the center and had coaxed Glenn into an accelerated routine of leg therapy. His right leg had developed perfectly, but his left leg would always need added support, because a large portion of his leg below the left knee had been smashed into small pieces. He had undergone an operation to implant a metal rod in the knee to increase rigidity and hold the foot more securely. The operation was successful, but Glenn was never comfortable without an external brace from his knee to his ankle. The brace worked well and made him feel more secure. The doctors told him that it was a variation of the same braces worn by President Franklin Delano Roosevelt. His progress had been rapid.

Fundamental differences began to crop up between Glenn and Jessica after she became pregnant. He was ready and eager to start earning a living, and had been spending much less time at the therapy center. She was adamant that his therapy workouts should have top priority. Eventually they had compromised, and Glenn began going to the center every other day. On those days when he was not at the center, he had managed to establish his own engineering consulting firm in downtown Philadelphia. He had recognized early on that the business needed a second in command and had turned to an old friend and classmate, Bob Smart.

It had been a wise decision on Glenn's part. Bob had been an army combat engineer serving throughout the European campaign. He was a demonstrative small-framed man of enormous energy and a genius with figures and specifications. When he showed up at a job site the construction foremen had better know what they were doing and be able to articulate why they were doing it in a certain way, or there would be hell to pay. Bob Smart looked much younger than he was. Those who hoped to snooker him were chewed up and spit out by the red-headed, freckle-faced engineer. Bob developed a reputation as a bad-tempered redhead, but to those who knew him well, he was simply a soft-spoken gentle man with an intolerance for incompetence. He himself was always well-informed about the subject at hand and if there were some alternatives, he usually researched them in advance. Bob was a perfect complement to Glenn and they got along very well.

* * *

That first night in the Portsmouth Hospital, Glenn phoned Bob in Philadelphia to bring him up to date on Glenn's situation.

"What hospital are you in, Glenn?" asked Bob.

"I'm in the Portsmouth, New Hampshire Hospital, Bob. I had an accident with the Hawk and probably totaled it."

"Where are you injured?" Bob inquired with concern.

"I got banged up some. A couple of broken fingers and two cracked ribs. I was lucky but man, it hurts in my chest when I breathe," Glenn told his friend.

"I'll bet you didn't take much for clothing with you," Bob surmised.

"Just what I'm wearing," Glenn replied. "It was a spur of the moment excursion. All I've got with me is my shaving kit. My bags were shipped home."

"Listen, Glenn. You've got this crew so well trained and brained washed that they can run things for a few days without us. I'm going to New Hampshire as soon as I can get a flight to Manchester or Portland. Then, I'll rent a car and see for myself what kind of a predicament you've gotten yourself into."

"But, Bob..." Glenn protested.

"No buts about it, Glenn. I'm coming," Bob stated firmly. "I'll see you when I get there. In the meantime, make up a want list and I'll go shopping for you. Hell, you could use some new clothes anyway and that old Stude was on its last legs no matter how much you babied it. I'll see you soon, old buddy, listen to the nurses," demanded Bob Smart glibly.

"Okay, okay," answered Glenn with a smile. The blustering orders were typical of his best friend and right hand associate.

* * *

Later that same night, when the hospital corridors were quiet, Glenn lay on his hospital bed thinking about Jessica again. It had been such a bittersweet time in his life, and the memories were still sharp. Jessica was not well during much of her pregnancy. Her energy dwindled, and her usual positive outlook gave way to chronic complaining as the months dragged on. She blamed him for her increasingly awkward physical condition and they argued a lot. Jessica ceased to encourage him with his therapy exercises as her pregnancy progressed, and thought only of herself.

Jessica had called the company office to tell Glenn that she was in labor. Glenn nervously took the call and asked Bob to drive them to the hospital. He was still in a wheelchair and could not use his legs well enough to drive an automobile. Jessica's water broke before they arrived at the maternity ward and she was very uncomfortable. Her contractions were getting closer and closer together when they pulled into the emergency entrance. The nurse that met them was a friend of Jessica's and was able to calm her down as she was being wheeled into the delivery room. Jessica turned from the wheelchair to give Glenn a hopeful wave as she disappeared around the corner.

"It'll be okay, Glenn." Bob laid an encouraging hand on his shoulder. "I've been through this twice. The first is the worst believe me. If that's any comfort."

Glenn smiled wryly. "It's not much, but I'll take it. Thanks for coming along to help out. I was ready to call an ambulance."

"No trouble, Glenn," answered Bob, taking a seat next to his wheelchair in the waiting room. "Listen, I've been meaning to talk to you about Jessica and the new baby. If you two find it difficult, you're welcome to move in with Anne and me for a while until you settle in to the baby's schedule. Believe me, the baby will rule the household like a tyrant. My two girls would love to have another baby in the house and I know I speak for Anne too."

"I appreciate the thought, Bob. I really do, but I think we should gain the experience by ourselves. It's not fair to invade your lives, and I think Jessica will do better on her own. She's pretty strong-headed. But, I sure would welcome a helping hand from Anne for a few hours a day at the beginning. I know I'll be exhausted and Jessica will need to build up her strength."

Bob shook his head. "You've got it. She'll be happy to drop by. Good Lord, she may even get the idea that we should have another baby around our house. If that happens I'll blame it all on you, Buddy Boy."

"We'll just have to see," laughed Glenn. "How long does this usually take?"

"That depends," answered Bob, checking his watch. "Sometimes it can take all night. What do you say if we check out the coffee shop down the hall?"

"Sure, why not." Glenn was grateful for anything to divert his attention from Jessica's labor.

They drank coffee and puffed cigarettes for several hours in the smoke-filled coffee shop. Finally, about midnight, a doctor in a white coat entered the cafe and took a seat at the table across from Glenn.

"Mr. Hastings, I have some news for you," said the doctor in a calm and measured tone. He seemed to be searching for the right words. "Your wife has delivered twin boys..."

"Twins!" Glenn and Bob exclaimed. Their joy quickly turned to fear when they noted the distressed look on the doctor's face.

The doctor continued. "The boys are fine, but your wife started bleeding internally. We gave her a transfusion and were able to temporarily stabilize her, but she suffered a heart attack moments after delivery. I'm sorry, Mister Hastings - your wife is dead."

Chapter Five

When Glenn heard about Jessica's death, he gathered his head in his arms on the table. Tortured sobs wracked his frame, as Bob tried in vain to comfort him. What was he going to do without Jessica and two new babies in need of a mother's care? While Glenn was venting his grief, Bob Smart had quickly reviewed what was ahead for his friend and came to the inevitable conclusion that, for the immediate future, Glenn and the twin boys should move in with him and Anne. The Smart's small house in the suburbs of Philadelphia was well suited for his wheelchair. All that had to be done was to build a short ramp on his porch, a project Bob had been intending to complete anyway.

Bob and Anne had been high school and college sweethearts, and had married immediately upon graduating from college. Bob had taken a job with the City of Philadelphia in its engineering department, but after Pearl Harbor, he had quit to join the Army. Their two children were four and two years old when Glenn and the twins moved in with them. The Smart household adjusted well. At first it was hectic for everybody, but once a routine had been worked out and the newness had worn off, life at the Smart household continued at an energetic pace. It didn't take Glenn long to figure out a system whereby he could serve as the twin's main caretaker and still maintain a high level of input at the business. He hired a nanny to come to his apartment while he was at work, and Anne and other friends volunteered to help out those times that the nanny could not be available or was ill. The system had worked out well for everybody, and allowed Glenn time to continue with his rehabilitation program.

* * *

The day after Glenn was admitted to the Portsmouth Hospital, Bob Smart entered his room unannounced.

"Well, it looks as if you've survived your ordeal," said Bob, glad to see his friend.

"Bob," exclaimed Glenn, happy to see a familiar face. "Actually, I'm doing quite well considering."

"I called the police station to find out where your Studebaker was and ran out to take a look at it. I'm afraid your estimate is correct, it's a total basket case. The frame is severely wracked."

"I'm not surprised," Glenn replied. "I haven't heard back from the insurance company yet. I called them this morning when I first woke up."

"What are you going to do for an automobile? Rent one?"

"I'm not sure, Bob," answered Glenn absently. "I suppose I should return with you..."

"Have you resolved anything on this trip, Glenn?" he asked. He knew all about Glenn's affair with Kathleen Cohen and he had always known that at some time or another, Glenn would return to the State of Maine. "I don't want to put words in your mouth or tell you what to do, but at some point you've got to stop looking backwards and reach out for tomorrow, which may hold more for you than you imagine."

Glenn sighed. "God, I've thought about it so often. A part of me understands that what you suggest is sound advice. But, I just can't turn those memories off, Bob. They're too strong to ignore." Glenn had that detached look that Bob knew all too well — as if he was thinking of something he refused to divulge.

Bob grasped his hand. "Listen, Glenn, we go back too far not to be honest with each other. You don't owe me an explanation and I'm certainly not wise enough to tell you what to do. I'm just concerned for your well-being, old buddy."

Glenn smiled warmly. "I know that, and I value your friendship more than I've ever been able to express. It's just that this accident has complicated things for me."

"What did you really expect to discover on this trip, Glenn?" Bob pulled a chair next to the bed. He had always been a good listener.

"You're asking me to describe my feelings, which is impossible," Glenn replied. "The simple answer is that I have a strong desire to physically and emotionally revisit a part of my life that held more joy and contentment than anything I'd ever known before or since."

"We can't ever go back to yesterday, Glenn," Bob cautioned his friend. "We can revisit the memories in our hearts but they don't exist in the real world. I'm concerned that you're tormenting yourself needlessly over what doesn't exist. It was over twenty-five years ago and everything and everyone has changed, including you and me."

"I know that what I'm hoping and praying for is illusive and irrational, but something inside of me is driving me to get to the root of my feelings. I can't explain it any better than that, Bob. If I were to return with you it would only be a short time before I would have to make the trip again. So, I feel compelled to stay here until I find the courage to face the source of my feelings. Of course, that means facing Kathleen Cohen or whatever her name is now. She holds the key to my future."

"Have you considered that she must have a different life now and may not want to see you?"

Glenn hesitated a moment and continued, "Yes, I think of nothing else. I know these feelings are selfish and self-serving on my part, and I've tried to suppress them, but I can't help what I feel..."

"Then it's settled," said Bob, considering Glenn's words. He rose to his feet and began pacing back and forth beside the bed. "I'll set you up with a rental car for now. If you decide to purchase a new one, that'll at least give you mobility to do so.

Prices here in New England aren't much different than prices back home in Philly, so you decide on what is best for you. I'll also buy you some new clothes and bring them to the hospital." Bob stopped pacing and asked Glenn. "Do you want me to stick around or would you prefer to handle this thing in your own way?"

"I appreciate your coming, Bob, I really do, but I've got to finish what I've started on my own. I'll be fine, just be patient with me, okay?"

Bob had expected Glenn's response. "It's your life Glenn, and I understand your need to do it alone. I guess I'd feel the same way. That being the situation, I'll just take care of your shopping for you and return to Philly later this evening if I can get a flight, provided you promise to keep in touch with me or the office. You've got a lot of good people that care for you."

"You're right, Bob," said Glenn sincerely. "I'm a lucky man in many ways. Thanks for being there whenever I needed a lift. I don't know what I would have done if it hadn't been for you and Anne after Jessica…"

"You would have managed, old friend," Bob stated with certainty. "All right then, I'll see you later. I have a feeling you're going to be surprised at the colorful clothing I select for you. You need something bright to jazz up your life." Bob chuckled on his way out the door.

"Keep it conservative," Glenn called, having second thoughts about giving Bob free rein in selecting his clothing.

Shortly after Bob left the hospital, Glenn was dozing off when the phone beside his bed woke him.

"Hello," he said, uncertain as to who could be calling.

"Hello, Dad, this is Melvin. I'm so glad I reached you. I've been worried about you. Uncle Bob called and left a message for me here at Fort Bragg. I was out in the field on training exercises and just received it. How are you?"

47

"It's nice to hear your voice, Son," Glenn replied. "I'm fine, the accident could have been much worse. In a couple of days I'll be back as fit as ever. I would have let you know but I didn't want to worry you. I know how busy a young platoon leader can be."

"I'm never too busy for you. When are you getting out of the hospital, Dad?" Melvin asked.

"Probably tomorrow, if all goes well. They just want to keep me under observation for a few more hours, that's all. Tell me, Son, how do you like being attached to an active regiment?"

"I'm thrilled to be with troops. As you know, Dad, it's where I always wanted to be. We're still in a staging area at Fort Bragg and we're accepting men and equipment at an accelerated rate."

"How long before the regiment is up to its full table of organization status?"

"A few weeks at most," Melvin answered. "By the way, Dad, I've got a free weekend coming to me, and a friend of mine in the Air Force invited me to join him in a flight to log some flying time this weekend. We could fly to Pease Air Base in Portsmouth."

"I can't think of anything in the world I'd rather do than be with you, Son. If I'm not here at the Portsmouth Hospital, then I'll be at the Snug Harbor Inn at York Harbor, Maine, less than ten miles from Portsmouth. I don't expect to be doing much except resting up for a few days."

"Then it's decided," Melvin announced. "I'll see you when I get there, Dad. Rest well."

"I promise, Melvin. Thanks for calling."

Glenn replaced the phone on the receiver and laid back against his pillow, wondering what Melvin was going through at the large Army training center. The greatest achievement of his life were his two sons, Melvin Allen and Marvin Alfred. They were identical twins in looks and mannerisms, but they were opposites in temperament and personalities. Glenn frequently mistook the boys if they were dressed similarly. Throughout their childhood they were competitive with each other, but they were always quick to lend support when outside interference threatened either of them. Throughout their lives, they were comfortable when they were together and uneasy when they were separated for any extended period of time.

* * *

Glenn and the twins lived with Bob and Anne for four months after they were born. He would not have been able to do anything with his business if it had not been for the generosity and graciousness of Bob's wife, Anne. Energetic, small of frame, Anne had the instincts of a mother hen, and she won everyone's heart in no time. A bond that has stood the test of time was established during that period. However, Glenn was too independent to be comfortable imposing on his good friends, so he and the twins moved into the roomy apartment he and Jessica had shared.

The twins grew up under the watchful eye of Amanda Grimshaw, the elderly lady next door whom he had hired as the boy's nanny. She was a short, matronly looking lady with white hair neatly pulled behind her head into a tight knot. The boys could not pronounce her last name so they called her Mrs. Grim. She did not have any children and was glad to take the nanny job Glenn offered to her. While she was not destitute, money had always been scarce since her husband had been killed in the war. She had a gruff, no-nonsense manner about her, but beneath that thin shield was a warm caring person who was thankful to fill her lonely days taking care of the twins. She cared for the boys and Glenn as if they were her own, and they in turn loved and admired her as if she were a revered grandmother.

Generally, Mrs. Grimshaw would come by the apartment before Glenn left for work in the morning. Though she was devoted to the boys and Glenn, he made a point of never abusing her generous nature. He understood and appreciated

49

that Mrs. Grim was no longer a young woman and that she was entitled to have a life of her own without being saddled with the continuous care of small children. Frequently Glenn adjusted his schedule at the office in order to return home early in the afternoon to relieve Mrs. Grim. Fortunately, he was able to do a lot of his work in his small study at the apartment.

The first ten years had flown so quickly. Glenn's business had prospered from his intense attention. Rarely did he take any time off except to be with the twins. His life was balanced between work and his two sons. Both had needed him, and for years he had given little thought to his own personal needs. Looking back, Glenn realized that his life since the end of the war had been one of denial of the past. He had considered that, but only in terms of how it would affect the welfare and education of the twins.

As time went on, Glenn's business had provided them with the financial resources to purchase those extra things that made their life more enjoyable and rewarding. He had also set up a trust fund for Mrs. Grim to draw on, and told her to use it at will. The only concession he made for himself was the purchase of the 1956 Studebaker Hawk.

Bob Smart was always suggesting that Glenn purchase a house where they could be more comfortable and have more space. Glenn consistently refused to follow the advice. He agreed with the reasons Bob advanced for owning a house, but deep inside, he realized that a home would only highlight the fact that he and the boys were alone. He had reflected grimly that a house without a mother or wife was only a house, not a home.

Over the years, Glenn had had a number of opportunities to date and be with women whose company he enjoyed. Some even became close friends, yet he had never allowed them to pierce the veneer of privacy in which he had wrapped himself protectively, to maintain something he wasn't able to define. Some women had tried to become an integral part of his life; whenever he had felt his inner isolation threatened, he had simply walked away from the relationship without a word of explanation. If he had faced reality with the same integrity that guided his conduct with others, he would have come face to face with a simple truth: though he had mourned Jessica's passing, it was Kathleen Cohen who had filled his heart to capacity with love. Time had never diminished his yearning for her.

Melvin and Marvin had grown into responsible young men with a strong sense of the same values by which their father lived. As children, they frequently had accompanied Glenn to the office during summer vacations and holidays. When they had turned twelve, he had made them responsible for all of the janitorial services in the office complex until they graduated from high school. They had worked diligently and maintained the area with a high level of excellence. The boys had also developed a large newspaper delivery route in their section of town, sharing the same entrepreneurial spirit as their father. Glenn was not only a caring father, he was their friend and buddy as well. Their devotion to him was one of his greatest joys, and he was supremely proud of them.

Glenn had always planned to send the boys to a college of their choice. However, he had also encouraged them to think for themselves. Glenn distinctly remembered the day that Marvin had told him he wanted to join one of the armed services after high school graduation. He was alone in the apartment when a large manila envelope was delivered. It was from the Coast Guard and addressed to Marvin. Glenn had watched Marvin as he walked down the sidewalk from school that afternoon, tall and slender with an easy going manner about him. Both boys were as tall as Glenn, and both looked a lot like him, especially at a distance.

"Hi, Dad," Marvin had greeted him.

"You've got some mail today, Son," Glenn said from the large kitchen table. "Looks like something from the Coast Guard."

Marvin rushed to the refrigerator to get a cold glass of milk and answered him. "I expected something from them. All of the service recruiters visited the school to tell us about the advantages of their services. Boy, I'm starved." He quickly made himself a peanut butter and jelly sandwich, then sat down at the table across from his father.

"What do you think about the Coast Guard, Dad?"

"I think they're a fine organization that has served this country with honor and distinction for over two centuries."

"I was hoping you'd see it the way I do. The Coast Guard recruiter that came to our school was great. He didn't get all cocky or puffed up, but you could tell he was proud to be part of the small force. There was something more down to earth and kind of warmer about him than the other recruiters. That appealed to me."

"Well, they've got a long tradition of saving lives at sea under all kinds of conditions, and I'm sure that's reflected in the way they take pride in their service to our country. Their traditions are noble ones and they train hard to maintain a high standard of excellence. If you've made up your mind that one of the military services is right for you after high school, the Coast Guard is a fine choice, and I'll support your decision."

"They really impressed me. Thanks, Dad, I knew I could depend on you," answered Marvin, pouring himself another glass of milk.

"Are you sure you've explored other alternatives as thoroughly as you've checked out the Coast Guard?"

Marvin nodded vehemently. "Oh yes, I'm just not ready for college. Maybe Mel is, but I'm not. The Coast Guard station down at the port is such a lively place and the cutters are works of art," Marvin explained excitedly, referring to the sleek Coast Guard ships.

"I agree," Glenn had said. "In fact, I remember when our convoy enroute to North Africa was escorted and supported by several cutters. They were like charging mustangs the way they rode herd on our slow ponderous troop ships. Whenever we were threatened by German submarines, the cutters nimbly inserted themselves between us and the most likely direction that the German torpedoes would be launched. I can tell you, we never forgot that act of courage and loyalty. Yes, no question about it, I have some deep-seated reasons for admiring the Coast Guard."

"Tomorrow I'll bring home the applications, and we can plan on my joining up when we graduate this spring," concluded Marvin proudly.

Glenn fervently believed that any of the services would be a good place for an adolescent to grow into manhood if that was what he chose. He remembered, with pride, the men in his company during World War II. They were no older than his two sons when they were a part of the team that successfully forced two of the most militaristic nations the world has ever known to surrender on the field of battle. He had every right to be proud of them.

Marvin joined the Coast Guard that spring. Glenn attended his boot camp graduation ceremony at Cape May, New Jersey. He was bursting with pride as he watched his son raise his hand to take the oath of allegiance to defend his country. His young son Marvin was fast on his way to becoming a man. That spring had been a time of pride in past accomplishments, as well as a time of sadness that an innocent era of Marvin's life had passed and would never be the same. It was also a time of apprehension and worry for Glenn, who was all too aware of the potential for disaster.

* * *

Glenn rested in his hospital bed at Portsmouth, recalling the last time he had seen Marvin. It was 1968, four years after his enlistment in the Coast Guard. Marvin had just earned his promotion to chief petty officer, the highest rank an enlisted man can attain. Twenty-two years old with four years experience, Chief Marvin Hastings was no longer a carefree adolescent, but a seasoned veteran of the war in Vietnam. After the war had started, the Coast Guard was attached to the Navy where Coasties brought their wealth of knowledge and skills of seamanship to bear in the shallow waters off the Indonesian coast, and in the multitude of rivers surrounded with fetid jungles where the enemy could hide indefinitely. The Coast Guard's shallow draft vessels were the only viable mode of transportation for the vast areas of swampy slow moving waterways.

Marvin had served on an eighty-foot Coast Guard Cutter heavily armed with machine gun mounts with attached eighty-one mm mortars beneath them. The mounts were capable of awesome rates of fire that could destroy any craft in just a few seconds of sustained fire. The cutters were stationed up and down the length of the Vietnam coast.

Marvin had returned home on leave from Vietnam a changed man. Gone forever was the easygoing young man ready to embrace the world. Instead, he was a combat-seasoned veteran, matured beyond his twenty-two years. Combat left its mark on every participant, and it endured for a lifetime.

Melvin came home from the University of Pennsylvania immediately upon Marvin's arrival. The two boys had had a lot to catch up on. They took time for a couple of movies and visited with old friends. Marvin had wanted to pack his leave time with as much activity as possible.

There was a sober restlessness about Marvin that Melvin could not understand, but Glenn knew. It was a difficult thing to describe to those who have never been baptized to combat. So Glenn never tried to enlighten Melvin. The memory of that last day, just before Marvin jumped aboard a train bound for the large Coast Guard base at Portsmouth, Virginia, was indelibly engraved on Glenn's soul.

It had been a balmy day with a soft drizzle. Melvin and Marvin had chatted incessantly all the way to the station. Glenn listened to their banter savoring every word. He had always hated good-byes, and lately, he had been suffering from sleepless nights and vague premonitions of tragedy. Glenn could still visualize Marvin standing on the station platform, proud and handsome in his chief's uniform, trying to act indifferent and relaxed as he made his farewells.

"You know, Mel," Marvin had said quietly, embracing Melvin. "I want you to know that I could never ask for a better brother than you've been to me. If you weren't my brother, I would have been proud to call you my friend. Study hard and take care of Dad."

"You take care of yourself, Marv," Melvin replied, his eyes glittering with tears. "I promise I'll write often." The twin boys silently embraced again. Marvin gave Melvin a hard squeeze, then turned to Glenn.

"As for you, Dad, I've always been proud to call you my father. Hopefully this mess in Vietnam will be cleaned up before too long, and I'll have a chance to be a part of the team that does the job. So don't worry about me okay? I've got a job that I've been trained to do and the quicker we get it done, the sooner we'll all be able to come home and get on with our lives. You know, before this, I never fully appreciated the sacrifice you made in the war. Now that I've had a taste of what it was really like, my respect for your silent courage has only grown."

Glenn had hugged his son tightly. "If I had my choice, Marvin, I'd give anything to prevent you from going back. But I understand how you feel. We're proud of you, Son. May God watch over you and safely bring you back to the ones who love you," he had whispered, unable to contain the tears that had flushed his burning eyes.

Without another word, Marvin had jumped on the train, taking a seat near a window where he waved good-bye until his father and brother were out of sight.

Two months later, Glenn was sitting in the study of his apartment when the doorbell rang. He opened the door and was greeted by a Captain in the Coast Guard.

"Mr. Hastings, I'm Captain Homer Olmstead. May I come in, Sir?"

"Yes of course," Glenn had answered in a wavering voice.

"I have the unfortunate duty to inform you, Sir, that your son, Chief Petty Officer Marvin A. Hastings, was killed in action against a superior enemy force."

Chapter Six

Glenn had immediately lapsed into a state of shock. His son was dead! Captain Olmstead continued speaking. Glenn listened to his words, barely comprehending their significance.

"Your son was piloting a small river craft on a routine patrol when the ship was taken under fire from heavy shore batteries of the Viet Cong. Your son and the three members of his crew were killed instantly. We were unable to retrieve any portions of their bodies. I was a witness to the strike and I can assure you that the end was quick and complete, if that's any comfort to you."

Glenn simply stared at the young captain. He had known that this day would come; a ghostly premonition had been haunting his soul for weeks. There was no way he could lessen the pain that accompanied the notification of Marvin's death. The fact that his body was never recovered added a surreal and inhuman element that was impossible to accept.

A part of Glenn died that day. The change was complete and instant. He ceased to be the same man that had taken ideas and built them into a prestigious engineering firm with projects all over the globe. The business simply ceased to be a driving force that filled his days with intense activity. Marvin was gone forever, as if he had never even existed other than in his father's heart. Melvin had recently graduated from college with a degree in civil engineering and military science and joined the Army. He had been promoted to the rank of first lieutenant. Glenn was proud of Melvin's accomplishments, but the war in Vietnam still continued, and the troubling possibility that Melvin might be sent there was a regularly recurring nightmare. Still he recognized that his only son had his own life to live, and that fact positioned Glenn right back where he had been before the twins were born — alone.

During those torturous weeks after Marvin's death, Glenn had been so distraught and withdrawn that Bob Smart feared for Glenn's mental welfare. Life had dealt Glenn blow after blow without relief, and he simply retreated into himself to the point where he would sit for hours staring at the walls or empty space without moving a muscle. Whenever Bob or Anne stopped by, they found Glenn incapable of carrying on a conversation. On several occasions, Bob had tried to obtain some input about important company-related decisions, but Glenn remained unresponsive.

In his heart, Glenn had been asking a God whom he had embraced all his life, why he was being punished. His faith in a loving God was fading rapidly — all he could see was the work of a vindictive God, and he wanted no part of Him. His faith failed to sustain him at his hour of greatest need, causing him to sink ever deeper into darkness and despair.

Bob Smart stopped by the apartment one morning prepared for a sink or swim showdown. Either Glenn started to take better control of himself, or Bob would have him taken to a hospital where he could be properly cared for. Walking through the kitchen door, Bob recognized that this confrontation was going to be the supreme test of their friendship, and he was ready to risk it for Glenn's sake. Bob had found the house in an advanced and uncharacteristic state of disarray. Glenn, sitting at a table in the kitchen, was in a more disheveled state than ever. His hair hung sloppily down over his ears badly in need of trimming, and his beard was grotesque. He hadn't shaved for several weeks. The person who stared blankly at Bob was not the same man who had the guts to defy medical science by learning to walk and talk, and whose courage had earned his country's highest and most respected award for valor — the Medal of Honor.

"Well, old Buddy Boy," Bob began insultingly, feeling sick about what he was doing. "I see you haven't shaved yet and I bet you pissed your pants, too. I could smell it before I opened the door, but don't let that bother you. There's no sense in getting yourself cleaned up, you'll just soil yourself all over again." Bob watched Glenn closely for some response. There was none and Bob had to force himself to continue.

"You know, the person I once knew, and respected would never have let himself sink to the level of this stinking shell of a man who has jumped off the deep end and exited from the human race. He had more guts than that, but, then again, you're no longer the man you used to be, so why should we care what happens to you?" Still no response from Glenn. Bob desperately grasped Glenn by the shoulders and shook him. "Listen to me. Don't you think this has gone on long enough? Don't you think Marvin is watching in disgust at what you've become? You're not hurting anyone except yourself and a lot of people who depend on you. Are you going to crap out on them too? Are you going to continue wallowing in your own filth feeling sorry for yourself?"

At that point, Glenn stood up from the table, wrenching his shoulders free of Bob's grip, kicking the chair out from under him. The torment and agony in Glenn's bloodshot eyes, sickened Bob. "Who made you God?" screamed Glenn, swinging his right fist at his friend. Bob easily dodged the blow and stood his ground facing Glenn, eyeball to eyeball.

"Who are you to come in here and mouth off to me?" Glenn demanded. Then he flung himself at Bob with fists flailing and a menacing look on his face.

"Go ahead, Glenn," Bob retorted. "If it makes you feel better. Go on, take another swing at me, I won't stop you this time."

Glenn froze at the words. A painful realization of what he was doing became clear, and he wrapped his arms around his friend, clinging to Bob. Cries of torment echoed from his very

59

soul. Bob supported him and held him tightly, and for a long time the two men clung to each other. Glenn's body writhed with uncontrollable anguish. Slowly the fury within his soul was vented. The catharsis had left him weak and dripping with sweat.

Bob guided him to the couch in the living room and gently positioned him so that he could rest comfortably. Biting his tongue, Bob reluctantly left Glenn to his own thoughts. Some journeys, Bob knew, could only be made alone, and he prayed that his friend could muster the strength to complete the pilgrimage.

Early the next morning, before the regular staff started work, Bob Smart quietly unlocked the door of the engineering office to work up a set of figures for a proposed project. He liked to work alone and generally managed to accomplish more in an hour at that time in the morning than he did all afternoon when the place was filled with people. To his surprise, Bob noticed that the door to Glenn's office was open and a light was showing on his desk. He peeked in to see Glenn bent over the desk, checking a set of plans for a bridge over the Delaware River. He noted that Glenn's hair was well-trimmed and he was clean-shaven, and wore neatly pressed brown pants and shirt.

Bob experienced a sharp sense of joy and relief. "Nice to see you at your desk, Glenn," he remarked cautiously, not sure of the reception he would receive.

Glenn turned towards the doorway. "It's nice to be back," he replied soberly. He had lost some weight, and his eyes were shrunken and set more deeply in their sockets, but Bob also noted a glimmer of that old determination and persistence that had served Glenn so well in the past.

"I've decided to join the human race again," Glenn continued. "You were in pretty good form yesterday." Bob figured that he was in for it now. "There's just one thing I want to say about that episode, and then we'll never mention it again.

If you ever, I repeat ever, tell anyone that I pissed my pants, I'll never speak to you again. Understood?"

"Understood," Bob had answered quickly.

* * *

Bob had kept his word. Now, from the perspective of his bed in the Portsmouth Hospital, Glenn couldn't help smiling about the incident. It had been a turning point in his life and had deepened his relationship with Bob. Glenn was gazing at the setting sun when Bob entered the room all smiles.

"Boy, are you going to love my selections, Glenn!"

"I hope you won't embarrass me," Glenn warned him. He knew from experience that when Bob Smart smiled he was being devious and mischievous. He had a puckish sense of humor and it wouldn't have been above him to purchase something outrageous like an orange suit with purple pin stripes. But to Glenn's relief, Bob laid out on the bed a very respectable set of casual pants and shirts and an assortment of socks and underwear.

He grinned at Glenn. "I was tempted, you know, but I was afraid you'd disown me if I picked out what I really liked. Instead of carrying the stuff around in a paper bag, I also bought you a small suitcase. That old one you've been using for years has seen better days, so you needed one anyway." Bob pulled a set of keys from his pocket and added, "Oh, I almost forgot. Here are the keys to a car I rented for you. It's a green Jeep Wagoneer parked close to the building in the hospital parking lot. At least you'll have wheels when they let you out."

"Thanks, Bob," said Glenn, touched by his friend's thoughtfulness. "I'll settle with you when I get back to Philly. By the way, Melvin called and sends his love. He's hitching a ride in tonight with an old classmate in a fighter plane. They plan to land at Pease Air Base in Portsmouth. It'll be nice to see him. I've seen him only once since Marvin's death."

"That's fabulous. A visit from Melvin is just what you need." Bob paused a moment. "Since you'll have company, I'm going to return home tonight. You'll be in good hands with Mel. Tell him his Uncle Bob loves him and wishes him well. If I can do anything else for you, just give me a holler."

"You've done enough, my friend," Glenn said seriously. "Sometimes I feel guilty thinking of what a terrible burden I've been to you and Anne. I didn't plan for things to happen that way, but they did. My life seems to be traveling a roadway full of obstacles. I want you to know how much I appreciate your loyalty and friendship."

"I know you do, Glenn" Bob replied. "That's what friends are for, and it's been a privilege to call you one. In fact, over the years I've sometimes felt guilty about the easy life Anne and I have had together compared to what you've been saddled with. You've had a steady stream of crises and setbacks that would have gotten anybody down. I hope you find whatever it is you're searching for, Glenn. Rest assured that all of us are betting on your success. Don't worry about the business, we'll keep it running until you're ready to return and take over the reins again. There are a lot of things in life more important than money or business. Actually, this trip you're taking back to yesterday may be the most courageous thing you've ever undertaken. I wish you luck in your search, old friend."

Glenn smiled warmly. "Thanks, Bob. I really am grateful for your support."

"Be sure to give my love to Mel when he comes. Anne and I will continue to write as often as we can. So long for now," said Bob, squeezing Glenn's left hand.

With some misgivings, Glenn watched him leave. Bob had a gift for bringing a breath of fresh air to any situation. His endless energy and optimism were contagious. Glenn smiled at the assortment of clothes beside the bed and was thankful again for his friendship.

It had been a busy day and Glenn was tired. His chest hurt every time he took a breath. Though he hated to be idle, he had to admit it felt good to rest quietly. That evening a nurse entered his room with the contents of his jacket and pants that had been cut off him in the emergency room. She placed them in the drawer of the stand beside the bed. He checked to see that nothing was missing. The first thing he noticed was an old well-worn letter from Kathleen. He carefully removed the letter from the envelope and read it one more time. He could recite it word for word, but he derived pleasure from viewing the words Kathleen had written in her flowing artistic penmanship:

June 6, 1944

My Dearest Glenn,

The radio and newspapers are full of accounts of the Normandy invasion of France. I shudder at the magnitude of the battles taking place. I know that your regiment is part of the initial landing force and I pray that God will watch over you and keep you safe. I will never be able to sleep comfortably or truly enjoy my life until I know that you are safe. I can't wait till you're back home and we can pick up our lives again.

I think often of all the wonderful times we've had together. Remember how you were a little shy at first with my mother and father? But you soon won them over completely, dearest Glenn. Dad speaks often of the day that you two went out to pull lobster traps. As a matter of fact, he's already hung an official tea cup with your name on it on the board in the fish shack. Dad must have told you about the fishermen's tea-drinking tradition which means a great deal to them.

Not much happens in this small town that is newsworthy. We've got a couple more weeks of school before the summer vacation. I plan to take a refresher course in teaching remedial reading this summer in Portland to maintain my certification. I'll have to live at the school while it's in session. It would be impossible to get the gasoline for the commute. But I'll still be able to get your letters and, of course, I'll always write. My days are not complete until I've shared some time with you.

We were informed yesterday that my brother Philip has been wounded. We don't know all of the facts yet, but the Coast Guard informed us that his ship was hit by a torpedo or a mine while escorting a convoy of freighters to Murmansk, Russia. The last we heard he was in a hospital in Greenland or in Iceland. The fact that he's in a hospital and out of harm's way gives us some comfort. Isn't that a selfish sentiment? I'm ashamed to admit it, but it's true nevertheless. We'll be even more relieved when the guns are silent and all of you men are safe back home. The safest place for you is in my arms, but until that time comes, my love, I will hold you in my heart and pray for you.

I'll say goodnight now, my dear Glenn, and send my love across the sea to you. There's a beautiful moon out tonight. I hope it's shining on you too, wherever you are. Come back to me soon, for I need you so very much.

All my love,
Kathleen.

Even though he had read it countless times, the letter never failed to send emotional spikes throughout Glenn's body. Lying on his hospital bed he remembered how it had been with them. A day never passed that he did not think of her. After all the years, his feelings for her now were as strong as that day he had said good-bye in 1942.

* * *

He found it easy and comforting to escape to that happier time of his life twenty-five years before.

One day after his first visit to the Cohen residence for supper, Glenn was returning from a joint patrol with the Coast

Guard on the York River when he spotted Kathleen at the far end of Sewall Bridge beside the road with her father's pickup truck. The truck was pulled off the road next to the river with a flat tire. Glenn pulled his Jeep in front of the truck. Kathleen was struggling to change the tire.

"Hello, Miss Cohen," said Glenn pleased to see her again. "Can I give you a hand?"

"Hello, Lieutenant," Kathleen greeted him cheerfully. "You certainly can. I can't budge the wheel bolts with the wrench. My father must have set them, and he's a lot stronger than I am. Maybe you'll have better luck."

"Here let me have the wrench," said Glenn, making sure that the truck's wheels were blocked and that the jack was secure on solid footing. Then he took the four-sided wrench and braced himself. It took every ounce of his strength to loosen the six wheel lug bolts. "You're right," he said. "Your father set them tight. I'll put your spare tire on and have you back on the road in no time. Where were you headed?"

"I'm on my way back to the dock after delivering a load of lobsters to a wholesaler at York Harbor. Dad is still at sea checking the traps. I'm sure glad you came along."

"Soldiers always rescue damsels in distress," Glenn laughed in that easy-going way he had of doing things.

She grinned at him in return. "I try to help Dad when I can. There's so much work to be done with so few hands that it's difficult, but we don't complain. It's frustrating to find tires for the vehicles. Dad bought these tires from an old truck that had been scrapped, but the new ones aren't much better than the originals. Dad keeps patching and repairing them to get by." She fell silent as Glenn tightened the last bolt.

Glenn had straightened and smiled at her. "May I see you again, Kathleen?"

"I'd like that. I'm free most any evening. We could go to a movie."

"That sounds great. I'll call you beforehand." Glenn removed the jack and placed it in the rear of the truck bed. "Say 'hi' to your Dad for me. I'll see you on the first evening I can get off."

"I'll look forward to it," she had answered softly.

* * *

Glenn's reflections were interrupted by a nurse making her final rounds before the evening shift changes. "Would you like me to move your TV so that you can see it better, Mr. Hastings?" asked the young nurse.

"No thanks, nurse. I don't care to watch it tonight."

"I expect the doctor will release you tomorrow," the nurse told him. "He left instructions for your medication, and if you need relief from the pain he authorized morphine. Is there anything else I can get for you?"

Glenn shook his head. "As long as the pain remains the way it is now I can handle it without stronger medication. A couple of aspirin would be adequate. I'm more tired than hurt."

"That's natural, Sir. I'll be right back." The nurse returned with aspirin and a glass of water, and helped him raise his head to drink. "I hope you sleep comfortably, Sir. Is there anything we can do about your brace?" she added hesitantly.

"No, it's fine. It's a souvenir from the war and I wear it all the time, night and day, like I would a pair of socks. Sometimes it itches and irritates my skin, but it has become a part of my body now. Thanks for asking though."

"My father was killed in the battle for Bastogne," said the nurse. "If he had lived, he'd be about your age…"

Glenn listened knowingly. "A lot of fine men, the best this great nation could produce, never came home. You must be proud of him. Keep his memory alive so that your children will be able to appreciate what was given up and sacrificed for them. We must never forget that freedom has a price, and it was purchased by courageous soldiers like your father in a land far from our shores."

The nurse smiled sadly back at him. "Goodnight, Mr. Hastings. You'll probably be gone when I come on duty tomorrow. I wish you well."

"Thank you, young lady. Your father would have been proud of you."

Glenn watched the evening shadows lengthen. The lights from the Portsmouth Naval Ship Yard lit up the sky in sharp contrast to the days he remembered during the war. At that time, along the coastal communities, lights were not allowed anywhere outside. Interior lights could only be used if the windows were covered with shades. People were cautioned not to open outside doors from rooms that were illuminated, and they soon developed the habit of turning off all lights before opening the doors.

The purpose of the ban on lights was to deny German U-Boats, lurking off the shore, any reference points to aid them in navigating the coast. Headlamps and taillights on cars and trucks had to have the top half of the illuminated lens shaded with black paint or covered with black friction tape.

Glenn dozed off to sleep with his head full of memories of the war years. Even though some of the memories were filled with terror and misery, it was still collectively the time to which he felt most connected. Visions of Kathleen laughing the way she often did brought a sense of peace and warmth to his heart. Sometime during the night, he had a dream so real that he broke into a sweat and awoke excitedly. In the darkness of the room, he imagined that he saw Kathleen bending over him, gazing intently into his face as if she wanted to say something. He could hear her breathing, she was that close to him. The apparition was so vivid that he reached out to touch her and called her name — "Kathleen, is that you?"

Chapter Seven

Very early that next morning, Lieutenant Melvin Hastings was a passenger in an Air Force jet fighter plane landing at Pease Air Force Base. As soon as he landed, security personnel ushered him to the main gate in a Jeep, where he grabbed a taxicab to the Portsmouth Hospital. Melvin wondered if the hospital would allow him to meet with his father at such an early time in the morning. Within a few minutes, he was inquiring at the main entrance desk.

"I've just arrived in Portsmouth. I know it's earlier than your normal visiting hours, but would it be possible for me to see my father, Mr. Glenn Hastings?" Melvin asked. "I believe he was admitted two days ago when he had an auto accident.

"Just a moment, Lieutenant Hastings," answered the nurse, thumbing through an index file. "Oh yes, Mr. Hastings is in room 412. It would be awkward for you to go up there now. The nurses are going through a shift change on all of the floors and they're finishing breakfast. Why don't you wait about a half hour or so before you visit your father? There's a cafeteria down the hall to your right. A cup of coffee might help you pass the time."

"That sounds like a good idea, nurse, thank you," he answered.

The cafeteria was busy. The smell of sizzling bacon and brewing coffee filled the room, making him hungry. Melvin had not eaten for twelve hours, so he loaded his plate with scrambled eggs, sausage and blueberry muffins, his favorite, and carried his tray to an empty table near a window with a view of the Piscataqua River. He was occupied eating his breakfast watching the heavy boat traffic on the river. The boats made him think of his brother Marvin.

Suddenly, Melvin was startled by a high-pitched scream from a nurse walking past his table carrying a tray of food. Melvin glanced at the source of the scream just in time to see the nurse drop her tray. It landed with a splash on the floor beside where he was sitting, part of the contents landing on his shiny shoes. His pants would certainly have been the recipient of some of the food flying through the air if he had not reacted quickly enough to tip himself out of the way. Nevertheless, Melvin was caught off guard by the mishap and was speechless for a few seconds.

"Oh, my!" exclaimed the nurse, kneeling down on the floor to clean up the mess. "I'm so sorry, Lieutenant. It was terribly clumsy of me and I apologize. Oh, your shoes are spattered with coffee..."

"It was an accident, Nurse," Melvin added, not wanting to be the object of a scene in the crowded cafeteria. Several people were already helping the embarrassed nurse pick up the spill.

"Here, let me clean your shoes," pleaded the nurse holding a damp towel in her hand.

"You don't have to do that, Ma'am. Here, give me the towel and I'll take care of it. See? No harm done," Melvin replied good-naturedly. "I'm glad you missed my uniform, it's the only one I have with me." The nurse was extremely agitated and he expressed his concern. "Is there anything wrong?"

"No...no," exclaimed the nurse, breathing heavily, and nervously avoiding his discerning glances.

She was an attractive woman. Melvin guessed that she was slightly older than himself. She was slender in build, with angular facial features, and her light brown hair was pulled back over her ears and held in place by her white cap. Her dark brown eyes betrayed the fact that she was still upset, even though she was trying hard to compose herself.

"Since your breakfast was lost may I get another tray for you?" Melvin offered. "It would be my pleasure."

"I think I'll just stick to coffee," she replied with an uneasy smile.

"Why don't you have a seat," suggested Melvin. "I'll be glad to get us some coffee. I could use another cup myself."

"If you don't mind," the nurse agreed, relieved to sit down. She removed her cap and placed it in the large shoulder bag she was carrying, all the time watching Melvin cross the room carefully balancing two full cups of coffee on a tray. "You did a better job than I did. I can't tell you how embarrassed I am about all this."

Melvin smiled and offered her his hand. "My name is Melvin Hastings. Most people call me Mel. May I ask what your name is, Mrs....?" asked Melvin, noticing the wedding band on her finger.

"I'm Mrs. Andrew Richards," the nurse answered quickly. "Thank you for the coffee. I don't know what got into me. I just finished my night shift. It was a difficult one and I'm tired."

"I can understand that, Mrs. Richards. I'm waiting to go upstairs to see my father. He had an automobile accident a couple of days ago. I just flew in from Fort Bragg with an Air Force friend to Pease Air Base. I wanted to make sure he's going to be all right."

"Is your father Mr. Glenn Hastings?" Mrs. Richards asked curiously.

"Yes, were you on his floor?"

"I didn't have his floor, but the nurse that did told me that he was a nice gentleman."

"I'm biased of course," Melvin grinned. "But they don't come any better."

"Does he live around here?" asked Mrs. Richards casually.

"No, he has an engineering firm in Philadelphia. It's been weeks since I last saw him. I hope the accident didn't bother his legs. He was badly wounded in the war and still wears a brace on his left leg, but he never let it slow him down."

"Well, the doctor that attended him is the best in the area so you can be assured that he's in good hands," volunteered Mrs. Richards, gathering up her bag to leave. "Thank you for being so understanding about the accident and thanks for the coffee. I hope your visit is a happy one, Lieutenant."

"Thanks. It was nice talking to you." Melvin could see that she was still uncomfortable about something. "Mrs. Richards, may I take the liberty to ask a personal question before you leave?"

"Yes," she answered hesitantly, her eyes alert and bright.

"I'm a stranger to this community, yet I have a feeling that I'm the cause of your discomfort. Am I correct?"

Mrs. Richards sighed. "You're right, but it doesn't mean anything. I mistook you for someone else, that's all. I'm sorry if I seemed unfriendly."

"I accept your apology," answered Melvin watching her walk away. He sat at the table for several minutes longer, analyzing what took place between him and the nurse. Finally, unable to attach any significance to the encounter, he finished his coffee and went to look up his father.

A short time later, he found his father in good spirits walking around the hospital room to exercise his legs.

"Mel!" cried Glenn when his son walked into the room. "I'm so glad you could make it. I didn't want you to worry about me. My goodness, you look great in that uniform."

"You look none the worse for the wear yourself, Dad," said Melvin, holding his father at arms' length. "So tell me, what happened to you?"

71

Glenn described the accident in some detail, lamenting more about the demise of the trusty Studebaker Hawk than about his own personal injuries.

"It's time for a new car, Dad."

"Your Uncle Bob said the same thing. He left here last night after going shopping for some clothes for me and getting me a rental car. It's in the parking lot of the hospital," said Glenn, searching for the keys to the car on the bedside table. "They're discharging me this morning. Here, take the keys, Mel. It's a Jeep Wagoneer. You can bring it around to the main entrance as soon as we're ready to go."

"Are you sure you're ready to leave so soon? What about that cut on your forehead?" Melvin questioned.

"I'll return in a few days to their outpatient clinic to have the stitches removed. The nurse just told me that the doctor has signed my release papers, and I'm anxious to get out of here. All hospitals are pretty much the same. It's a policy of the hospital that they wheelchair me out to the rotunda where you can park the car. Incidentally, how do you like my new clothes?"

Melvin smiled. "Uncle Bob bought them, didn't he?"

"Yes, how can you tell?"

"Because your pants are blue and your shirt is multicolor, Dad. You've never bought anything except brown or tan pants and shirts," Melvin replied with an amused shake of his head.

"In fairness to Bob, he did purchase a set of my colors, but I thought it would be nice to be a little bolder today."

"You're living dangerously, Dad," commented Melvin, giving his father another hug.

The first thing father and son did after leaving the hospital was take a tour of the coastal regions of southern Maine. Glenn was especially excited to show Melvin the beach area around York where he had been stationed during the early months of the war. He pointed out the location of sentry posts and gun

72

emplacements along the beach and at the mouth of the York River. By noontime, Glenn was getting tired, so they drove to the Snug Harbor Inn, where they enjoyed lunch together in a quiet relaxing setting.

"So how long do you have before you need to get back, Son?"

"I've got to be at Pease Air Base by nine in the morning, Dad," Melvin replied. "Airman Dave Fellows is an old college friend of mine. He needed to log some flying time so he volunteered to bring me up here. He'll be waiting to take me back to Fort Bragg."

"That isn't a lot of time, but I'm grateful for what we've got. You know I'm a little more tired than I expected. What do you say about us going up to the room? I can take a short rest and then we can spend a quiet afternoon together."

"Sounds fine to me. I could use a hot shower. I forgot my shaving kit so I'll have to borrow yours."

"That's about all I did think to bring," admitted Glenn sheepishly. "You can use some of the new underwear Bob picked up. We're still close to the same size."

Melvin walked along the shore while his father took a short nap. After returning to the room he showered and felt refreshed. They were both in good spirits that evening as they lingered over a late dinner in the inn's dining room.

"When I leave for Pease in the morning, are you going to stay here in Maine, or are you going to return to Philly?" Melvin casually inquired.

"I plan to stay a while longer, Son. I really haven't resolved anything so far."

"Just what is it that you're looking for, Dad?" Melvin asked, knowing how well his father defended his privacy. "What needs to be resolved? What was different about your tour of duty here in York that made it more significant than all of the other duty stations you must have been assigned to?"

Melvin realized that he was broaching very personal territory that he and Marvin had always avoided. The fact that he would be departing in the morning made him hope to elicit an answer he could understand without prying too intrusively.

"I don't know how to answer that, Mel. A lot of things happen in a person's lifetime that can't be explained easily, and you more than anyone else know how private a person I've always been. I'm not trying to hide some deep dark secret from anybody. It's nothing like that," reflected Glenn, getting that far-away-look on his face that his sons had frequently seen over the years.

"Does it involve Mother?"

"No, I didn't meet your mother until after I was wounded in France."

"Is it another woman?" asked Melvin on a whim, and instantly regretted the choice of words. "I'm sorry, Dad. Forget that I asked that question. Whatever your reasons for bringing you to this particular time and place in your life is nobody's business, least of all your son's. I'm not questioning you, I'm only concerned about your welfare. I want you to be happy. You're reaching a time in your life that should be the most rewarding of all. Your business has prospered over the years, and you should take advantage of that and reward yourself in any way you desire. God knows you've earned that right."

Glenn clasped his son's hands across the table. "I appreciate your concern, Son," He looked deep into Melvin's eyes and saw images of the two boys when they were small. "I don't know what I'd do if anything should happen to you."

"Now, Dad, you know better than to think things like that. I'm a soldier, and I'll do my duty just the way you did yours. There are risks, sure, but there are risks in crossing the street or driving an automobile, as you've found out. Would you want me to deny my responsibility to the men in my care?"

"Of course not, and if it sounded as if I implied such a thing, forget it. I didn't mean that. I've been following the latest

74

events in Vietnam. I certainly hope and pray that President Nixon will be successful in bringing the war to an end. But to get back to your questions, this may sound strange to you, but I simply have a strong impulse to take this journey back in time. When you boys were growing up there wasn't time to think about anything else," Glenn casually reflected with that same distant look. "Things started to happen to me when I went to our regiment's reunion in France with some of my old buddies. It triggered this feeling of urgency that I don't understand, and can't put off. I guess what I'm trying to tell you is that I'm going to stay here until I find a new direction for my life and I can successfully come to grips with the feelings that have been dormant for so long."

Glenn continued to explain. "Marvin's death has been hard on all of us. I understand how difficult it has been for you, Melvin. You two were inseparable for all those years."

Melvin's eyes mirrored the pain of his loss. "My life was ripped to shreds when I heard about his death. I still expect to see him come through the door at any time. A part of me died that day, Dad. Marvin and I shared so much, the same dreams, same hopes, and the same youthful secrets. It's going to take time Dad, but I'm making progress. I've found comfort in the fact that we had him for as long as we did. The memories we have are priceless and I return to them often when I'm feeling sad and want to be comforted. God, I've missed him so much!" he burst out with a sob.

"I know, Son," said Glenn reaching out to comfort Melvin. Tears of disbelief that Marvin was gone, still gripped father and son.

"You mentioned finding comfort in the deep recesses of your memory," continued Glenn. "In a way, that's what I'm trying to do here on the coast of Maine. I loved your mother very much and I mourned her death. I tried to be a father she would have been proud of, and I've tried to be faithful to her memory. However, there is another part of my life that is completely unrelated to you two boys or your mother. For a

75

while in 1942, when the war was raging all over the world and it seemed as if the nations would tear themselves apart, I found contentment for the first time in my life. I thought I had discovered the true meaning of life here at this place. All during the terrible campaigns of North Africa, Italy and ultimately France, the one thing that sustained my sanity was the world I'd left behind here in this tiny coastal village. Every day I hoped and dreamed to return to this world. It gave me the courage to continue when it would have been easy to give up.

"Months, even years disappeared from my life. After I was wounded, my link to Maine was broken by the severity of my injuries and I let the rupture become permanent. I don't know why I let it happen, but it's a fact of life and nothing is gained trying to figure out why. I was not the same young soldier that I had once been..."

"Who was the woman, Dad?" Melvin asked softly. "I'd like to know, but if you want to keep it a secret I'll understand."

"It doesn't matter what her name is, Melvin. Some day I'll let you read the letters she sent to me. They span twenty-four months of the war years and have become very precious to me. Now, twenty-five years later, something has gone off in my head that demands an explanation and I'm determined to search until I find the answers before I come home. Does that make any sense, Son?"

"More sense than anything I can think of, Dad."

"It was a different time and place, unrelated to any other periods of my life. It was an island of serenity in a sea of chaos. The truth is, Mel, I've never found the same peace of mind that I experienced those few months I posted guards on the coast of Maine. It wasn't just the young woman, it was her family too. Maybe I'm looking at that episode of my life through rose-colored glasses, but I can't help it. That's how I remember it.

"To put it in simple terms," Glenn continued with his monologue. "I guess I'm still trying to recapture that same feeling of well-being. I don't kid myself that circumstances and people change. I can handle that. I won't know what I'm looking for until I find it, Son. Maybe it isn't here and I'm looking in vain, but this is where I'm beginning the search. Time is an important factor for me. I know that I'm not old by contemporary standards, but two-thirds of my life is over. The shadows are getting longer and soon they will fade completely. If this journey has to be taken, then it must be done soon or it will never be."

Melvin sat spellbound, listening to his father sharing what was in his heart. Throughout the years, neither he nor his brother ever dreamed that their father had carried such vivid memories for so long in silence. Tonight Melvin was seeing a side of his father he never knew existed, and he was bursting with admiration and respect for his Dad's inherent decency and integrity.

"I'll be able to return to Fort Bragg tomorrow comforted that you're in full command of your actions. Reach for the stars, Dad, and if you need any help along the way, just say the word."

"I will, Son. Thanks for the vote of confidence. When and if I find what I'm seeking, you'll be the first to know, after me."

The next morning Glenn and Melvin shared a leisurely breakfast at the inn. Melvin insisted on calling a cab to take him to Pease Air Base so that his father could stay at the inn and rest a while longer. They said good-bye embracing each other so tightly that Melvin was afraid of hurting his father.

"Take care, Dad. Good luck in your journey and keep in touch," Melvin said in a wavering voice, and climbed into the taxicab.

"I will, Son. Thanks for coming. You've helped me clarify a few things." Glenn waved, reluctant for his son to leave. He had waved the same way to Marvin less than a year ago...

Glenn abruptly picked up a newspaper in the lobby and returned to his room where he took a seat at the window and watched the relentless assault of the waves against the granite shore. The *Portsmouth Press Herald* newspaper's front pages were filled with stories covering President Nixon's efforts to stop the war in Vietnam. The local communities section of the paper started on the second page. Instantly a small insignificant notice shook him to the depths of his soul!

"Engagement announcement between Kathleen Cohen and James Farley. Wedding plans are not firm but both expect it to be early June."

Chapter Eight

The simple announcement registered with Glenn like a powerful blow, leaving him with more questions than answers. His first thought was that her name was still Cohen. If she had never married could he assume that she had been waiting for him all those years? To assume too much could be dangerous to his mental stability. Suddenly, he felt like an intruder. What right did he have to return to Kathleen's hometown, after an absence of twenty-five years, just as she was starting to build a new life for herself?

A few hours earlier, Glenn had laid out, analyzed, and substantiated his motives for returning to York to Melvin. The notice reinforced an impulsive urge lingering in the recesses of his mind to return to Philly. Perhaps he should simply leave the area and calmly start to pick up the threads of his life where he had left them. After all, if Kathleen was engaged to marry, it meant that she was happy and looking forward to the future. He had no desire to jeopardize her chance for happiness with someone else. Maybe he would be an unwelcome ghost from a distant past, rekindling issues that were best left unvisited. Common sense told Glenn that the feelings, and the love he was chasing had long since evaporated. Glenn believed it would be cruel to return to open up old wounds that had been so long in healing.

Normally Glenn's thought processes were predictable and methodical, a by-product of his pragmatic engineering training which assessed situations on the basis of facts and formulae rather than emotion or sentiment. If he looked at the present situation honestly and without bias, it was clear he should leave the area as soon as possible; the chances of anything positive developing from conditions as they now existed were slight. The more he allowed himself to reflect upon that fact, the more relieved he became. For him to leave would be the easiest thing for all concerned. After all, what did he expect to do when he ultimately confronted Kathleen? It was a distinct possibility that she loathed him for breaking off their relationship the way he had never warned her or offered her any explanation. His life had been so consumed by a desire to walk and talk again that he had chosen to exclude her from his life without ever soliciting her thoughts on the matter. The decision had been cowardly and selfish, and he was ashamed of it. He was paying for that decision now.

When Glenn stopped receiving letters from Kathleen, he had been angered and hurt because he had needed her more than ever. Pride and hurt made it easy for him to rationalize that she would not want him in the condition he was in anyway. His analysis of the situation could have been wrong. Glenn never dwelled on that aspect of his choice. He had never determined, to his satisfaction, if he had detached her from his life because he loved her, or, if he feared rejection on the basis of his severe physical injuries. Probably, it was a little bit of both. A small voice inside of him still cried out for some clarification. Was the engagement announcement the answer he was searching for? Would this give him the closure he had been craving, or was it all the more reason to continue the search? The more he thought about it, the more confused he became. Nevertheless, to leave town without even speaking to Kathleen would be a cowardly act of denial contrary to all that he had hoped to accomplish on this nostalgic trip. His deepest instincts told him that at the very least, he ought to congratulate Kathleen, and, finally, that was what he was resolved to do.

Glenn spent several days reviewing the situation, searching his mind for solutions while he rested and took brisk walks along the shore feeling better with each passing day. He did not want to drive the rental automobile until he felt stronger. There was no reason to rush the healing process so he let Nature do her work while he patiently waited. The stitches on his forehead and shoulder would be ready for removal at the end of the week, when he would be able to better evaluate his situation.

Five days after his discharge, Glenn drove the Jeep Wagoneer to the Portsmouth Hospital to have his stitches removed. It was the first time he had driven the vehicle and was impressed with its quality and sturdiness. His Studebaker Hawk was much faster, but the Jeep combined the ruggedness of a truck with the comfort of an automobile. It was a remarkable compromise vehicle that was fun to drive.

Glenn parked the Wagoneer in the parking lot next to the out-patient clinic, and went in to register with the receptionist at the desk. He spoke briefly to the nurse and was directed to a waiting room until his name was called. The room was full of patients. He anticipated a long wait so he selected a magazine from the table and started to browse through it. He noticed that the nurse on duty was the same one he had talked to the day he was discharged.

Within an hour she called his name. "Mr. Hastings, the doctor will see you now."

"It's nice to see you again, Mr. Hastings," she greeted him. "How are you doing?"

"I'm doing fine, thanks. It's nice to see a familiar face. Hopefully, this will be my last trip to the hospital," Glenn remarked, following her into an examination room.

"I hope so, too," the nurse smiled at him. "The doctor will be right in to see you. Before he comes I'll take your vitals. Would you please remove your shirt to expose the wound on your shoulder? How's the chest cavity, sore?"

Glenn shrugged "At times it hurts but it's not a constant thing. If I stretch too much or bend over too far, like tying my shoes, it hurts. I still have some shortness of breath. That seems to be slowly diminishing though."

"That's all normal," the nurse acknowledged. "The pain and shortness of breath will disappear completely as your ribs continue to mend." She took his temperature and blood pressure and then asked him to stand on the scales.

"You've lost five pounds since you left the hospital last week, Mr. Hastings. How is your appetite?" she asked with concern.

"I've been eating a little less than usual," admitted Glenn offering no further explanation.

"Well, if you have any questions you can direct them to the doctor. Good luck, Mr. Hastings. I wish you a speedy recovery."

The same doctor that had treated him the day of the accident now gave him a thorough examination and removed the stitches from his two cuts. He did ask the doctor about the time required for his ribs to heal, or about any exercises that could aid the healing process. Glenn knew from experience that a good physical therapist could work almost as many miracles as a doctor.

"I wouldn't overdo the exercise for the next couple of weeks," the doctor recommended. "You should continue to walk and stretch to the point of being painful. Slowly increase your level of activity every two days until you can maintain a level of exercise commensurate with your normal routines." The doctor paused a moment. "Mr. Hastings, when you were brought to the hospital, we were struck by the severity of the injuries you received during the war. It looks like a miracle that you're alive and walking unassisted."

"It was a long struggle, doctor," Glenn admitted.

"By the way, I spoke to the policeman who investigated your accident, and he told me that you're a Medal of Honor recipient. Is that true?"

"Yes, it's true. I was at Normandy," Glenn answered.

"I served in Korea with the Army Medical Corps and I just wanted to shake your hand, Sir."

Glenn offered the doctor his hand. "I wear the Medal with great pride, but there were a lot of men who did more than I and were never recognized for their valor, so I wear it in their memory and I'm honored to do so."

"Good luck to you, Sir. It's been a privilege to serve you," dismissed the doctor. "By the way, you should have your regular doctor remove the cast on your fingers a month from now."

After leaving the outpatient clinic, Glenn crossed the Memorial Bridge over the Piscataqua River which connected Portsmouth, New Hampshire with Kittery, Maine. He took the coastal route back to York instead of the more direct Route one. His duties in 1942 did not extend to any area south of York Harbor with the exception of the York River access roads. The street Kathleen Cohen lived on branched off from the coastal route. Without thinking, he turned on the road leading past the house and down the hill to Sewall Bridge.

As he approached the house, his heart beat faster. He slowed a little, but not enough to become conspicuous. Every nerve in his body was alert and observant as he scrutinized the back yard and front of the house. No one was visible. A couple of toys were on the porch — a Radio Flyer cart and a red tricycle. The small Cape Cod style house with natural cedar shingles looked exactly as he remembered it. The trim boards, windows, and doors looked freshly painted, and the home still possessed an air of informality and neatness. There was no evidence of odds and ends scattered around. Glenn was struck with the desire to turn into the driveway and run into the house just as he had years ago. Overcome by a sense of loss, he continued driving past the house, rationalizing that since there were no automobiles in the yard, most likely, no one was home.

Beads of sweat trickled down his forehead and into his sideburns. The Sewall Bridge still pounded and clattered whenever a vehicle ran over it. From the bridge, Glenn could see Ernest Cohen's dock and fish shack beside the river. A lobster boat was tied up at the dock where someone, a much smaller and younger man than Ernest Cohen, was unloading traps. Glenn continued on past Mrs. Marshall's general store and into the village square. He was suddenly hungry, so he went directly to the inn, which served excellent food, and took his favorite seat near the window with an ocean view. A waitress brought him his customary cup of coffee.

"Thank you. I guess I'm predictable," Glenn smiled. He had just ordered a sandwich and was quietly sipping coffee when a figure suddenly appearing beside his table, gave him the shock of his life.

"My God, Kathleen!" Glenn cried involuntarily.

The young woman smiled at him. "No, I'm not Kathleen. She's my mother. May I join you, Mr. Hastings?" The young lady looked about the same age Kathleen had been when he last saw her. In fact, she looked almost exactly like her mother, with that same tilt of the head when she spoke and the same luminous brown eyes.

"Please do," Glenn stammered in reply, unable to keep his eyes off her. He noticed a wedding ring on her finger. "I must say this is an unexpected surprise."

"You've been quite a shocker to me also, Mr. Hastings," the young lady admitted nervously. "I recognized your name when you were admitted to the Portsmouth Hospital. I knew that you had to be the Glenn Hastings I've been hoping to meet for a long time. I saw you one evening in the hospital."

Suddenly Glenn recalled. "I remember that night clearly."

"Yes, that night when you reached out for me and called my mother's name I was certain I had found you at last."

Glenn was confused. "Found me?"

She smiled softly. "Yes, Mr. Glenn Hastings. Try to relax and be as calm as you can," she reached across the small table and gently grasped both of his hands. Her face was flushed with excitement and exultation. "I never dreamed that this moment would ever come for me…"

"What's wrong, young lady? I don't understand." Glenn exclaimed. "What moment?"

"Mr. Hastings, I'm your daughter!"

Chapter Nine

Glenn was slow to grasp the significance of what she said. His daughter? How could that be? "Is this some cruel joke?" he finally asked. "I…"

"No cruel joke, believe me," the woman replied, still holding his hands tightly. "My name is Glenis Cohen Richards. Please let me explain as best as I can. I know this is a shock to you. It was to me, too, when I first saw you. I only hope that this revelation is going to be as pleasant for you as it has been for me." She smiled and continued. "I just had a terrible argument with my mother, whom I love dearly. She disagrees with my announcing the news to you so suddenly. I'm not sure whether I'm right or wrong, but I feel strongly that you have a right to know that I'm your daughter, just as I have a right to know who my father is. My mother never kept your identity from me. I've known about you from the day I was born. In fact, the first picture I had in my room as an infant was an enlargement of you in your uniform standing on the front porch of our house, Mr. Hastings. Your face has always been a part of my life. I'm so thankful now to know that the picture represents a real live person."

Glenn was still flustered. "Forgive me if I'm not responding to your revelation in the way you'd hoped. Please believe me, I'm not displeased, I'm simply unprepared to hear such profound news. I never dreamed of anything like this. Your mother never told me. I swear I never knew. If I had only known about you, so much of my life would have been different…" The realization that he had a daughter finally hit him. Tears of joy clouded his view of his daughter, Glenis, named in his memory. Suddenly, he felt uncomfortable in such a public place. "Would you mind if we have our discussion somewhere else?"

"Why, certainly," Glenis replied beaming. "Wherever you choose, lead the way."

"These warm sunny June days are wonderful after a long winter. There's a lovely walkway in front of the inn with magnificent views of the ocean. That might be a more appropriate setting for us to continue our chat."

"I agree," Glenis answered, her voice filled with excitement and pride. She felt like shouting to the world that the mystery of her life was solved at last. As they left the dining room, she noticed his walk and remembered what her nurse associate had told her about his leg brace.

"This morning I went to the hospital to have my stitches removed," Glenn told his daughter. "In a short time I'll be as good as new."

She grinned. "I have to confess that I've been keeping close tabs on your activities since I first saw you. I felt guilty spying on you like that, but I couldn't help myself. I wanted to make sure you were all right. Ever since that morning I met your son, Melvin, I made up my mind to confront you at an appropriate time and place."

"You met Melvin?" Glenn asked surprised. "He never mentioned it to me and we talked a lot about personal things after I came out of the hospital." They walked a short way and stopped at a bench situated at a prominent point where the cliffs jutted into the ocean, creating a panoramic vista of water and shore on three sides.

Glenis studied the lines in his face. "That picture I've always treasured of you in your uniform is all I had to go by. Then, when I saw your son in the hospital cafeteria I couldn't believe my eyes. He looks just like you when you were younger."

Glenn smiled at her. "The twins do look like me. I'm not sure if that's good or bad."

"The twins…?"

"Yes, Melvin had an identical twin brother, Marvin. Marvin was killed in action in Vietnam. We received the notice of his death a short time before I came to Maine."

"Oh, I'm so sorry," she said sincerely, touching his arm. "What a terrible thing for you and Melvin and your wife to have to live with."

"Their mother died giving birth," Glenn explained. "I never remarried."

"My God, and I used to think that I had a difficult life," exclaimed Glenis. "You've certainly had your share of tragedy, Mr. Hastings." She hesitated, and then asked, "I realize it's sudden and unexpected, but may I call you Father?"

He was consumed with emotions, and reached out for Glenis. She fell into his arms. They embraced in silence holding each other close to their hearts, each desperately needing the other and thankful for this moment when the mysteries of the past were unraveled. Glenis unleashed the flood of tears that had been stored for years. The search for her father had been a treasured and secret desire for most of her life. Now that her search was over, she could finally relax while her heart sang for joy. It was a milestone by which all other events would be referenced.

"It's a miracle that I found you," she sobbed quietly. "A friend of mine at the hospital was talking to me about you. When she mentioned your name, I just had to check if it could possibly be you, and it was." Glenis wiped her tear-streaked face with a tissue.

"Now I know why this trip had become such an obsession for me," said Glenn, his face flushed with emotion. "To think that I almost left York a few days ago. My daughter… I still can't believe it's true. You must hate me for not being around to support you and to share your childhood dreams. If I'd only known!"

Glenis looked him in the eye. "No guilty thoughts, Father, please," she requested. "I never hated you. Mother always told me how kind and gentle a man you were. We all make choices and most of the time those choices are correct. But sometimes they turn out to be bad ones, and we can't change the past, so we salvage what we can and get on with our lives. I don't blame you or Mother for not being together. I would have preferred that, of course, but I don't blame either of you for the circumstances that made it impossible."

"Young lady, that kind of wisdom and maturity reminds me of your mother. How is she, Glenis?" Glenn asked in a shaky voice.

"She's doing well. She still teaches school in the village. She's in good health and is as youthful-looking as ever. People sometimes mistake us for sisters instead of mother and daughter."

"I'm not surprised to hear that," Glenn drank in every word she spoke.

"She continues to work hard. Almost every summer she enrolls in some course to improve her skills and certification as a teacher. She has a large reservoir of devoted former students that keep in touch with her. She's very intelligent and I'm proud of her. We get along well. She's not comfortable trying to be 'one of the girls' like some mothers who are afraid of aging. She prefers to remain what she is, a mother. She's been a wonderful confidante and advisor, and I love her very much for her simple honesty."

Glenis continued, gazing out at the ocean. "Right after I was born, this small town, like most small towns anywhere, was just buzzing with rumors about her. Some of them were lurid and had her pegged as an immoral woman, as you might expect. For a young unwed mother to bring up a child in a small New England town is an act of courage and determination.

There are a lot of mean-spirited people who thrive on gossip and love to condemn others. My mother stood up to all of them with great dignity. I never appreciated how difficult it must have been for her until I was older. The hardest question for her to answer was 'where was my father'?"

"I feel so guilty about that."

Glenis shook her head. "Don't. She promised me that you would have done the right thing if you had known. She made a choice that maybe, in retrospect, wasn't a good one. She did not want you to return simply because of me. She wanted you to return of your own free will for her love. She loved you very much, you know."

"I never doubted that for a minute," Glenn whispered, touched by her words. The thought of Kathleen needing him at the time he had consciously turned away from her, filled him with remorse and regret.

"Her stock answer to the townspeople was that she had fallen in love with a soldier who never came back from the war. It was true, as far as it went, and she never elaborated on the statement to anyone. She told the local school board that if they wanted her to continue teaching school they would have to accept the fact that she gave birth to a child out of wedlock. She refused to be ashamed of it, or to confess any further details. She was terrific and they have never questioned her once in all these years. She's a remarkably strong-willed woman. I hope I have half the courage she does."

"I'm guessing that you do," Glenn replied. "Those characteristics were what attracted me to your mother the first time we met."

"Was that the time you brought your Jeep to the school and talked to the students?"

"Yes, it seems a long time ago," Glenn answered, shaking his head. "So you've heard that story too? I hope this isn't a dream. I don't want to wake up tomorrow and find you gone. I've searched all over the world for the peace and wellness that

I felt when I was stationed here years ago. You must understand, Glenis, your mother was not an immoral woman. She was honest and respectable and I loved her with all my being. The reason I didn't return was not that I didn't love her; on the contrary, I loved her too much. Maybe that doesn't make any sense now, but at the time it seemed to be the best way. It was a bad choice on my part. Then, after I was wounded, I fell in love with, and married, another woman. I've never been able to reconcile the fact that I loved them both at the same time. I don't apologize for that because the boys she gave me have been a joy to my life. Without them I probably would not be here."

Glenis smiled gently at him. "No judgments will ever come from me, Father. Those boys were lucky to have you. Growing up without a mother had to have been hard for them."

"It was," Glenn answered, pleased by her accepting nature. "I tried to be mother and father at the same time, but it's impossible. You and your mother can relate to that."

"Yes, but at least I had my grandfather Cohen. He did all he could to make up for your absence."

"How is he?" Glenn asked curiously. A shadow passed over his daughter's face.

"Grandfather passed away five years ago. Right to the end he worked every day. He died on the boat one day, pulling traps. Another fisherman close by saw him slump down and came to check on him. He had died instantly."

"I'm sorry to hear that. He was a fine man." Glenn could picture the proud fisherman, and was filled with sadness. "I spent a day on his boat pulling traps. I never forgot the experience. I remember him as a large man with a big heart."

"He was as gentle as a lamb too. During the summer months when school was out I often helped him on the boat. A few times Mother and I went out alone and pulled the traps. I have many fond memories of him."

91

Glenn enjoyed listening to her youthful energetic expressions. "Please, tell me more about yourself. Fill in some of the blank years for me. I notice that you're married."

"Yes, I'm married to a wonderful man, Andrew, Andy for short. He's serving in Vietnam right now as an Army helicopter pilot. We met in college. I went to the University of New Hampshire at Durham because it's closer to York than any other college and I wanted to be able to commute from home. The commutes cost less than it would have cost to stay at the school. Grandmother and Grandfather pitched in with Mother and Uncle Philip to buy me an economical automobile. It was a 1962 Studebaker Lark. I sure put a lot of miles on that car."

"That's interesting," Glenn was amused. "I just totaled my Studebaker Hawk in Kittery. It was a great car. The Lark was a good car too, economical and reliable."

"My Lark had the six cylinder champion engine. My Uncle Phil said that it was all the power I needed. He used to joke that if I had the V/8 engine I'd be getting speeding tickets all the time."

Glenn chuckled. "Your Uncle Phil sounds like a nice guy. I never met him. He was in the Coast Guard when I met your mother. She wrote me that he'd been injured in the north Atlantic. How did he come out of that situation?"

"He spent a long time in the hospital before he finally came home. Mother told me that the family was shocked the first time they saw him. He had lost one leg and was still recovering from extensive burns. He's recovered completely. The burn scars aren't too noticeable, except on his left cheek. The government fitted him with an artificial leg. Now he gets around as well as anyone. He's still running the family lobster business that Grandfather started and does great. It's amazing to see him move around on the boat in rough waters. He's married and has two children. They live out on Kittery Point Road."

"My son, Marvin, was in the Coast Guard. I have a lot of respect for that service," Glenn remarked in a tense voice.

"You know," said Glenis putting her arm around his shoulder. She had a little-girl quality about her that was infectious. "I've been doing a lot of the talking, Father. I like to say that word, Father. I'm so glad I came today. I was scheduled to attend a two week seminar in Portland, but, at the last minute it was canceled. That's how I ended up at the hospital when you were admitted. Just think, if that seminar had not been called off, you would have come and gone without my ever knowing about it."

Glenis and her mother shared that same gift — the ability to make people around them feel special. He was bursting with pride and thanksgiving watching her talk about her life. Yet, a feeling of guilt lurked in the deep recesses of his mind. He couldn't help thinking that he had missed a lot by not being around to watch this lovely girl grow into womanhood. An hour had gone by since he first discovered that he had a daughter. Already, in that short period of time, Glenis had succeeded in enriching his life and making him feel important and needed. Kathleen and her family had done a wonderful job with her. His prayers had been answered. That small insistent voice inside him that had led him to this miraculous discovery of his daughter, was one that he would listen to from now on.

"Tell me about yourself, Father," Glenis requested. "I've thought of you almost every day of my life. As a young girl I used to imagine that you would return to Mother and me. You would show up in your uniform and I could tell all of my friends about you. It was a dream I frequently had. Every night at bedtime, Mother would come into my room and we'd kneel and pray together. We always included you in our prayers." She smiled radiantly at him. "Now, those prayers have been answered, later than I'd hoped for, but you're here at last. Is it difficult for you to talk about what happened after you met Mother?" She noted Glenn's emotional expression and exclaimed, "I'm sorry."

"My dear daughter," answered Glenn, taking her slender hand in his. "If I can help you lay to rest some of the impressions and thoughts you've had about the father you never knew, I'm pleased to share my story with you. Perhaps you'll understand me a little better once you've heard it. I owe you and your mother an explanation. I've never been completely certain how or why things happened the way they did, but I will tell you the truth. I'm a very private person and I've never been comfortable sharing my thoughts or feelings. After you've heard my story, you may not feel the same way about me, but you're entitled to the truth. It's a chance I'll have to take."

Glenis placed a finger to his lips. "Shh, remember what I said about guilt feelings? I really meant that. If you're comfortable telling me what happened to you after my conception, I promise to be truthful in telling you how I feel once I've heard you out."

"That's a fair statement," Glenn nodded, inhaling deeply, thinking back to those days so long ago. "It was in the early fall of 1942 when I said good-bye to your mother for the last time. I can honestly tell you that a part of me died when that parting took place. I was a young first lieutenant assigned to an infantry company at Fort Dix, New Jersey, as its executive officer. Back then, we were assembling formations as fast as the recruiting depots could train the men. Late in September my company shipped out for North Africa where we landed in Algiers. Our outfit was badly mauled during the first week of combat. We lost half of the men. I was promoted to captain and took over the company as its commander.

"The fighting in North Africa was brutal. I buried a lot of good men in the blowing sands of Algiers and Morocco. After Africa, in July, 1943, my regiment went on to Sicily and continued up the toe of Italy across the Messina Straits. By February, 1944, we were pulled out of the line and sent to England to prepare for the Normandy invasion in June, 1944.

"My company was one of the first ashore. We fought our way inland, but we were slowed by hedgerows of impenetrable vegetation that surrounded the fields on the flat coastal plain. The Germans were waiting for us behind these shields. It was the most bitter fighting I've ever experienced, and our losses were heavy. I had assembled a couple of squads of riflemen to assault a German stronghold that was holding us up and inflicting terrible losses on our regiment. We managed to silence the machine gun posts with a rocket launcher and some satchel charges before I was hit by a mortar round that almost killed me."

"Was that where you were awarded the Medal of Honor?" Glenis inquired softly, not wanting to interrupt with his train of thought. The hospital was all abuzz at having a MOH recipient as a patient. The Medal was no surprise, Glenis had known about it for years.

"Yes, that was where I earned the MOH, but I didn't know anything about it until months afterward. I was a human wreck. Both of my legs had been shattered and my lower jaw was splintered. For some reason your mother's letters stopped coming at about that time. For over a year I was unable to walk or talk. I almost went out of my mind. Finally, after months without any word from your mother, I made a conscious decision not to contact her. I had the feeling that she had found someone else and was afraid to tell me. I didn't want to tell her how badly I was wounded because I did not want her to pity me."

"You should have told her," Glenis protested gently. "That was a bad choice on your part, Father. Your injuries would have made no difference to her."

Anguished at the notion of all that he had lost, Glenn answered in a wavering voice. "Deep inside I knew that too, but prospects for my recovery and physical pain clouded rational thinking. For months, operations were almost a daily routine for me until I started therapy, my life centered around my efforts to walk and talk again. That's where I met Jessica, the mother of the twins. She was my physical therapist."

Glenis smiled in understanding. "A classic case of transference, Father. It's understandable and perfectly human."

"Jessica died in childbirth a year after we were married. After that, I shut out the rest of the world to complete my therapy and raise the two boys. Looking back, I probably needed the twins more than they needed me. Well, that's a quick summary of my life during and after the war." Glenn leaned back against the bench and stared at the horizon, anxious for her verdict.

Glenis sat in silence, and tried to imagine what it had been like for her father. "It's a miracle that you're here and able to walk and talk. You and Mother were the victims of a cruel foul-up in addresses and forwarding procedures. What a shame and a terrible waste of such a beautiful love!"

"Perhaps now you can understand why I wanted to return to Maine. Ever since Marvin's death, I've been desperately seeking some direction for my life. I just couldn't continue the way it was going, and I felt more and more uncertain about the future. Something inside of me guided my footsteps here."

Glenis reached into her hand bag for an envelope. There was a big smile on her lips. "Father, I have something to show you, these are some pictures of four-year-old Ernest Richards, your grandson.

Chapter Ten

Glenis held the pictures for her father to examine. The first showed a laughing four-year-old Ernest Richards wearing a pair of corduroy coveralls sitting on a Radio Flyer cart with his feet dangling happily over the edge. He looked like his mother and grandmother.

"Young lady," said Glenn calmly. "You've managed to turn my whole world upside-down in just a few hours. First I discover that I have a lovely daughter, and now you present me with a grandson. I'm overwhelmed. I don't know what to say except that I feel very fortunate."

"We named him after grandfather."

"That's nice. It would have made him proud."

"Ernest is a dear child," said Glenis with a broad smile. "What else would a mother say about her son? Mother takes care of him those evenings I have to work. That's why I was able to take the night shift at the hospital. I live at home with Mother and Grandmother while Andy is overseas. As soon as his tour is complete we plan to buy or build a house. He's a mechanical engineer."

"I saw that same Radio Flyer cart on the porch of the house earlier today," Glenn mentioned nervously. "I probably would have stopped, but I didn't see any vehicles in the yard and continued on my way,"

Glenis noticed his nervousness at broaching the subject. "You haven't gotten over Mother, have you?" she asked, looking into his sad eyes.

"Is it that obvious?"

"I'm afraid it is," Glenis replied.

"Is she happy with this James Farley?" Glenn asked cautiously, wondering if it was prudent for him to try to see Kathleen. "I'd like your advice on something. Am I going to dig up a painful part of your mother's past if I show up at her door now? Would it be better for me to just leave and send congratulations on her wedding plans? God only knows that I don't want to bring any more pain or hardship to her life. If I'm going to be a source of unhappiness, then I won't see her."

"It's impossible for me to give you a simple answer to something that has been a part of your lives for so long. Who knows, maybe your visit will give both of you some closure to that troubled period of your lives and allow you to start fresh without any commitments to the past. I'm not sure, it's just a thought. The past can never be redone, but the future is ours to shape."

"You have a nice way of putting things, after all, I never expected to find a daughter or a grandson. I hope that I can be a positive part of your lives from now on. I have a whole lot of years to make up for."

"Well, you've started already," Glenis squeezed his arm affectionately. "Now, what do you really want to do about Mother?"

"I want to see her again, and tell her how sorry I am for what might have been," Glenn answered resolutely. "My life will never be right unless I have an opportunity to talk with her one more time."

"Then it's settled," Glenis nodded her approval. "I think it would be better for the two of you to meet on neutral ground. I know, you could meet her at the school this afternoon. She'll be in class until three o'clock and with luck, she'll be ready to leave by three-thirty. She's now principal of the school and always locks up the building, so there won't be any other people around to bother the two of you."

"That sounds like a good idea," Glenn agreed.

"Do you want me to prepare her for it?"

Glenn considered her question. "Does she know that I'm in town?"

"I told her about your accident and… yes, she knows."

"Then I'll be at the school when she's ready to leave," Glenn said firmly. "Don't bother telling her. What kind of a person is this James Farley?"

"He used to work at the Portsmouth Naval Yard as some kind of a technician before he started teaching at York High School. He's lived in York for about five years and has been courting Mother for most of that time. He's a little younger than she is. Most people that know him seem to like him. I haven't found any reason to object to James Farley. He's most attentive to Mother and I believe he genuinely loves her. If she did not love him in return, I'm positive she would not consider marriage. Your visit may help her close a chapter of her life. Nothing can be gained by assigning blame for the past, so it's important that the two of you bring down the curtain on the past."

"Where did such a young lady as you get so much wisdom?" asked Glenn, pleased with the turn of their conversation. "You're right though, we owe each other an explanation."

"You don't have much time to make it to the school, Father. I should be going now. I wish you luck. If you need to call, this is our number at the house," she said, kissing him on the cheek and pressing the paper with her number in his hand.

"This number is different. The old one at the house was 288J," Glenn recalled. "Thank you for coming, Glenis. I'll be in touch with you."

Glenis left her father to himself. The possibility of seeing Kathleen in a few minutes gave him the shakes so bad he had trouble placing the keys in the ignition of the Jeep Wagoneer.

99

He drove slowly through the center of town. The closer he drew to the elementary school the more dissembled he became. The school was as he had remembered it. Glenn turned into the driveway up a slight grade and brought the Jeep to a stop beside a black Rambler station wagon in the parking lot behind the building. Two possibilities ran rampant through his head. Would she reject him without a word or would she demand an explanation he might not be able to give?

He saw her coming through the door. The Jeep was parked on the opposite side of her Rambler so that it was not readily visible when she first came out the entrance. Kathleen was carrying an armful of books and walked wearily toward her car. She noticed the Jeep with a puzzled look on her face. Glenn quickly opened the door of the Jeep and walked around the vehicle to intercept her face to face. He felt like taking her into his arms and pleading for an opportunity to remove all those years of hurt. Kathleen had grown older with remarkable grace. Her gray and white streaked hair hung loose over her shoulders. She was as lovely as ever. She walked as if it had been a long day's work, but there was still that sparkle in her eyes that seemed to look inside a person. At first, she glanced at Glenn and was uncertain, and then, like a bolt of lightning, she recognized him. A look of trepidation and disbelief filled her eyes. In a state of shock, she dropped some of the books and leaned against her automobile for support.

She challenged him in a wavering voice. "Is that really you, Glenn?"

"Yes, it's me, Kathleen," he replied gently. "Are you all right? I didn't mean to startle you."

"What did you expect?" she replied in a clear voice. "Have you spoken with our daughter?"

"Yes," Glenn answered, staring all the while into the eyes he remembered from long ago. "She's a lovely girl, Kathleen. I never knew. Why didn't you tell me?"

Kathleen sighed and closed her eyes just for a moment. Finally, she answered, "When I found out that I was pregnant, Glenn, you had already left for overseas duty. I was afraid that the news would be a burden to you. So, I made the decision to keep it to myself until you came home to us after the war was over. By mid-1944 my letters were returned with no forwarding address available. I didn't know what to expect. I checked the killed-in-action lists and could not find your name, so I knew you weren't dead. And then, at about that same time your letters to me stopped. I could only conclude that what we had was over. My world collapsed, and terrible years followed!"

"I was badly wounded," cried Glenn, anxious to explain as best he could. "When your letters stopped coming I was devastated, but I decided not to contact you because I didn't want you to know how serious my wounds were. I didn't want you to pity me, Kathleen. I thought it was best if I didn't write..."

Upon hearing his explanation, Kathleen reached out and slapped him hard across the face. The sound rang across the school playground carrying with it all the frustrations, anger, and pain of the past twenty-five years, never knowing where he was, or what direction her life should take. "How dare you make that decision on your own, without consulting me. How dare you!" Tears erupted from her eyes and streamed down her cheeks while Glenn looked on helplessly. Without a word, he picked up the books she had dropped on the ground, placed them in the car and relieved her of those still in her arms. Kathleen searched for a handkerchief in her jacket pocket.

Glenn felt helpless and tried, again, to explain his actions. "I don't offer any excuse for my decisions, Kathleen. The fact is, you're not the only one to have suffered. I spent that entire year learning to talk again, like a two-year-old child. It was another, before I could move my legs and still another five years before I could walk without a cane or crutches. I can't erase the pain you endured; all I can tell you is that the years have been far from easy for me, too."

Kathleen listened carefully. "I didn't know then that you were so severely wounded. After the war, Philip purchased a book with a list of Medal of Honor recipients and I saw your name on the list. It took some doing, but I was able to track down the therapy center in Philadelphia where you were relocated for surgery and therapy, and I started to write to you again. All of my letters were sent back to me with 'Return to Sender' written across the envelope."

"This is the first time I've heard that Kathleen, believe me," Glenn replied sharply, thinking back to that painful time. He had met Jessica by then. "Kathleen, do you still have those letters?"

"Which ones?"

"Those returned to you from Philadelphia."

"Yes, I have them at home. Don't you believe me?" she asked sharply.

"Of course I do," he answered in a softer tone. "Off hand, I'd say that it must have been about September of 1945. I'd like to see the envelopes if you don't mind."

"They're at home in the attic," said Kathleen, uncertain about his intentions. "Is this why you've returned after all those years, to retrieve those letters?"

"Not exactly," answered Glenn awkwardly, searching for the right words.

"Did you expect that I'd wait forever?" She demanded angrily. "Every time the phone rang I expected and hoped that it would be from you. Every time a car turned into the driveway I ran to see if it was you. Every time I saw a soldier with a build like yours, I'd stop to see if it was you. It was just one disappointment after another, year after year. Isn't twenty-five years of emptiness and confusion a long enough purgatory?" Tears continued to stream down her cheeks. Now they were tears of rage.

Her words cut through Glenn like a knife. "I'm so sorry Kathleen. Forgive me, I never meant to hurt you. My life has been a terrible ordeal since I left you. The war changed a lot of things and people, too. I'm the one responsible for not keeping in touch. My foolish pride has often gotten me in trouble, and this time it destroyed my life and hurt you in the process."

"Glenn, stop! Nothing can be settled at this stage of our lives if we're looking for a chance to place blame on each other. If we must blame something we should blame the war. It destroyed entire countries, entire generations of dreams, and hopes for the future. Honestly, I've never really blamed you, not deep down. Oh, I was terribly hurt when I saw that time was slipping away. I couldn't understand what had happened to us. I never knew..." She buried her head in her hands and softly wept.

It hurt Glenn to see Kathleen so distraught. He wanted to hold her like he had long ago. He spoke to her in a calmer voice with his heart. "I have a hard time explaining it to myself, Kathleen. When I saw the announcement of your engagement in the paper, I was prepared to leave town. I would have too, if our daughter hadn't come to the inn to announce herself to me. I wish you much happiness and fulfillment, Kathleen. Surely nobody deserves it more than you."

"Jim has been good to me," she acknowledged. "We have many things in common. He's teaching at the high school now."

"Yes, Glenis told me a little about him. I am happy for you," said Glenn, checking his watch. "I'm glad I stopped by, Kathleen. I just wanted to see you one more time. Also, I'd like to be a part of our daughter's life, if she'll permit me. But don't worry, it's not my intention to intrude or make a nuisance of myself in any way." He paused and looked into her eyes. "You know Kathleen, you're as lovely as ever. I'll never understand why I stayed away."

Kathleen looked away. "We all have our share of regrets, Glenn," she said. "If you have some time, I'd like to show you something at the dock."

"My time is your time," he answered.

"Follow me then. It won't take long."

Glenn followed her Rambler in his Jeep to the familiar dock on the York River where a man was unloading the boat of its catch of the day. The man recognized Kathleen's car and walked over to greet her.

"Hi, Kathy," said Philip Cohen in that clipped peculiar Maine dialect of his. He was not a big man like his father had been, instead he had a thin wiry frame with angular facial features like Kathleen. He had those same deep-set eyes that could practically look through you. He looked like Kathleen and her mother. Glenn noticed the walk and recalled how Glenis said he wore an artificial leg.

"Phil, this is Glenn Hastings, Glenis's father," Kathleen introduced him. "He's come to Maine for a visit. The first since the war…"

"I'm glad to meet you. Glenis stopped by a little while ago right after she left you, Glenn. She was happier than I've seen her in years," Phil said, looking Glenn over closely. "She's a great girl. She's more worried about Andy in Vietnam than she lets on to any of us. He's a helicopter pilot and is at more risk than the riflemen on the ground. I'm glad you gave her something to help take her mind off the war."

Glenn liked his straight-forward attitude. "Her mother and the rest of you have a right to be proud of her. She's a wonderful girl. I'm sorry to have missed out on so much of her life. Life's too complicated and too short as it is."

"She told me about your son being killed in Vietnam. I'm sorry for you," Phil said sincerely.

"Your son was killed?" Kathleen asked with a puzzled expression on her face.

"Yes," Glenn nodded. "I told Glenis about my two sons. They were twins. Melvin is in the Army. He came to visit me in the Portsmouth Hospital the other day, and Glenis ran into him in the cafeteria. My other son, Marvin, joined the Coast Guard right out of high school instead of going to college. He was killed in Vietnam. His patrol boat came under fire from heavy shore batteries and was disintegrated by a direct hit."

Kathleen was struck with the pain of Glenn's loss. She impulsively reached out to grasp his hands and held them tightly in hers. "I'm so sorry, Glenn."

"The Coast Guard has quite a contingent over there in Vietnam. You must be proud of him," added Phil visibly unnerved at the details of Marvin's death.

"I was proud of him," Glenn murmured. "The last time I saw him he looked so strong and sturdy in his chief's uniform. His death has been hard to accept. A lot of good men have died for this country. I only hope that the people are worthy of their sacrifice." He looked away, lost in thought. "Still, God works in strange ways. He took my son away from me, but now He's given me a beautiful daughter I've just discovered. That's something to be thankful for."

Philip saw in Glenn that same spirit and determination common to most combat veterans, regardless of age. It was a difficult quality to define or describe to the uninitiated, but those who had been to the edge of the volcano recognized that look in others when they saw it. It was a shared experience of a select band of brothers.

"The docks here haven't changed much from when my father took you out to sea back in 1942," Phil commented, breaking the sober tone of the conversation. "The boat may look the same, but it's heavier and slightly larger than the old one you rode in, and much more seaworthy."

"If I remember correctly," said Glenn, examining the boat more closely, "the old one had a six cylinder Chevrolet engine."

105

"This one has a small diesel engine," Phil replied. "I was glad to eliminate the risk of gasoline fires at sea. The potential for fire is a lot less with diesel fuel."

"Phil," Kathleen interrupted. "I wanted to show Glenn something in the shack."

"Sure, I've got to finish unloading the boat anyway, so I'll say, 'so long' to you Glenn, for now. It was great meeting you. I'm glad for you and for Glenis."

"Thanks, Philip. It's been a pleasure," assured Glenn, walking towards the shack with Kathleen.

The old equipment shack was the same as Glenn remembered it. The tea-drinking ritual before and after a trip out to sea to harvest lobsters, had touched him when Ernest Cohen introduced him to the tradition. It was a select and exclusive group of individuals who were allowed to be part of the ritual. Glenn recalled that Ernest Cohen had offered him a guest mug to give thanks for a safe passage and a bountiful harvest. The peg board holding the cups looked exactly as he remembered it in 1942.

Kathleen opened the door wider and placed a wedge beneath it to hold it steady. She then reached for a mug at the top of the board the same color and size as the others. She held it carefully in her two hands before passing it to Glenn.

"This one was made especially for you. Father was so proud the day he received it from the store. It was his way of letting you know that he'd accepted you completely. He was hoping that someday he'd have the chance to share a toast with you again. It's a small symbol of how he felt about you."

Glenn accepted the mug and turned it so that the light picked up the inscription: "For Glenn Hastings, an honorary crew member of the *Santa Maria*.

Chapter Eleven

The simple message of acceptance and inclusion reached out and struck Glenn with the force of a heavy blow. He struggled to restrain his emotions. He had waited too long to return! He had hurt not only himself but also others like Ernest Cohen, who had been so kind to him. He could still picture the powerful, self-reliant fisherman on that day they had pulled traps together. He had failed Kathleen and her family, all of whom had welcomed him into their hearts. His hand shook as he replaced the mug on the wooden peg. A deep feeling of sadness consumed him.

"It's yours, Glenn," Kathleen informed him in a calm voice.

"If you don't mind, I prefer to leave it where it belongs," answered Glenn, losing the struggle to remain calm.

"Are you all right?" she asked in a soft voice.

He replied in a tremulous voice. "No, I'm not all right, Kathleen. I haven't been right since I said good-bye to you in 1942. I didn't expect to react this strongly and I apologize. Too much time has passed. We're not the same people anymore. I'm not sorry I came back, but I expected too much and was only thinking of myself. I think it's best that I leave. I didn't mean to bother you." Glenn abruptly turned away from the shack and walked as fast as he could toward the Wagoneer.

Kathleen hurried after him. "Glenn, I'm so sorry. I didn't intend to upset you by showing you the mug. I was hoping that it would reassure you that others cared for you, too."

Glenn reached the Jeep and turned toward her. "Kathleen, I really do thank you and your family for caring. I can't believe it would hurt so much, just a simple mug, it's hard to imagine."

Kathleen saw that same empty stare that had so alarmed Bob Smart. Horrified at what she saw in Glenn's eyes, she reached out for him as he was getting in the Jeep.

"I'm sorry, Glenn, please don't leave like this."

His view of her was clouded by tears he did not want her to see. "Kathleen, if I had the power, I'd turn back the clock to yesterday, but it's impossible. Your father was a good man, and I could have loved him like a son loves a father if I'd had a chance. This trip has been worthwhile because I've found a lovely daughter whom I want to get to know better. I was not a part of her life as a child, but maybe I can be for her son. I wish you and your fiancé all the happiness you've been denied for all those years. I regret the worry and heartache I've caused you. Can you forgive me, Kathleen?"

"Of course," she replied without hesitation.

"With your forgiveness, I'll be able to leave York with fewer regrets." With that, Glenn closed the door of the Wagoneer and rolled the window down.

"You can't leave now without seeing your grandson or Mother," Kathleen cried. "She would be crushed if you failed to see her, Glenn. Please, she's old and fragile, and her support and loyalty to you deserves some acknowledgment."

"Well, what do you suggest, Kathleen?"

"Perhaps you could come to the house for supper at say, seven o'clock? Glenis is staying with us while Andy is overseas. Little Ernest will be there and you can see him then." Kathleen made the offer, feeling powerless to comfort Glenn.

"Okay, I'll be there," answered Glenn, starting the Jeep.

The pain in Glenn's eyes stung Kathleen, and tears of frustration formed in her eyes. She watched the Jeep as it pulled up the driveway out of sight. Philip saw her standing alone and motionless in the yard and approached her.

"Is anything wrong, Kathleen?"

"Everything is wrong, Phil. It's been over twenty-five years since I saw him and then, when he finally had the courage to return, all I could do was berate him for his absence."

"Kathleen, this is the first time I've met Glenn. It's certainly not long enough to know the man, but I can tell you something about him."

"What do you mean?" she asked, feeling a sudden restlessness in her heart.

"I never said much about what happened during the war. When I came home and started my recovery process for this artificial leg, I had to erase a lot of ugly images from my heart. You and all the other family members who were physically safe here at home can never know how horrible some of those memories are to us vets who experienced the terror. I saw that same terror in Glenn's eyes. They tell you a lot about a person. He's been to the brink, Kathleen, and he's searching for something, anything that will ease his pain."

Kathleen understood what her brother was saying. "Yes, I did notice something different about him. He wasn't the same person..."

"My God, Kathleen!" Phil burst out. "How could he possibly be the same person? A few minutes of sheer terror on the battlefield can change a man forever. Remember, Glenn earned the Medal of Honor, and the accompanying citation is impressive. While others were doing their duty, he rose above personal concern and out of responsibility and love for the men in his command, he rose to the challenge and did what he thought was necessary without any thought of his own safety."

"I know," Kathleen answered, recalling the citation in the book Philip had given her. "I was proud of him when I read it

109

too, but I wasn't surprised. He always had a gentle strength that I found reassuring."

"The wounds he suffered, and his recovery from them may have been a more frightening ordeal than anything else." Phil knew what he was talking about. "Who knows? I don't know Glenn well enough to judge him, but I can tell you one thing. Any person who has earned the Medal of Honor has won my respect."

"It's so strange," Kathleen sighed. "Glenn shows up the same week Jim and I announce our engagement."

Phil eyed her sharply. "Are you having second thoughts, Kathleen?"

"No, no I'm not. It's just that I'm shocked to see him again after so long."

"What do you think Jim will think about his showing up at this time?" asked Phil. "He has a tendency to be rather possessive of you."

"Oh, Phil, you exaggerate his attentiveness to me. I've told Jim all about Glenn and we'll just have to handle his presence like mature adults. Besides, Jim and I have started to build a whole new life together. I never had one with Glenn except for a few months when both of us were still so young and the terrible war interfered with everyone's plans for the future."

"I didn't mean to upset you, Sis."

"You haven't really, Phil. I've got to get ready for supper, Mother's home alone with Ernest."

"Here, take some lobsters for tonight's meal," Phil offered. "Say 'hi' to Mom, and tell her I'll stop by tomorrow."

"I will," Kathleen answered, accepting the basket of lobsters from Phil.

Glenn had left Kathleen with mixed feelings. He drove slowly along the beach and turned up the hill to the Nubble Lighthouse. He needed some time to be alone, to reflect on what he was doing and where he was going. The lighthouse sat solidly on the granite cliffs flashing its signal day and night to ships at sea, ensuring a safe passage to those who heeded its beacon. He had to bring his emotions under better control for the remainder of his visit in York. His outbursts were not only unsettling to him, they had the potential of straining his meeting with Kathleen and Glenis. He had to dig deeper into his reservoir of determination and curtail what he always viewed were signs of weakness. He watched the churning sea breaking upon the cliffs again and again, without any measurable progress, and was reminded of his own inability to let go of the past. He and Kathleen had come often to the lighthouse where they had sat in silence and listened to the ocean. He could still see her gazing out across the water, a sea breeze combing her long hair. His vision of her had remained alive, never diminishing with the passage of time. Tears suddenly swept away all his efforts to stop them. At last, once again, he had found her, only to lose her to somebody else!

Later, Glenn returned to his room at the inn to change clothes and shave in preparation for his visit to the Cohen household. On his way there, he stopped at a florist to buy a bouquet of red roses. Turning into Kathleen's driveway seemed so natural. With some apprehension, he climbed the steps to the porch and knocked on the door.

A smiling Kathleen opened it. "When you say seven o'clock you mean seven, don't you?" she greeted him. A long dormant feeling of excitement made her feel warm all over when she saw him standing at the door. "Thank you for coming, Glenn."

He held out the flowers to her. "I bring a peace offering of red roses for a lovely lady." Glenn felt much more at ease and in control than he had been earlier.

"Thank you, they're beautiful. Come in. Glenis is giving Ernest his bath and getting him changed into his pajamas. They'll be down in a few minutes. Mother's in the living room; she's anxious to see you." She led the way into the large living room with a view of the river. Mrs. Cohen was sitting in a Boston rocking chair near the fireplace. A small fire was crackling merrily on the hearth. Mrs. Cohen's milk-white hair hung loose about her shoulders. She was a small-framed lady with angular features like Glenis and Kathleen. She hadn't changed much, Glenn thought when he saw her. She still had those bright sparkling eyes that seemed to light up when she talked. Most of the family inherited that characteristic from her.

"Mother, you remember Glenn Hastings," announced Kathleen.

"I never forgot you," Mrs. Cohen replied, reaching out for him. "Welcome back, Glenn."

"It's good to see you, Mrs. Cohen, it's been a long time and I apologize for my absence." Glenn eagerly grasped her long frail hands with both of his. He had always liked Kathleen's mother. She was a hardworking, plain-talking lady who devoted herself to her family.

"You're forgiven, young man."

"I'm not so young anymore," Glenn returned her smile.

"I can use the term because it's relative," she laughed, still holding his hands tightly. Glenn was enveloped with the same feeling he had long ago. Warmth and harmony filled the room.

"You know, I never forgot this room and your family," Glenn reflected, remembering how it had been. "I carried that same feeling of peace and tranquility with me throughout the war. It sustained me more times than I could ever tell and it's still here. It's a warmth, from people who care, that fills the heart." He nodded as if to himself, murmuring, "Yes, I've been away too long."

"Glenn Hastings, you're going to make me cry if you don't stop." exclaimed Mrs. Cohen, pleased with his remarks. "The years have been kind to you. You haven't changed much. But I must say that you looked better in your uniform than you do in civilian clothes."

"Mother," Kathleen scolded. "Don't pay any attention to her, Glenn, she says the same thing about Phil. Ah, here comes the youngest member of the family." Kathleen saw Glenis and Ernest coming down the stairs and went to check on dinner.

"Hi, Father," said Glenis, obviously glad to see him. "This little boy is your grandson, Ernest. Ernie, this man is your grandfather, the same one I showed you in the photograph."

Four-year-old Ernest Richards was dressed in a one piece pajama suit with Walt Disney characters printed on the front. He was a shy child with the same bright eyes that ran in the Cohen family. He clung to his mother, watching Glenn carefully and wasn't too sure of him.

"Hi, Ernest," said Glenn, gently kneeling down to his grandson's level. "This is the first time I've seen you. Your mother and grandmother tell me that you're a very good boy."

Ernest tugged at his Mother's hand. "Is he the same man in the picture, Mom?"

"Yes, he is," Glenis replied.

"He doesn't look the same," Ernest whispered to her.

Glenn laughed heartily. "Aha, a child who speaks the truth. Well, Ernest, that picture was taken a long time ago when I was much younger. I may not look the same, but I hope that you and I and your mother have a chance to see each other more often from now on. I promise to be your friend. If you want to be my friend, we can be pals and have lots of fun together. Do you think that would be possible?"

He thought about what Glenn had said, and looked up at his mother, then answered, "Yeah, I think so."

"You look comfy and cozy in your pjs," said Glenn. "You're lucky, you get to go to bed before the rest of us." He looked up at Glenis with a questioning look on his face.

"I'm afraid he fights bedtime like the plague," Glenis teased. "But the women in his life eventually win out. His father gives him a lot more liberties."

113

"Well, us guys got to stick together, don't we?" Glenn winked at him.

"Are you a soldier like my dad?" Ernest asked Glenn.

"Yes, I was a soldier once when I was young. You must be proud of your dad. I haven't met him, but I'm proud of him, too. While he's away, do you try to be Mom's little man about the house?"

"Sometimes," admitted little Ernest.

Kathleen called from the kitchen. "Come everyone, the lobsters are ready. I hope you brought a good appetite with you, Glenn,"

"I certainly did," he called to her. "May I escort you to the table, Mrs. Cohen?" offered Glenn.

"I'd like that if you don't mind."

"It'll be my pleasure," he answered, helping her out of the rocker.

"I don't get around as well as I would like," she admitted. "It's my knees mostly. Kathleen watches over me as if I was one of her pupils."

"And I'll bet you like it that way." grinned Glenn.

"If I did, I'd never admit it, young man!" answered Mrs. Cohen briskly, a gleam in her eye and a determined tilt to her chin.

Glenn took a seat beside Glenis with Kathleen opposite him and Mrs. Cohen at the end of the table next to him. Ernest sat at the other end of the table opposite his grandmother.

"I took the liberty of cracking the lobster claws and cutting the tails so that they would be easier to eat. The Cohen family has probably eaten more lobster than any other food, yet, we still enjoy them," said Kathleen, serving vegetables and potatoes.

"Nothing beats the Maine lobster," Glenn declared. "The lobsters of the warmer southern waters are a pale imitation in comparison." Kathleen smiled and nodded in agreement.

The meal progressed smoothly. Everyone ate their fill and Glenn found the fellowship at the table comforting. Mrs. Cohen chatted happily about the days when she and her husband were first married and settled in York. She took delight in teasing Kathleen about how shy she had been on her first date as a junior in high school. It contributed to a feeling of well-being. Glenn had forgotten how soothing the atmosphere at the Cohen household was. He felt accepted and elated. This was what he had been searching for! The simple peace and serenity of a loving home where people cared for each other and supported one another. It made him think about his two sons.

"Is Melvin scheduled to go overseas soon?" asked Glenis. "I told Mother and Grandmother about my visit with him. He looks so much like you in that picture I have of you in uniform."

"Melvin is at a staging area, so I believe he'll be leaving soon. I'm thankful for the time he was in college, that kept him out of the war for a few years anyway. Marvin, on the other hand, went into the Coast Guard right after high school and served two terms in Vietnam."

"Glenis told us about his death," announced Mrs. Cohen in a clear voice. She placed a sympathetic hand on his arm. "What a horrible thing for you to go through. You have our prayers and sympathy."

"Without reservation," Kathleen reiterated, glimpsing the hidden anguish in Glenn's eyes.

"I really appreciate your prayers," he said. Sometimes just the mention of his son's name would trigger despair. Glenn continued in precise measured tones afraid that he would break down in front of the Cohens. "Marvin was a fine young man. You would've liked him and been proud of him, too, if you'd known him. Yes, it's been difficult. But, time is slowly healing the wounds. I think often about the twins. They were extremely close and supportive of each other. I'm thankful that we had Marvin for as long as we did. Nobody hates war as bitterly as an old soldier."

Touched by Glenn's loss, Kathleen added, "Philip told me the same thing in different words this afternoon."

Kathleen announced that dessert would be apple pie and vanilla ice cream, a sweet and simple compliment to a good meal like the last bars of a symphony. Everyone asked for a piece.

"This meal has spoiled me. I'm not used to real home cooking," said Glenn, with an impish smile. Before they had finished their dessert, a knock came at the door. Glenis answered it.

"Hello, Jim." Glenn heard her say. "Come on in. You're just in time for dessert. Mother, it's Jim."

"Yes," answered Kathleen, excusing herself from the table to greet him.

Glenn watched with interest how Kathleen took Jim's hands and allowed him to kiss her briefly on the lips.

"Come in, Jim, there's someone I want you to meet," Kathleen said, leading him into the dining room.

"I wondered who owned the car outside," James Farley mentioned. He was a tall heavy set man with light blue eyes and blond hair. Glenn's first impression was that he was either German or Swedish. There was a formal air about him that discouraged friendly banter or intimacy.

"Jim, meet Glenn Hastings," Kathleen introduced them. "Glenn, this is my fiancé, Jim Farley."

"Well, how do you do," said Jim Farley taken aback by this sudden appearance of a man he'd heard so much about.

"Hello, I'm glad to meet you," Glenn told him warmly. "Congratulations on your engagement to Kathleen. I wish you much happiness."

"You two have something in common," added Kathleen. "You're both engineers."

"Where do you work, Mr. Hastings?" Jim asked.

"Please, call me Glenn. I have my own company in Philadelphia. We've specialized in designing and constructing industrial and manufacturing plants and the transport of their products to market. We also did a small railroad in Peru. Right now we're involved in building an aluminum plant in northern Quebec. Are you an engineer or a teacher?"

"I'm an engineer by trade but have been teaching for a few years. I like working with young minds and derive a lot of satisfaction in seeing them develop to their full potential. Money and power is not the only measure of success," claimed James Farley with a condescending air.

"A noble profession, Mr. Farley, I couldn't agree more. Still, the world needs builders with vision and the courage to dream," Glenn noted.

Mrs. Cohen listened to the conversation without comment and was impressed not only with Glenn's achievements, but also with his ability to stand his ground to Jim, who had a tendency to be opinionated.

Farley hadn't noticed Mrs. Cohen at the far end of the table. When he did, he acknowledged her.

"Hello, Mother Cohen," he said. "I thought I'd stop by to see how you were doing."

"Hello, Jim," she replied. "I'm fine and in good company."

"I can't stay too long, I've got a backlog of work that needs to be done. It was nice meeting you, Glenn. Are you going to be in town long?"

"I expect to leave within a day or two. This is the first time I've seen my daughter and grandson, and I plan to take advantage of the moment and enjoy them."

"Well, that makes sense, after all, you've been away for quite a while," said Jim matter-of-factly. Glenn detected a hint of sarcasm in the remark, but chose to let it pass. He decided then that James Farley was not going to be on his list of favorite people.

"That's true, nobody knows that any more than I do. I hope to make up for that in the years to come!" replied Glenn firmly. "It was nice meeting you. I wish you and Kathleen the very best."

"Well, very good. Goodnight, Mrs. Cohen. Good-bye, Kathleen, I'll see you tomorrow." Kathleen escorted him to the door. He gave a final nod of his head to Glenn who smiled in return.

Once Jim had gone, Glenis stated with authority, "It's that time of night, Ernie. Would you like to help me tuck him in bed, Father?"

"I'd love to," Glenn replied, reaching to pick up his grandson. "Uh, uh, Grandmother, someone's got a dirty face and he can't go to bed like that." Glenn held Ernest up for Kathleen to wipe his face with a wash cloth.

"There, little man," she said. "Give Gramma a kiss goodnight." Kathleen caught Glenn's expression as he held Ernest, and a feeling of relief came over her. She saw contentment in his eyes and was happy for him.

"Give your great grandmother a kiss goodnight, too," Glenn suggested. "You're one lucky boy, you have a lot of wonderful people who love you." He held Ernest for Mrs. Cohen to kiss.

"Goodnight, Ernest. Sleep tight and say a prayer for me."

"I know that you can go up these stairs better than I do, but it's been a long time since I held a little boy in my arms," said Glenn affectionately. "How about I carry you to bed. Is it a deal?"

"It's a deal," answered Ernest, wrapping his little arms tightly around his neck. Glenn interpreted it as acceptance of the offer. "Which way do we go," Glenn asked at the top of the stairs.

"That way," Ernest pointed to his room on the left.

"Reporting for bedtime, Mother," said Glenn, laughing out loud.

"Would you like to join us in an evening prayer?" asked Glenis, kneeling beside Ernest's bed.

"Yes, of course."

The three of them knelt beside the bed and folded their hands. They repeated a prayer Glenn had taught to the twins when they were Ernest's age:

> Now I lay me down to sleep,
> I pray the Lord my soul to keep,
> If I should die before I wake,
> I pray the Lord my soul to take.

Glenis added, "We also pray for God to watch over Daddy and bring him home safe as soon as possible, to watch over Grandmother and Great Grandmother and to thank Him for bringing your grandfather into our lives. Amen."

When they were finished, Ernest climbed into bed. Glenis pulled the blankets up around him and hugged and kissed him goodnight.

"Goodnight Mother, goodnight Grandfather," said the little boy.

It was the first time the boy had called him "Grandfather," and Glenn was moved by it and gave him a hug. "Good night, Grandson, rest well."

Glenis waited for her father at the head of the stairs and placed her arm around him. They walked down the stairs together.

Kathleen again noted the contentment on Glenn's face. "The roses you brought me tonight reminded me of something I want to show you, Glenn," she said, holding up a large encyclopedia book in her hands. "Do you remember bringing roses to me just before you left for overseas?"

"Yes, I remember buying them at the same place I purchased the roses today, between the village and the harbor."

"Well, this is one of them," said Kathleen, carefully opening the book to present a dried and pressed rose. She gently picked it from the book. "I'm surprised that it still holds together. I've taken it out of the book so many times." She caressed the dried petals with a longing look that touched Glenn. They were a symbol of the love he had for her.

"I'll be, it has retained its bright red color," murmured Glenn. It was what he would have expected from her. She was sentimental about a lot of things, but refused to let those around her know about it.

Mrs. Cohen bid Glenn a pleasant evening before retiring to her room. He reached out for her hand and held it for several seconds.

"Mrs. Cohen, the world has turned more times than I like to remember since I was last here. Much has changed since then, but one thing that has remained a constant is the harmony and peace that still reigns supreme within these walls. I want to tell you how proud I am that my daughter and grandson have been nurtured in such an environment. God bless you."

Mrs. Cohen embraced him, beaming. "Mr. Glenn Hastings, you have a gift for making people happy. I always saw the goodness that was in your heart. Come back to us as often as you can. Goodnight, thank you for coming."

"Goodnight, Mrs. Cohen. Thank you for having me."

Glenis had retreated to the kitchen table to write a letter to her husband. Kathleen noted the warm interchange between her mother and Glenn. She smiled and motioned him to the sitting room.

"Glenn," she said, once they were alone. "I have something to show you that we talked about earlier. It has been a source of wonder to me for a long time."

Glenn noticed that she had a stack of letters in her hand. "I was hoping you would find the letters."

"These are all of the letters that were returned to me. The first time you were transferred to a stateside hospital, the Army must have made a mistake in your address, because the letters I wrote were returned. They were all stamped with the familiar stamp of a finger pointing to the return address and the words 'return to sender' printed as if it was a part of the stamp. Twenty of your letters were returned that way."

"I had no way of knowing," Glenn said, astonished. "That was the lowest ebb of my life. I was like a vegetable. I couldn't speak or eat and I couldn't move my legs."

"I didn't give up then," continued Kathleen. "After a lot of searching and phone calls, I discovered that you had been sent to a civilian physical therapy center in Philadelphia, so I started to write to you again. I sent ten letters and they were all returned to me with the words 'return to sender' written by hand on the envelope. Here are the letters that came back to me."

Glenn accepted the letters and checked the address for the therapy center; it was correct. Then, the hand written notice on the envelopes grabbed his attention! The writing was the same on each one, a unique style of penmanship. He looked up at Kathleen, his face white as snow.

"It can't be," he said faintly. "The handwriting is unquestionably Jessica's."

Chapter Twelve

"What are you telling me, Glenn?" Kathleen asked sharply. "Was I wrong to be disturbed by the handwriting? I assumed that it was a woman's handwriting and the likelihood of its being the same person each time over a period of two weeks at such a large Post Office was improbable. In order to test my misgivings, I sent a letter to a John Doe at the therapy center. The post office returned it to me with the familiar stamp of the extended finger. This is the letter."

Glenn examined the envelope. "I can't explain it, Kathleen. The address is correct, I was there then. As I recall, Jessica did bring my mail to me, and I never thought anything about it. I couldn't do much except think about my physical condition and how I was going to get back to normal, if that was possible."

"Why would she do that to you, if she claimed to love you?" Kathleen pressed for some explanation. "Getting those letters back really hurt. The more I thought about it over the years, the more it hurt and the angrier I got. If Jessica is the one who did this, then I hate her for being so callous and selfish."

The torment in Kathleen's voice, stabbed at his heart. "I don't know what to say, Kathleen. I can't defend Jessica's actions. My God, she was dictating every facet of my life at that time. I interpreted her controlling behavior as love and I needed her more than I can ever tell you. It appears now that she thrived on my dependency. The more you think about it, the sicker it sounds." Glenn was stunned by the magnitude of Jessica's possessiveness.

Kathleen gazed back at him soberly. "My sentiments exactly."

Glenn released an anguished sigh. "I'm so sorry for the part I played in this horror story. Oh Kathleen, I never dreamed it would end this way. My God, what have I done to us?" Glenn looked at her with beseeching eyes. She was standing by the fireplace staring helplessly into the glowing embers. The flickering shadows danced across her face hiding the tears she held in check. It was all Glenn could do to keep from taking her into his arms. How he ached to hold her one more time. He whispered, "I never stopped loving you, Kathleen. I could never be a part of anything that would hurt you. You must believe that."

His words hung in the air as Kathleen paused to collect her thoughts. "I've always known it, Glenn." She continued in a low voice, choosing her words carefully. "Right after the war, there might have been a chance for us, but it's different now. We've changed and our lives have changed. The reality is, I'm not getting any younger. I want to share the companionship of someone I love and who loves me in return. I don't mean to be cruel and I don't want to hurt you, Glenn, but we've got to be honest with each other. I have a chance to live out the rest of my days with Jim and I believe we can be happy together. I want to live my life, not simply exist in anticipation of tomorrow. Tomorrow is already here for me. I hope you can understand that."

Her words were not unexpected, and yet they had cut him deeply and left him numb. "It's plain enough to me," answered Glenn. Whatever he and Kathleen had once shared, was now over. "I don't hold it against you. If you can find happiness with Jim, then, you two have my blessings. Life is way too short to not seize happiness when it's offered. I did, and though I have some regrets now, the twins have been a gift that I cherish. Sure, it's true, deep in my heart I was hoping, against all the odds, to find something for us. The embers glowed for a long time and it's only natural that when the flame flickers and dies it can't be recharged."

"Do you hate me for this, Glenn?" she asked.

"No," he looked at her sadly. "I blame myself if there's any blame to be placed. I'd give my life to shelter you from harm. It would be impossible for me to ever hate you." A cold tremor ran through his body and he felt a sudden urge to be alone. "It's getting late and I should really be going. Thanks for a memorable evening. It's been swell seeing you again," he said with a wry smile.

"I understand," Kathleen replied softly.

"Please say good-bye to Glenis and your mother for me. I'll be leaving York in the morning. Before I go would you promise me one thing?"

"If I can, I will."

"If there is ever a time in your life that you need a friend and/or a helping hand, no matter what the circumstances, promise that you'll come to me."

"Thank you, Glenn, I promise. Time has diminished what we once had, but my respect and admiration for you as a person has never faltered. I hope that God will guide you to the happiness you're searching for and so richly deserve. Good-bye, Glenn."

"Good-bye, Kathleen." Without a word she embraced him tightly, and quickly closed the door behind him. He looked back at the door wistfully, then walked briskly to the Wagoneer.

The next morning Glenn arose early, notifying the clerk at the desk that he would be leaving and went in the dining room for a cup of coffee. He reflected that his reasons for making the trip had been vindicated. All in all he had found more than he bargained for. Now, he had to let Kathleen go. It was all over, and the time had come to bow out as gracefully as he could. The key to his future was not in the past as he and Kathleen were painfully aware, their hourglass of time was two-thirds full and waiting for no one.

The hurt from the rejection was still there, yet, at the same time, there was an element of freedom and release from bondage that he had felt beholden to. The yoke of responsibility for Kathleen had been lifted by her own choice. It was a bittersweet experience and she still occupied his mind as he sipped his coffee. He was released from his reverie when Glenis unexpectedly showed up at the dining room and went directly to his table.

"Good morning, Glenis. I didn't expect to see you."

"I have to report for a day shift today, but I wanted to check on you first," she replied. She was in a serious mood. "You left the house in a hurry last night, and I wanted to make sure that you were all right. Mother was so quiet last night after you left. I don't want to pry into your affairs, but if there's some way I can help either of you, I hope you'll let me."

Glenn felt a rush of love for his newfound daughter. "Dear girl, I love you for your generous heart. There's nothing you or anyone else can do for your mother and me. What we had together was incredibly special and precious to me. I'll always treasure it, but love that's left unnurtured eventually withers on the vine, like the blooms of spring. Our time has come and gone. I'm not bitter; disappointed, yes, terribly disappointed, but not bitter."

"Oh, Father, I know how painful this must be for you. On the other hand, Mother and Jim have been happy together. I just didn't want you to leave York with a heavy heart."

"Don't worry about me," he smiled affectionately. "I'll be fine. I'm glad you came because I want to speak to you about something. My business has been relatively prosperous, and I've lived a frugal existence all of my life. I've never really used the financial gains my company has generated for my personal satisfaction. What I'm trying to say is if you and Ernest ever need any financial help, I hope you'll call on me. That goes for

125

your mother and grandmother as well. Please, don't think I'm trying to buy your affection, but what good is money if you can't share its benefits with the ones you love? What I have is also yours, Glenis."

"Thank you, Father. That's a very sweet offer, but right now we're doing fine." She stood up and placed a loving hand on his shoulder. He squeezed it firmly. "I'm sorry, I've got to run or I'll be late for shift change."

"I understand; thanks for dropping by. I'll be in touch, I promise. Rest assured that I leave with a happier heart than when I first came to town. Give Ernest a hug for Grampa and tell him I love him," said Glenn, hugging her.

"I will. I'm so glad you've become a part of my life. You're just the way Mom described you. I've loved you for a long time."

"I love you, too. You've made a lonely old man feel like singing again, young lady, now go take on the world."

"Have a safe trip to Pennsylvania." Glenis waved good-bye as she left the dining room.

Glenn finished his coffee and returned to his room to collect his things. It was still early when he left the inn, and the town was free of traffic. He drove directly to Portsmouth where he signed new papers for the rental Wagoneer, which he would turn in at a Philadelphia agency when he got there. Then, he turned onto Route 95 south and headed back to Pennsylvania.

The hours Glenn spent on the road gave him time to think about his current situation, and he came to the conclusion that his life would be better overall if he could get out of the stressful environment of Philadelphia. The site for the aluminum processing plant in Quebec sounded like an interesting place to visit, especially in the summertime. He could monitor progress as resident engineer and break away from the main office at the same time. The idea of returning to the small apartment in the city held little appeal for him.

Before he traveled to Canada there was something weighing heavily on his mind that he needed to address. He couldn't get James Farley out of his mind. There was just something about the man that did not ring true. His claim of suddenly becoming enamored with the ideal of dispensing knowledge to young minds in the middle of an engineering career, sounded suspicious to Glenn. Glenn was not certain if it was because he did not like the man, or if he was just plain jealous of Jim's relationship with Kathleen.

On his first day back, Glenn decided to investigate a few things. He was a member of the American Society of Mechanical Engineers and had presented a number of papers at the Society's annual meetings. The Director was a personal friend of Glenn's, and he requested the Society to find out, if possible, why Jim Farley stopped being an engineer so suddenly. He was acting solely on a hunch that all was not well. Once he had that information, Glenn was not sure what he would do with it, but for his own satisfaction, he had to quell the uneasy thoughts that lingered in his mind.

The second day after his return, Glenn wrote a letter to Glenis:

June 20, 1969

Dear Glenis,

A few lines to let you know that I arrived in Philadelphia safe and sound. The traffic was terrible, but then, it always is. I'm afraid Maine's leisurely pace has spoiled me. My broken ribs must be mending without complications because I don't hurt anymore.

I have returned with a more positive outlook on the future and am looking forward to getting back to work. I have warm memories of you and Ernest and, of course, your mother and grandmother. Please thank them, for me, for their gracious hospitality. I'm not sure when I'll return to Maine. Right now I have several projects that need my attention. Soon though, I plan to break away from here and spend some time in the wilds of Canada where we have an interesting project underway.

If things go well, I may even investigate the chances of building a new home somewhere that will give me more privacy and a chance to `get back to nature' more than I have been able to these past few years. I'm really a frustrated forester at heart. I've loved my engineering work, but if I had it to do all over again, I'd study forestry instead. I have a dear friend who is a forester. I've probably made more money, but he's had a richer life working in Nature's best handiwork — our nation's forests.

I received a phone call from Melvin. I told him all about my trip to York. You and your mother were, of course, the main topics of discussion. He has always known about my feelings for your mother, but he never knew who she was. I'm afraid that he'll be shipping out to Vietnam before too long. He mentioned that he might be able to get a few days off before his outfit leaves for the west coast, and he expressed a desire to meet with you and get to know you better. He admitted to me that he had received an unusual first impression of you and he was not surprised when I told him who you are. I didn't know about you spilling coffee all over his polished shoes until he told me over the phone, laughing. I love to hear him laugh, it comes from deep inside him and builds in intensity. I'm glad you two hit it off well. He was impressed to know that he has an older sister, (half-sister to be precise). You'll find him to be a gentleman and a kind, caring young man. It would please me a lot to know that the two of you had each other as mutual supports.

Tonight, my head man at the office, Bob Smart, is throwing a home-coming party for me. He and his wife, Anne, have been my best friends for a long time.

I love them both dearly, but they have a terrible habit of trying to match me up with an unattached lady acquaintance. Parties are not my favorite thing, but I don't want to disappoint Anne or Bob. They have always been there for me whenever I'm in need of a helping hand.

Goodnight, Glenis, goodnight, Ernest. I think often of you and it warms me to my toes. I love you,

Dad and Grampa.

Later that night, Glenn attended Bob's and Anne's party as guest-of-honor at their home. He hoped that it would be a simple gathering of a few friends. The Smart's two daughters no longer lived at home. Their departure was one of the reasons their parents entertained more often to help fill up their days and bring merriment to the empty household. When he turned into the driveway, Glenn was hopeful that his wish would be granted. Very few automobiles were parked in the driveway. That was a good sign. There were a couple of cars Glenn recognized as belonging to neighbors of the Smarts as well as a Ford Falcon that he did not recognize. As soon as he entered the house he was greeted by the Smarts and their neighbors, whom he had met before.

"Come in, Glenn." Bob welcomed him with his usual exuberance. "Let me introduce you around. Stan and Beverly Hughes and Don and Susan Mcleod. They all live down the street." Glenn warmly acknowledged the Hughes and the McLeod's.

"I also have a surprise for you, Glenn. I'd like to introduce Faith Hamilton. Faith, meet our boss, Glenn Hastings. Faith is our newest employee. We need a full-time hydraulic specialist for the site work at the aluminum plant in Quebec Province," Bob was pleased with the choice.

"Hello, Faith," said Glenn cordially. He recalled that Bob had mentioned the new addition to him earlier. "I'm glad to have a chance to get better acquainted with you."

"I'm pleased to meet you, too, Mr. Hastings," Faith replied. "Mr. Smart mentioned you might be coming tonight."

"In the past," said Bob, anxious to explain his decision to hire Faith Hamilton, "we've always contracted with consultants for water drainage and filtration studies when they've been required. Since we're getting more demands for them now, I thought we should have our own in-house expert. The Quebec contract is going to require an extensive evaluation of water distribution at the site before major construction begins, and the Canadians are also going to demand progress reports until completion, so we really require a full-time hydraulics person on site. We can pay Faith's salary and have her on the staff for other work locations for the same price it would cost us to sub it out, plus, we'll have more confidence in our figures."

Glenn was amused with his friend. "If Bob Smart checked your résumé I'm sure you're right for the job," Glenn reinforced Bob's decision. "By the way, I'll call you, Faith, if you'll call me Glenn. We're not that formal at the company."

"Please call me Faith," she agreed shyly. "Are you disappointed that I'm a woman?"

"Why no, of course not" he answered quickly, surprised at the question. "I'm not disappointed, it's just that Bob Smart moves rapidly and it never ceases to amaze me how often he's right. Where did you go to school?"

"I went to the University of Vermont. I'm really an agronomist, but hydraulics and its influence on the earth's surface inspired me to go back for my master's degree in hydraulic engineering at the same school in 1948."

"I'm sure you'll do fine," he said, comfortable with her straightforward answers.

Faith seemed reserved and slightly uncomfortable talking to her new boss. She was a little younger than Glenn and as the evening wore on, Glenn noted that she was capable of defending herself and articulating her ideas in a coherent manner. She was attractive without being showy. Her sandy blonde hair pulled up on top of her head made her look taller than she actually was. Her light complexion and hazel green eyes were accented by the dark green pantsuit she wore. There was a no-nonsense attitude about her that Glenn found refreshing.

"Couldn't your husband make it tonight?" asked Glenn, noticing the wedding band on her finger.

"My husband was killed in action in Korea at the Chosin Reservoir in 1950. He was an Army infantry officer," she answered without any further explanation.

"I'm sorry," said Glenn. "It must have been rough."

"Yes, it was," she offered with a wry smile. "Our son was born at the same time his father was killed."

"He must be a young man by now." Glenn had calculated the years mentally.

"He's nineteen and is a freshman at the University of Vermont," she proudly told him.

"You still live in Vermont, then?"

"Yes. I answered your ad for a hydraulic specialist because I was interested in making a change. While my son was in high school I worked with the Soil Conservation Service in Vermont. Now that he's in college, I thought it would be a good time to move into the private sector. Your job offered more money, so here I am. I'm staying at a motel for now, but I'm prepared to take up field residency at the job site in Quebec when it becomes necessary."

Glenn was pleased with her obvious sense of team spirit. "I'm beginning to understand why Bob Smart hired you, Faith. Welcome to our team. I'm sure Bob told you about how we operate and conduct ourselves as representatives of the company."

"He's been quite thorough," she grinned. Glenn could relate to her amusement. Bob Smart never left anything to chance. His detailed description of duties to employees were well known to everybody in the company.

"We respect and insist on professionalism. If you disagree with us on any topic, please let us know. I promise that no one will ever hold it against you if you can defend your position against mine or Bob's. I can't stand 'yes' people. If you can prove to me why my premise on anything is wrong, you'll have my gratitude for preventing me from making a mistake and looking like a fool."

"I appreciate that," said Faith hesitantly. "I've run into problems on occasion enforcing certain regulations that are important and unchanging simply because I'm a woman."

"The next time you run into that situation, Faith, you let Bob or me know about it," Glenn emphatically told her. "When you act as our agent, you carry our full support, and we'll back you with all the resources of the company without exception. I promise you that."

"Even though I'm a woman?" she asked.

"Even though you're a woman. You're a professional engineer, you speak as a professional engineer, and you have a right to be treated as a professional engineer without exception. If that is not reciprocated we'll find out why in a hurry and correct the situation."

"You feel strongly about this, don't you?" Faith observed.

"You bet I do. It's the way my company has always done business and it has worked without complications for years. I'm not about to change a winning combination when my name is at stake."

"Thank you. I appreciate the vote of confidence," she added. "And I promise to do my best. Whatever I do has my name on it, too."

With that, the tone of their conversation lightened as they moved onto the extensive buffet table. Glenn and Faith had just sat down at the kitchen table to eat, when Bob Smart interrupted them.

"I'm sorry to interrupt you two. Could I have a word in private with you, Glenn?"

"Is it worth eating my food cold?" asked Glenn, looking at Bob.

"I think you'll agree that it'll be worth it."

"All right. If you'll excuse us, Faith," said Glenn, following Bob outside onto the porch.

Bob spoke in a low voice. "I just got a call from the office of the executive director of our Mechanical Engineer Society about your inquiry into James Farley."

"Does he have anything for me?" Glenn's eyes lit up.

"Well, it's only preliminary, but he was able to determine that Farley was on a job site near Syracuse. He was a partner in an affordable housing development company. It seems that the company was dissolved by the State of New York for fraud. Farley forged signatures on several water tests in order to obtain occupancy permits."

Chapter Thirteen

"I knew there was something." exclaimed Glenn.

"The investigator will document the evidence within a couple of days and send it along to you. Evidently, Farley was heavily fined and black-balled from the Society of American Mechanical Engineers for failure to maintain their code of ethics."

"Thanks, Bob. You're right, it was worth interrupting a good dinner. Say, your choice of Faith looks like a good move. I think your judgment was sound."

"Of course, that's what you pay me for. She's highly qualified," Bob grinned, escorting him back to the table in the kitchen.

Anne and Faith were talking with each other when Glenn and Bob returned. "Sorry to have interrupted your conversation," Glenn apologized.

"What conspiracy are you two hatching up now?" Anne asked suspiciously, recognizing the smug look on her husband's face.

"Just some business details," reported Bob affectionately, grabbing his wife around the waist.

"I'll bet," Anne shot back with a shrug of resignation. "You aren't very clever at keeping secrets, you know. I may not know what it's about, but I know that it's a secret nonetheless."

"Someday we'll let you in on this one, Anne," promised Glenn. "Right now it's better left with Bob and me."

"Men!" proclaimed Anne breaking away from her husband's hold to check the buffet table. "Sometimes they're impossible, Faith."

Bob followed behind his wife and called back to Glenn, "I'll let you continue with your lunch, Glenn. See that he eats all of his veggies, Faith. He has a habit of bypassing them when he can."

"They're a nice couple," Faith remarked.

"They've been very dear friends to me. He's one of the most organized persons I've ever known, and a perfect complement to me. I'm a concept person who's occasionally off base from reality. Bob is a superb detail man who helps to keep me on track. His ability to work a slide rule still amazes me."

"That must be how you two have built the company you have today. It has a very good reputation in the professional engineering world. That's one of the reasons I responded to your ad. Detail men with facts at their finger tips are necessary to implement ideas, but the world around us has been shaped and influenced more by those with the capacity to dream and conceive bold theories that originate from the heart. Mechanics are plentiful in our society, true visionaries are rare."

Glenn wasn't sure if Faith was being philosophical or if she was giving him a compliment. Something about this new engineer continued to impress him. She seemed to always be in control and projected an air of serenity. She was obviously comfortable with herself, and Glenn envied people who had reached that level of inner strength. "I think you're going to be a fine addition to our team," he told her again.

"Thanks. I'll do my best."

The evening passed quickly for Glenn. He bid the Smarts goodnight shortly after Faith thanked them for an enjoyable evening and said good-bye. That night Glenn was preoccupied with thoughts of Jim Farley, and the newly uncovered information. He didn't sleep well. Questions cropped up that he was unable to answer and uncomfortable with. His main reason for investigating Farley had been personal, not professional. What right did he have to expose the man's transgressions when the information would cause nothing but unhappiness? Would revealing it advance Glenn's personal standing with Kathleen, or would she simply resent him for it and call him deceptive and small for being so selfish? Who was he to be judge and jury?

Several days later, Glenn was in his office studying plans for the Quebec plant when confirmation of the information on Farley was received from the ethics committee of the Society. Nothing new was added or detracted from what Bob Smart had already told him. However, it was indisputable evidence that Farley had violated the Society's code of ethics and potentially endangered the health and welfare of the new occupants of the structures under his supervision.

Evidently, reasoned Glenn, the York school board had not checked too deeply into Farley's background or they would have uncovered the same information Glenn and Bob had. The confirmation of the information did not resolve the issue of what Glenn should do with it, and he reluctantly decided to put it aside for the time being. He was certain that if Kathleen had knowledge of the incident, she would be extremely hurt and her feelings for Farley might be affected in some way. Glenn simply did not want to be responsible for making her unhappy.

* * *

In the meantime, while Glenn was orienting himself in Philadelphia, Glenis returned home early one morning after an exhausting night at the Portsmouth Hospital to find her mother doing laundry.

"You have a letter from your father, Glenis," announced Kathleen as soon as she came through the door.

"What a pleasant surprise! Is Ernest up yet?"

"No, he's still sound asleep," she answered handing Glenis the letter. "Would you like a cup of coffee?"

"Thanks, I'd love one." Glenis opened the letter and read it quietly. Kathleen placed two cups of hot coffee on the table and sat across from Glenis. When Glenis finished reading the letter, she passed it across the table to her mother. "That's a nice letter. He's everything I ever hoped for in a father. You always said he was a good person and it's true."

Kathleen read the letter slowly without comment. Then she carefully folded it and inserted it in the envelope. "I'm glad for you dear."

"Mother, tell me honestly, aren't you glad to see him again?"

Kathleen avoided the perceptive glance of her daughter and responded guardedly, "Yes, of course I was glad to see him again. He's older and more mature than I remembered him, but he still has that same quiet strength of character which defined him even as a very young man."

"I'm proud to call him my father," Glenis claimed solemnly.

"You have every right to be proud."

"Jim and Father didn't hit it off so good, did they?" Glenis inquired, anxious to hear what her Mother thought.

"No, I suppose they didn't," answered Kathleen, searching her heart for a suitable answer. "They're two very different personalities, so it's just possible that they would never be the best of friends under any circumstances."

"Meaning what?" Glenis saw a far away look in her mother's eyes.

"Young lady, don't forget who you're talking to," Kathleen warned. "Jealous feelings and bruised egos could have a lot to do with how Jim and Glenn perceived each other. I'm not sure I'm capable of making an objective comparison."

"I don't mean to hurt you or pressure you into something that's none of my business, Mother. It's just that I saw a look in your eyes when you were talking to Father that I've never seen when Jim was around."

"I'm engaged to Jim and I've given a lot of thought to that fact. It became more complicated when Glenn showed up, but it hasn't altered the reasons Jim and I got engaged. Do I have to justify what I do to you?"

"No, of course not," Glenis assured her. "I'm sorry I pressed so hard on such a personal subject. I didn't mean to upset you. I want your happiness as much as you do."

Kathleen sipped her coffee. "I'm looking forward to spending more time with Jim this summer vacation. It'll be good for the two of us. When you write your Father, give him my regards and tell him it was nice to see him again." With that, Kathleen dismissed the subject.

"I will, Mother."

* * *

Back in Philadelphia, Glenn and Bob spent several days at the office working on the Quebec project. Glenn planned to be a part of the initial design and construction crew. He hoped to hear from Melvin before he traveled to the Canadian wilderness where transportation was not easy to come by.

Melvin finally called with news of a definite timetable for his outfit's departure. The regiment was going to be shipped by train to the Presidio at San Francisco for naval transport to Vietnam. Melvin had been granted four days leave before he had to report to the Presidio command post. He had already made arrangements for a seat on a Military Air Transport aircraft out of Pease Air Force Base the last day of his furlough. He intended to spend a few days with his father in Pennsylvania and planned to go to York to visit with Glenis on the last day of his leave.

Glenn was delighted with Melvin's plans. With a definite itinerary available, Glenn reserved a rental car for himself and Melvin to drive to York. Glenn would then continue on to

Portland where he could pick up a flight to Quebec City and ultimately to the wilderness location. Living accommodations at the plant site were being prepared by the land clearing teams already at work. He had instructed Faith to take a few days off to prepare herself for the trip north, and suggested that she make her trip on the same shuttle he would be taking. She agreed to the schedule and promised to meet him in Portland on the assigned date, and left for Vermont to spend some time with her son.

Melvin arrived in Philadelphia as scheduled and spent two days visiting old friends and classmates. He spent some time with Anne and Bob Smart the day before he left for Maine with his father. Melvin was excited about the prospects of getting to know Glenis better. He drove the rental car from Philadelphia to York in six hours. It gave them a chance to visit with each other. Melvin asked a lot of questions about Glenis and the life she had lived with the Cohen family. He detected a wistful note in Glenn's answers.

"I've always known that a part of you was somewhere else, Dad," Melvin remarked thoughtfully. "I've been thinking a lot about the conversation we had the last time I saw you. Can you tell me more about Glenis's mother than you were able to then?"

Glenn shrugged. "I haven't tried to deceive you boys about my past. It just wasn't relevant to your lives, so I chose not to share it with you. I don't mind telling you about Kathleen Cohen now. I met her when I was a young soldier about the same age as you, Son. Maybe it was the war or maybe it was the two of us, but there was no guarantee of planning a future or even surviving the war, and we were caught up in that stark reality. It was a different time and place that this country will likely never see again. I loved Kathleen as completely as any man ever loved a woman. You know all about what happened to me after I was wounded. As crazy as it seems, I guess I loved your mother and Kathleen at the same time." Glenn watched the passing scenery and remembered how it had been.

139

Melvin had listened respectfully and asked, "Do you still love Kathleen, Dad?"

"She's engaged to another man and seems to be happy with their prospects for the future," Glenn answered calmly.

Melvin shook his head. "You haven't answered my question, Dad. Do you still love her?"

"That's a very difficult thing to answer, Son. To be brutally honest, yes, I still love her. I expect I'll always love what we once had, but time has a way of changing things. The truth is she doesn't feel the same way towards me that she once did. That's only natural. I love her enough to want her happiness, even if it's with another man," answered Glenn firmly. Melvin reached across the car seat and squeezed his father's arm.

"I haven't found the right girl that I could love the way you've demonstrated. Yet, I can understand how difficult it must be to carry the same feelings for so many years only to find that you're too late."

"I'm not that depressed about it, Son. After all, I've gained a daughter who promises to help dispel my disappointments. Glenis is a lot like her mother when she was younger, you're going to love her."

"When I called Glenis to tell her that I could come, she sounded really happy. She invited me to stay with them for the night and promised to drive me back to Pease in time for my flight to San Francisco."

"That's great. I'm so glad the two of you will have some time to become better acquainted before you ship out."

It was about two o'clock in the afternoon when Melvin turned the rental car into the Cohen's driveway. He switched off the ignition key and turned to Glenn.

"I'm a little nervous," Melvin confided. "I'm glad you're with me, Dad. This is a big day for me... a sister I never knew I had."

"Seeing you and Glenis together will gladden my heart."

Before they had even reached the top of the porch steps, the front door burst open and a jubilant Glenis met them with open arms. She embraced her father with tears of joy running down her cheeks, and then he introduced her to Melvin.

"Glenis, this is my son, Melvin, your half-brother. Mel, this is my lovely daughter, Glenis," Glenn's heart swelled as he witnessed his two children's reunion.

"Welcome to our home, Melvin!" Glenis hugged him tightly for several seconds until she regained control of herself.

Melvin embraced her as warmly. "I had a premonition about you when we met at the Portsmouth Hospital. It's nice to call you my sister." Melvin was excited and a little unsettled about the sudden discovery.

Kathleen stood quietly on the porch, observing the scene with a lump in her throat. The sight of Melvin standing straight and tall, just like his father, triggered a silent cry that sprang from her soul. Long buried memories were unleashed. She struggled to control the gush of feelings that rapidly engulfed her. Glenn saw her standing alone in the door and walked over to greet her.

"Hello, Kathleen. I'm back sooner than I expected."

"Hello, Glenn," she answered, holding out her arms to him as if it were the most natural thing in the world. Glenn accepted her warm embrace in silence. He could feel her tenseness. After a moment, he released her to introduce Melvin.

"Kathleen, this is my son, Melvin. Mel, meet Glenis's mother, Kathleen Cohen."

"How do you do, Miss Cohen," said Melvin, offering his hand to her.

"My lord, you look just like your father when I first met him," exclaimed Kathleen, brushing his hand to one side and hugging him.

Glenn's face was flushed from the emotionally-packed meeting. "I can only stay for a short time. I'm on my way to

141

Portland, where I'll pick up a flight for Quebec City," Glenn announced to Kathleen and Glenis.

"Come in, please. We've still got time to talk for a while before you have to leave, Father. Too bad, you'll miss Ernest. He's with Uncle Phil for the day."

The four of them made themselves comfortable in the living room. They talked a lot about the things that had touched their lives. Kathleen soon excused herself and insisted on making coffee before Glenn left for Portland. Several minutes later, she was serving coffee in the dining room when the phone rang.

"Hello, is this the Cohen residence?" asked Faith when Kathleen answered the phone.

"Yes it is," answered Kathleen, failing to recognize the voice on the other end of the receiver.

"I'm Faith Hamilton, and I'm calling to see if a Mr. Glenn Hastings is still there."

"Yes he is, just a moment please," responded Kathleen, motioning for Glenn to take the receiver. "It's Faith Hamilton."

"Hello, Faith," Glenn said into the phone. "What's going on?"

"I apologize for calling at this time, but I received word from the airlines that the flight to Quebec has been delayed a couple of hours. I thought it would give you more time for your visit in York. Bob Smart gave me the Cohen number."

"I appreciate it. Thanks for calling. I'll meet you at the airport in Portland. Is your son driving you from Vermont?"

"Yes," she replied.

"Have a safe trip then."

"I'll see you in Portland."

"That was our new engineer we just hired," Glenn explained to those present. "She's going to the Quebec plant site with me as one of our field representatives." Glenn took his place at the dining room table where Kathleen had served warm apple pie with the coffee. "Wow, that smells delicious, Kathleen."

"It certainly does. Home cooked food is a treat compared to Army rations," Melvin eagerly agreed. "When your husband comes home, Glenis, he'll probably eat you out of house and home. I've heard stories of veterans returning and almost overnight gaining a few pounds. Milk seems to be a food that most veterans crave."

"Yes, I've been keeping a close watch on the battles taking place in Vietnam," said Glenis. "My husband Andy helps by giving me information that the censors haven't cut out. I've been able to keep abreast of most of the activity. Mother showed me the flow charts she used to keep during World War II."

"Really? Do you still have them, Kathleen?" asked Glenn.

"I do, would you like to see them?" she offered.

"If you don't mind, I would like to see what you have."

"Okay, I'll get them," said Kathleen, leaving the room.

She returned a few minutes later with a bulging file of clippings from newspapers and magazines, and several rolls of maps, and spread several of them on the table. "I kept a lot of the battle and campaign clippings that involved your division, Glenn. You can see how the fighting progressed from North Africa, to Sicily and Italy, and finally, to the invasion of France at Normandy. I never knew when you were wounded, so I maintained a tracking record until Germany's surrender on May 8, 1945, VE-Day. The truth is, I lived each day's battle while the war was on."

"This is an amazingly accurate record, Kathleen," congratulated Glenn. He took his time to examine each sheet one by one, impressed with the detailed information Kathleen had collected. Afterwards, he watched her meticulously roll the maps and place them in their appropriate tube holder.

"Well, it helped to fill my days with some activity. Never knowing for certain what was happening was very hard." Glenn noticed a slight tremor in her voice, but she recovered quickly. "Would you like more coffee?"

"Not for me," answered Glenn, looking at his watch. "I'm afraid I have to say good-bye, Son. I happily leave you here with your sister. I hope the two of you can find some comfort in knowing that you have another family member to share your lives with. I hate good-byes and I pray that God will keep you and Andy safe from harm. I'm so proud of you. I love you with all my heart," proclaimed Glenn almost crushing his son.

"I'll be okay, Dad. I promise to take care of myself and do the best I can for the men in my command. No son could ever be more proud of his father than I am of you."

Next, Glenn hugged and kissed Glenis. "Take care, lovely daughter. I'll see you again, hopefully, before the summer ends. I promise to continue writing."

"Good-bye, Father, thanks for coming."

Glenn followed Kathleen toward the door to the porch with a heavy heart. He waved to Melvin and Glenis as he closed the door behind him. "Good-bye, Kathleen. Thanks for opening your home to Melvin. He needs all that you and Glenis can give him, so he has something to hold on to when it gets rough over there. He's got a hard job ahead of him and it's easier when you have support behind you. Nobody knows that any more than I."

"He's a fine young man, Glenn. You've done a good job with him. It will be as easy to love him as it was to love you," Kathleen watched him through tear-filled eyes. "Now… please go, before I embarrass us both."

"What a fool I was…," Glenn gasped, pulling Kathleen to him and kissing her trembling lips. After, he ran blindly to the car.

Chapter Fourteen

Kathleen sat on the top step of the porch watching Glenn's car travel down the hill, across Sewall Bridge, and out of sight. She felt like running after it and shouting that the feelings she had nurtured for him all those years were still real. Seeing him again and meeting Melvin for the first time, brought back all the memories she had tried so hard to suppress. She could not deny them any longer. She cried alone on the porch until there were no tears left to shed. Glenis and Melvin were silent witnesses to her grief. They quietly joined her on the porch, sitting on either side of her offering what comfort they could. Kathleen glanced at Melvin and, once again, she saw his father as he once was. Time had not dimmed the intensity of her feelings. She laid her head on Melvin's shoulder, closed her eyes, and dreamed again of yesterday.

Melvin put his arm around her, feeling helpless in his inability to console her. "I'm glad I came. My brother and I always knew that Father held someone close to his heart. He guarded the memories faithfully, sharing them with no one, but they were powerful enough to sustain him for a long time and carried him through some extremely difficult periods. Now that I know who that special person is, I understand why he loved you so dearly."

* * *

Faith waited nervously at the Portland Airport for Glenn near the plane boarding ramp. Its departure was scheduled for minutes away and he still hadn't shown up. The flight attendant suggested that she take her seat on the plane, when she saw Glenn walking rapidly toward her.

"You're just in time, Glenn," Faith said, relieved that she would not have to make the trip alone. She expected the construction site to be a relatively primitive affair, a condition she did not object to, but in such an isolated area the presence of a woman engineer might be resented by some of the workmen. With Glenn on the site, she felt more comfortable that there would be fewer problems.

"I didn't think I was cutting it so short," confessed Glenn, following her on the plane. They found seats together at the rear of the cabin.

"Did you have any trouble on the road?" asked Faith, after they strapped themselves in. She noticed that he seemed quieter and more reticent.

"I was a little late leaving York, that's all," Glenn responded vaguely. "It was hard to say good-bye to Melvin. He's going to Vietnam." He was not in a talkative mood and was glad when Faith made herself comfortable and started to read a pocket book as soon as they took off.

Glenn adjusted his seat backwards a few notches and closed his eyes. Faith casually lifted her eyes from the book to watch Glenn. She was glad to see him resting. He looked utterly exhausted. Glenn could not get the image of Kathleen standing on the porch watching him drive away, out of his mind. She had looked alone and dejected, and he wondered what would have happened if he had gone back to her in that moment.

When he had seen Kathleen, he had forgotten about Jim Farley and their engagement. It was as if the years had been rolled back and they were young again. It was a dangerous place to linger. He had been held hostage to his memories for far too long. He had to stop reliving yesterday. He caught a glimpse of himself reflected in the window beside Faith. An older man looked back at him. The once sandy-brown hair was now thinner, and more gray than brown. Youth had passed him by. He had been so consumed in living a small part of his life over and over again, that he had lost track of the fact that the remaining grains of sands in his personal hourglass were limited. The shadows were getting longer whether he liked it or not.

Faith's perception of him was correct, he was exhausted, and in a few minutes he fell asleep. The same dream that often plagued his nights revisited him.

* * *

It was early in the war in North Africa. His infantry company was at the point position, responsible for securing the flanks of a column of tanks on a push toward German positions in the mountainous regions of Tangiers. The column circled around a high cliff that obscured the road ahead, when the lead tank was hit by a single round from a German 88 artillery piece. Glenn was up front and off to the side of the tank when it was hit. The air was filled with gunfire and the smell of burning flesh and gunpowder. Sergeant Marcel Snyder, a small wiry North Dakota farmer, frantically motioned him to the opposite side of the road. Glenn ordered his radio man to hold the column until they had cleared the opposition, and then dashed across the road to Sergeant Snyder.

"The bastards are in that draw to our left, Sir. I could take a squad and hit their left flank if you can pin them down for us."

"You've got it, Snyder. Give me a few minutes to gather more fire power. I'll keep you in sight. When I give you the raised fist, you and your squad move out. Good luck."

Glenn ordered every man within sound of his voice to give the covering fire to Snyder. Several browning automatic rifles and an assortment of M-1 rifles and Thompson submachine guns let loose on the suspected stronghold. Glenn raised his clenched fist to signal Snyder to start his flanking movement. But, in the heat of combat, they had miscalculated the location of the Germans. Snyder's squad was wiped out by several concealed machine gun positions farther to their left.

147

Watching with horror what was happening, Glenn ordered the covering team to pull their fire to the left and concentrate on the muzzle blasts that were spitting death from the undergrowth around them. The company couldn't change their field of fire without hitting what was left of Snyder and his men. Glenn ran as hard as he could toward Snyder, screaming for him to take cover. The dream always ended the same way. Glenn witnessed the small body of Sergeant Snyder being lifted into mid-air by the force of the bullets hitting him. It was as if it happened in slow motion leaving his inert body suspended in space.

Glenn led the charge past the bloodied bodies of his squad and wiped out the Germans in a desperate frontal attack. He kept firing until his M-1 Carbine was empty and the Germans were all dead. The silence that followed after the firing stopped always woke him up.

* * *

"Are you all right, Glenn?" asked Faith, watching him tremble and raise his fist in the air. It alarmed her and she tried to wake him. "You frightened me. Can I get you something?" She was holding his left hand tightly so that it wouldn't hit her.

"I'm so sorry," Glenn answered, his face flushed and momentarily disoriented.

"Here, you're all covered with sweat," Faith handed him a clean handkerchief from her jacket pocket.

"I don't do this very often," Glenn apologized, accepting the handkerchief.

"My husband was also tormented by things he would never talk about. He was just beginning to deal with his memories of World War II when the Korean War started and his reserve unit was activated. He went off to war for the last time," Faith told him, remembering what it had been like.

Glenn appreciated her understanding. "Again, I'm sorry, Faith. I just dozed off for a short time…"

"That's all it takes, Glenn. You don't need to apologize to me. I've been through it before. It's okay."

By the time they arrived over Quebec City, it was dark and the city below sparkled like diamonds. The plane circled along the Saint Lawrence River above Château Frotenac, which was ablaze with lights and pennants flying in the wind that continuously swept through the river channel.

"Oh look, Glenn, that's Château Frotenac down there," Faith exclaimed. "It's larger than I expected. I've been to Montreal several times. This is my first visit to Quebec City. It's beautiful," Glenn smiled at her enthusiasm. There was a little girl quality about her that was becoming to a woman her age.

The company staff had made the travel arrangements for Glenn and Faith. They were scheduled to stay the night in the Chateau Frontenac, and fly out on a charter plane the next morning to Lac St. Jean, where the shuttle helicopter would lift them to the plant site. It was executed like Glenn would have planned a military operation, and he had organized the staff to do things the same way with contingency plans automatically taken into consideration. A taxi took them from the airport through the ancient parts of the lower town near the water's edge, up the hill to the terrace in front of the hotel.

They were assigned two adjoining rooms on the top floor. "I would never be able to afford such luxurious accommodations," commented Faith, exiting the elevator, her voice brimming with excitement at the extravagant beauty.

"That's one of the advantages of being on an expense account. As an employee away from your home, the company is depriving you of the personal leisure time you're entitled to. Consequently, it's only fair to reward employees by providing them with the best available. It's not luxurious when you factor in the normal after-work hours that they miss."

"That's a fair way of looking at it," admitted Faith. She checked the door numbers and announced, "Here we are."

149

"Are you as hungry as I am?" asked Glenn, unlocking his door across the hall from Faith's.

"Yes, the candy bar I had in Portland didn't quite replace a full meal."

Glenn grinned at her. "How about dropping off our bags and checking out the French cuisine at the hotel? We've got to eat somewhere."

"Sure, I'd like that," answered Faith. "Give me five minutes to comb my hair and change my blazer."

"Just knock on my door when you're ready."

The elegant hotel dining room looked out across the terrace that surrounded the cliffs above the Lower Town, offering a beautiful view of the river and waterfront. Glenn and Faith took seats next to a large picture window.

Faith smiled impishly. "I'm tempted to try out some of my high school French on the waiter, but he would probably not understand and I'd be embarrassed, or I'd say something rude without realizing it, and get us kicked out of the restaurant."

"You could give it a try," Glenn chuckled. "I'm too hungry for that, so maybe you'd better not risk it."

Faith ordered broiled salmon in English. Glenn chose a medium rare sirloin steak. They were hungry and ate heartily with a minimum of talking. While they were eating, they watched a beautiful white United States Coast Guard cutter approach the quay below them and tie up at the dock, a large American flag fluttering from the tallest mast of the ship. A smaller flag snapped furiously from the fantail. The ship's solid white color with the fire-red slash across the bow, gave it a sleek appearance of speed and endurance even though it was standing still.

"It's beautiful, isn't it?" remarked Faith. "It makes you feel proud to be an American."

Glenn shook his head. "My son Marvin always admired the sleekness and beauty of the high endurance cutters. They are graceful vessels, that's for sure. It does make one feel proud, especially when you're a long ways from home in a foreign country. The young men and women on the ship are the best our country has to offer. They do a great job of showing the flag and representing what our country stands for."

"I feel the same way about our young men and women in the armed services. My sister was a naval nurse in World War II and the Korean War. She died last year of cancer."

"I'm sorry for you and your family. It must have been difficult," said Glenn sincerely. He noticed that Faith didn't talk much about herself or her past.

"We've dealt with it, and life goes on," she answered in a sober tone.

"I do have a lot of respect for those who serve our country. Where else do you find young people who place their lives on the line for things like duty, honor and country? I never see our flag without thinking of the thousands of men and women buried in foreign soil, and I think of Marvin, who will always be a part of Vietnam. Sometimes I question whether the citizens are worthy of their sacrifices. However, I believe the principles set out by our Founding Fathers will always be worthy of any level of sacrifice. Nothing is more noble than the sanctity of the human spirit and the freedom to let it grow." Glenn felt Faith's eyes on him while he was talking and grinned at her. "I better stop my soap box speeches."

"No, what you said is fine," Faith replied warmly. "I feel the same way. My son is taking ROTC (Reserve Officers Training Corps) while he's pursuing a degree in forestry. Now that he's growing older, I'm beginning to see a genuine commitment to our country's ideals in him. It makes me proud, even though the thought of his going off to war frightens me."

"You're not alone, Faith," Glenn said gravely. He pushed his empty plate away and looked around the half-filled dining room. "It seems like a nice night. What do you say if we take a walk on the terrace outside?"

"That would be nice. I'm filled to the brim and a walk is just what I need," Faith agreed.

The evening was clear and cool, with a soft breeze laced with the subtle scent of spruce and cedar forests. The red sun had recently set in the west, promising fair weather for tomorrow. The terrace and waterfront were well-lit and lights glittered as far as they could see. Ships traversing the center of the St. Lawrence channel were also awash with lights. The Citadel was a fortress built to maintain the French influence in Canada.

"I know so little about Canadian history," Faith confessed.

Glenn was familiar with the history of the region and was glad to tell her about the significance of the area. He told her that the French influence in North America had reached its zenith in 1759 when French troops were routed by the English on the Plains of Abraham, a short distance from where Glenn and Faith now stood on the banks of the St. Lawrence River south of Quebec City. The defeat ended French military domination, but by then the French language and culture had already been firmly entrenched. British General Wolfe had commanded all of the English troops in the battle, while the honor of France was defended by the young French General Marquis de Montcalm. Both generals were killed in the battle.

"I remember the story now," remarked Faith once her memory had been stimulated. "The prevailing sentiment in French speaking Quebec today wants to break away from the Canadian Federation and become an independent state. I'm hardly a political expert, but that strikes me as a foolish move. The arrogance and elitism behind the movement to preserve their cultural heritage also rubs me the wrong way. They've already prevailed upon the rest of Canada to have French on all sorts of things like labels, signs, etc. Many of the English-speaking citizens of Quebec Province have been here as long as the French, and they've been harassed by those who desire to perpetuate French culture. If I lived here I'd resent their underhanded tactics."

"I get a feeling that you don't think much of the independence movement, do you?" he smiled at her. "To be honest, I haven't given the issue much thought. The company we'll be dealing with is an Irish company, and they've obtained all the necessary permits and approvals from the provincial authorities. The most important phase of the operation, as far as dealing with the province is concerned, will be the negotiations regarding the cost, construction and maintenance of the main access road to the plant. I'm sure that most of the supervising engineers for the province will be of French extraction. The company owners have told me that it was a reasonable negotiation, since the province is interested in opening up more of the northern lands to forestry and mining operations. The production of electric energy is also high on the Canadian agenda for the future."

They walked leisurely about the terrace as far as the Citadel, the walled fortress southwest of the hotel. Looking back at the city from that perspective highlighted its vitality and excitement. The massive structures of this century mingled with the ancient architecture of the early years of settlement creating a gentle mixture of tradition and progress.

As they strolled closer to the hotel, they could see that the Coast Guard cutter was getting ready to leave the quay. They rested against the iron railings to watch the ship get underway. The cutter pulled out to the center of the channel and set its course for the North Atlantic, its American flag proudly snapping in the wind. The ship was an island of light in a dark sea. Glenn leaned against the rail and watched it sail out of sight, quietly staring after it for several minutes once the ship had disappeared from view.

"I'm ready to call it a day," said Glenn, slowly turning his back on the river. "Tomorrow will be a busy one for us."

"That sounds good. I'm worn out," admitted Faith, taking one last look at the scene around her. "This has been a pleasant evening, Glenn. Thank you for having me come along."

"The pleasure has been all mine, Faith," answered Glenn, making their way toward the hotel.

The next morning, Glenn and Faith boarded the small charter plane provided by the large conglomerate responsible for construction of the aluminum processing plant. The plane was a two engine Cessna with single seats filled to capacity on each side of the fuselage. It was a clear sunny day with a scattering of white cumulus clouds in the cobalt-blue sky.

The plane set a course northeasterly at a relatively low altitude compared to that of the larger commercial flights. The rectangular parcels of land along the St. Lawrence River were clearly visible and they fascinated both Glenn and Faith. This was the land of the habitants. Each parcel varied in size from their neighbors, but they all conformed to a pattern of open tillage land, intensely farmed, close to the waterfront where farm buildings were located. The remainder of the tract remained forestland.

The steep cliffs and deep waters of the Saguenay River were visible for miles as the plane approached Lac St. Jean, about one hundred fifty miles north of Quebec. They landed at a small airport south of the lake, and were instructed to wait for the arrival of a helicopter under contract to carry supplies between Lac St. Jean and the plant site about one hundred miles farther north. Glenn scanned the airport looking for a coffee shop or restaurant, and found none.

"I hope you're not hungry, Faith," he remarked impatiently. "We could have a long wait."

Faith grinned. "I carry a few candy bars for emergencies just like this." She reached in her pockets and pulled out several Hershey chocolate bars, and a Payday peanut bar, offering them to him. "You're welcome to try some."

"You come prepared," he said, selecting a Hershey bar. "I'm a sucker for chocolate. Thanks, one should hold me until we get to the site. I hear something."

154

The helicopter arrived filled with supplies and equipment. While it was being refueled, the pilot and co-pilot gave the craft a thorough visual check before they resumed their seats in the cockpit. Glenn and Faith were the only passengers on the flight. They took the two single seats behind the crew.

The helicopter lifted off the runway and headed due north. They traveled very close to the treetops so that Glenn and Faith could catch glimpses of moose and deer on the ground. The interior of the helicopter was too noisy for communication so they didn't attempt conversation. The seemingly endless ribbon of green spruce and fir trees covered the earth everywhere they looked. In less than two hours they were over the plant site.

The pilot pointed below to their destination. The site had already been cleared of trees and stumps by the construction crews. Faith was instantly aware of the fragile nature of the soils in the area known as the Canadian Shield. The soil was shallow and even nonexistent where it was scraped clean by the large glaciers that moved through the area thousands of years ago. Those trees that managed to become established on the shallow soil were unable to grow roots deep enough to anchor them. Consequently, they were easily blown over by wind storms which lifted the shallow roots exposing the underlying bedrock.

The plant site was located adjacent to a mountain of rich deposits of bauxite ore. On a flat plateau across a drainage area they noticed the small village of tents already erected in two straight parallel lines. The pilot gently set the helicopter down on an oval concrete pad built to receive them. Drums of fuel and other supplies were neatly stockpiled beneath tent canopies close to the pad. People and supplies, alike, came in by helicopter.

Faith exited the helicopter first, a look of wonder and anticipation on her face. Glenn was pleased to see that the site was so well organized. Glenn counted three large tents used as mess halls. Several tents were also erected within the hub of numerous wood-framed modular cabins placed in concentric circles. The cabins resembled large boxes and were about two thirds the size of a normal mobile home. These were the quarters for the supervisors and foremen of the different crews. More cabins would be delivered, on an as-needed basis, by large crane helicopters that carried them in a sling beneath the aircraft and set them down on foundations.

The wooden cabins housed four people each, two on each end with individual private rooms. The center portion of the cabin contained a common kitchen-dining area and a bathroom that was shared by all four tenants. Glenn commandeered a cabin for himself and a supervisor who would arrive later when construction of the plant began. He could convert the two bedrooms at the opposite end into necessary office space. He assigned the cabin beside his to Faith with the understanding that she might have to share it with other women who happened to show up; currently, she was the only female on site. The cabins were spartanly equipped but clean and sturdy with self-contained gas-fired furnaces and bathrooms with plenty of heat and warm water. During the coming winter months, the most essential item for the people who worked at the site would be heat. The severe winter weather enveloped the area and those unprepared for its onslaught suffered grievously or perished quickly.

Glenn and Faith each carried two suitcases of necessary clothing and personal items to satisfy their needs for a week or so. Their additional luggage would be shipped later when the company's equipment and supplies made its way to the north country. Glenn had suggested to those who were scheduled for the project, that they should hold their belongings to a minimum. He had no objection to items such as radios and tape players or musical instruments if they would substantially contribute to the quality of life at such an isolated location.

Glenn placed his luggage in his cabin and knocked on Faith's door a short time later. "Faith, it's Glenn."

"Come on in, the door is unlocked," she hollered.

"What do you think? Will this do for field work?" he asked, noticing that she was getting settled into her temporary accommodations by placing a few pictures in the central living area. He saw a picture of a young man in an ROTC uniform. "Is this your son?"

Faith nodded proudly. "Yes, it was taken this year at school. The quarters are fine, better than I expected. I had visions of sleeping in tents for a while."

"They've come along much better than I imagined. I'm glad to be here. It's nice to get away from civilization once in a while. The air is invigorating. Say, are you hungry?"

"I'm starved," Faith replied. "Those candy bars can only carry you so far."

"Why don't we check out the mess tent next door," Glenn suggested, looking at his watch. "It's only four o'clock! It seems later than that. A light jacket feels good this far north."

"I'll be right with you. Let me grab a sweatshirt. You're right, it's getting chilly," Faith answered.

The mess tent was also organized like an Army operation. Kitchen facilities and storage areas were located in one small area of the tent. Serving tables took up twice as much space as the food preparation area. The balance of the tent was filled with picnic tables with attached benches. The canvas was draped over a wooden framework from which large fluorescent lights were suspended. The interior was bright and cheerful. The smell of food drew them to the serving tables where they were met by a young Canadian wearing a spotless white vest and apron.

"Good afternoon, young man. I'm Glenn Hastings and this is Mrs. Faith Hamilton. We're from Hastings Engineering Company and to be honest, we're starved."

"You're in the right place. Welcome to the Canadian north woods," the young attendant greeted them warmly. "We've been expecting you. We'll be ready to start serving in fifteen minutes. I just finished making coffee. Would you like a cup while you wait?" He pointed to the large coffee urns at the end of the serving tables.

"That sounds wonderful," Faith answered. The coffee was fresh and hot and they took a seat close to the serving line where they could relax and enjoy it. "I'm anxious to see what we have below the surface here. The Canadian Shield was scraped so close by the glaciers that not much soil was left. This area could never support agriculture even if it weren't in the more northern latitudes."

"Just what are you going to do first, Faith?" asked Glenn. "I understand the necessity of controlling run-off and erosion, but you go beyond that."

She paused a moment, and explained. "Water is one of our most valuable resources and the most universal solvent in the world. It's a necessity for all animal and plant life forms. Water distribution, either at the local or the regional level, is uneven at best. First, I'm going to make a master plan of the drainage patterns around the plant site so that we can account for every drop of water that falls via rain or from snow melt. Some filters into the ground and some runs off as surface water. The longer the distance surface water has to travel, the greater the chance for erosion of soil and contamination of the ground water, which tends to be of higher quality than surface water. We have pollution when absorbed elements such as the bauxite ore from the mining site leaches into waters originating from other sources such as rivers and streams from different watersheds.

"We'll take measures to intercept water travel with temporary sediment barriers and small reservoirs where it can be held indefinitely. In this case, contamination from the surface run-off of the mining area is very real. Therefore, we've got to isolate it as soon as possible. My main job is to quantify that potential and take the necessary steps to keep it to a minimum. In order to do that, I'll sink some test holes to map the presence of water below the surface and correlate it with the contours and irregularities of the land itself so that we know the carrying capacity of the subsurface to store water and at what rate it will filter through that surface. Then, I'll correlate it with the surface we have to deal with in the construction phase and ultimately redefine the area so that water movement, above and below ground, is similar to what it would be in an undisturbed environment. On that basis we shape the land to meet our needs in the production and maintenance of potable water regardless of what is taking place. Am I making any sense?" asked Faith, smiling at Glenn's blank stare.

He smiled back at her. "You lost me on the details, but conceptually I understand your position. You have an enthusiasm for your profession and that's nice to see."

His compliment pleased her. "I'm still learning, but I do like the work. I'm glad to be here, but if you really want to know the truth, I'm a little uncomfortable being the only female for miles around."

"Well, whatever you need, be it personnel or equipment, to do the job to your standards, don't hesitate to ask. Just ask and it's yours. You have the authority to demand it."

"I appreciate the support, Glenn. Let's see how things go," she suggested.

By the time they had finished their coffee the mess tent was half full of hungry men. Glenn and Faith took their turn in the moving line and were impressed with the quality and variety of foods. Standard food fare in the north country was moose stew and baked beans, available on the line every day at every meal. The kitchen staff also served spaghetti and meatballs, roast beef and moose steaks, along with a variety of fresh vegetables and fruits, and a section of warm freshly baked bread. The clean brisk air of the northwoods contributed to a healthy appetite, and the workmen ate enormous amounts of food, some four times a day.

Glenn and Faith carried heaping trays of food back to their table and eagerly began to eat. Before they had finished, a young well-proportioned man dressed in a set of light coveralls searched the tent interior for Glenn and Faith and once he located them, made his way to them.

"Hello, Glenn Hastings and Faith Hamilton, I presume! I'm Jeff Vail, the general supervisor of operations for the parent company. I've had correspondence with your company." He was a powerful, heavy-set man with bright red hair and a flushed complexion. He radiated confidence and authority without arrogance and spoke with a clipped New England accent.

"We're glad to meet you, Mr. Vail," said Glenn. "Mrs. Hamilton is our new hydraulics engineer."

"I'm glad to be here, Mr. Vail. Do I detect a northern New England accent?" she asked.

"Ah, it's impossible to deny it!" he said cheerfully. "You bet, I'm from Conway, New Hampshire. If you don't mind, I'd like to introduce you to the gang. I warned everybody that our designer and severest critic was coming, so we're on our best behavior. Maybe you could say a few words to our team?"

"Certainly, I'll be glad to, Mr. Vail," Glenn replied.

Glenn sized up his counterpart with the parent company and liked what he saw. Jeff Vail had that typical New England Yankee nothing-was-impossible attitude that inspired those around him. Glenn also suspected that that attitude might get him into trouble with some Canadians, who, occasionally, tended to lean back and take things a bit easier.

When all the men had made it through the serving line, Jeff Vail stood up on the bench seat and raised his arms to get everyone's attention. He announced the presence of Glenn and Faith and called upon several foremen and supervisors to stand and be recognized before he asked Glenn to say a few words.

"Gentlemen," Glenn also stood on the picnic table. "I'm pleased to be here with you in this beautiful country. This plant is going to be a challenge to our skills and to our perseverance if we are to complete it on schedule. If we work with a spirit of cooperation, it will go faster and easier. When it's finished we'll be able to point to it with pride and a sense of achievement. I'm proud to be a part of your team. Before too long I'll know each of you on a first name basis. My door is always open to discuss anything with anybody at any time. And now, our new hydraulic engineer, Mrs. Faith Hamilton, has got a few words to say."

Faith self-consciously stood before the all male group with some misgivings. "Thank you, Glenn, and all of you. This is my first job in Canada, and I have no doubt it'll be a rewarding experience. I look forward to the challenges that lie ahead. I echo Glenn Hastings's words about working in harmony and cooperation. I want you to know that my job will require assistance from some of you, and I hope that you won't have a problem working with a female engineer. I like working in a shared-responsibility atmosphere, but I think we also need to have mutual respect. You already have mine, I hope to earn yours."

The crowd clapped and whistled at the close of her short statement. She was blushing as she waved to the men. A tall lanky Irishman, Mike O'Leary, hurriedly made his way around the tent to where Faith was standing. He bowed to her and stood up beside her on the bench. He was the foreman of the heavy equipment specialists and had a reputation for running a tight operation. He held out his arms for silence.

"Listen you guys. You all know me. I just want to let you know that me and my boys are appointing ourselves as the personal bodyguard for our new engineer, Mrs. Hamilton. If anyone, I repeat anyone, steps out of line with her, they've got me and my boys to deal with. Now, is that understood?" shouted Mike. A rousing cheer filled the tent.

Faith continued blushing from all the attention, but she seized the moment and grabbed O'Leary's arm and thrust it in the air, pronouncing in a loud voice: "My Champion."

The mess tent erupted in cheers once again.

Chapter Fifteen

Glenn turned to Faith as soon as the crowd quieted down, "You were wonderful up there, Faith. You've won their support, good for you."

Shortly after the spontaneous reaction to Faith's pronouncement, the gathering at the mess tent broke up, and Faith and Glenn returned to their quarters. Faith was excited with her reception and laid in bed staring into the darkness. She thought of the home left behind in Vermont, and wondered what her son might be doing at that very moment. She could picture him in his dormitory room. Within a short period of time she had moved from an interview in Philadelphia to a work site in the forested wilderness of northern Canada beyond the civilized world. There was a dynamic energy at the plant site. A modern technologically advanced processing plant was being built where wilderness had once reigned. She felt a thrill at being a part of the team that would stand as a testament to man's achievement.

Somewhat overwhelmed by the swiftness of the events that had led her to this place, Faith was not unhappy to be in a strange land away from familiar surroundings. To the contrary, it gave her a feeling of security instead of isolation. For months, her nights had been filled with restless anxiety and uncertainty about the future. She needed a job to support her son and found it impossible to continue with the Soil Conservation Service. Faith had requested a transfer, but nothing was available for her as a soil scientist at the same pay grade. She had felt trapped, until the opportunity at the Hastings Company came along. It was a better paying job with greater responsibilities and, best of all, it would take her away from Vermont. She had kept the reason for her sudden move from Vermont to herself, determined to start a new chapter in her life.

In the early hours of that first night, Faith awoke to flickering lights streaking across her window. Frightened at first, she got out of bed and approached the window. It was the *aurora borealis*, the Northern Lights. She had seen them on occasion in Vermont, but never with such intensity. Quickly grabbing her bathrobe, she stepped outside to see the immense display of colored rays of light shooting across the sky in patterns of every description flowing in all directions. The heavens were alive with vibrant colors of every hue. At times the eccentric patterns resembled gigantic waterfalls of illuminated wires in red and yellow flowing over a cliff. Then it would disappear and move laterally with the speed of lightning. A subtle hissing and grating sound accompanied the evening show. The heavens were filled with energy and seemed to be alive. Faith leaned against the cabin and watched for a long time, mesmerized by the phenomenon.

Glenn's cabin was dark, so Faith assumed that he must be sleeping through the spectacular display until she heard his door open and saw him step outside.

"It's a dazzling show?" she asked, announcing herself to him.

"I thought I was dreaming again," he replied. "I've never seen the Northern Lights as active as this. I hope it's a good omen."

"I've been watching it for several minutes now, and it hasn't diminished in intensity" she told him. "This far north it's a common occurrence. I suppose we'll get used to it, but I'll remember this first one. Goodnight, Glenn, rest well."

"Goodnight, Faith, the same to you," answered Glenn, watching her shadow disappear behind the door. He watched the delicate electrical weavings above until he felt chilled and went back inside too.

Glenn was on the threshold of one of the most important operations of his professional career, and all he could think about when he climbed back into bed was Kathleen. The remote location, and the accompanying isolation and detachment, made him uncomfortable. He was surprised at his reaction since he had sought the withdrawal from civilization as a means of letting the past go. It wasn't working. A melancholic loneliness embraced his consciousness, and he half-heartedly regretted the commitment he had made to the project.

That same evening, some of his regular dreams came back to haunt him. In one, however, something had changed, the figure of a woman dressed in white linen and lace observed the battlefield scenes. The elusive and mysterious figure remained in the background, a white mist shrouding her identity. Then, just before he awoke, the mist cleared and the woman's grief-stricken face was revealed. It was Faith!

* * *

Two weeks had passed since Glenn and Faith had arrived at Trails End, the name given to the plant site by the first generation of workers. Glenn received his first letter from Glenis and walked to the privacy of his room to read it.

June 25, 1969

Dear Father,

I just returned from Portsmouth after bringing Melvin to Pease Air Base. We've had a wonderful time together. When I was growing up, I never gave any thought to the possibility that I might have a brother or a sister. I think Melvin enjoyed the visit as much as I did.

When I said good-bye to Melvin I had that same sinking feeling I had saying good-bye to Andy. There's something terribly heart wrenching about watching a loved one leave for a war zone. War is a curse to mankind. If we could expend just a fraction of the energy and effort into promoting peace instead of war, the world would be a better place. I suppose new generations have to learn the same lessons all over again.

I hope you had a safe trip to your job site in Canada. It was wonderful to see you again, even if it was for a short time. You looked much more rested and relaxed than the first time we met. I can't help wondering if you and Mother had words before you left. She was quite upset afterwards. She didn't say anything to me about what had happened, which is typical of the way she keeps things to herself. That evening Jim stopped by and she was more reticent than usual. I'm not trying to pry or intrude upon anyone's confidences, but it would be nice to see her happier. I love her very much and it hurts me to see her like this.

I've got to go now, Father. Duty calls. All my love,

Your daughter,
Glenis

The tone of the letter pleased Glenn, except for the part about her mother's mood after he left. He didn't know what to make of it. He had thought a lot about the kiss he gave Kathleen when they parted. Maybe it was uncalled for and maybe it shouldn't have happened. Either way, Glenn had no regrets. As far as he knew, her relationship with Jim seemed to be going well and he still had guilt feelings about the information he had obtained regarding Jim Farley. Glenn had left Pennsylvania before he had time to discuss it with Bob Smart. Would he be needlessly injuring Jim Farley's reputation by bringing up the misdeed? The dilemma still troubled him.

Glenn reread the letter and penned a short reply to Glenis so that it would leave the compound with the daily mail and supply shuttle at dusk. He truthfully informed Glenis that he had not had any words with her mother except to say good-bye, and that he had kissed her at the last minute. When he finished the letter it was too late in the day to return to the concrete foundation pouring, so he walked into the mess tent and went through the serving line before the dinner rush began. He took a seat off to the side of the mess hall near the coffee urns and quietly began to eat his meal.

Faith entered the tent and passed through the mess line as Glenn was pouring a second cup of coffee. She joined him. She was still dressed in her favorite field clothes, a set of light coveralls and a red kerchief wrapped around her head. The insect net she wore in the field was hanging loose at her back. Black flies were so numerous during the warmest part of the day that it was impossible to work without the protection of a net.

"I was looking for you," Faith said, as she sat down opposite him. She seemed content. "I've just completed the basic field work, mapping the soils and subterranean water system. Now I can put it all together and use it as a model for structuring the plant site watershed area. How did your day go? You look down about something."

"I'm glad you've completed your preliminary work, Faith. You're perceptive, I've been thinking about things back home. I received a letter from my daughter. She and my son, Melvin, had a pleasant visit before he left for the Far East."

"That's nice. I haven't checked my mail locker yet to see if anything came for me. I haven't heard from my son since we've been here."

"It makes it awkward to have our mail go to the office first, then by courier to Trails End."

"Oh, I'm not complaining," answered Faith, unfastening the red turban around her head allowing her hair to fall loose on her shoulders.

Glenn watched her rearrange her hair with a couple of quick movements of her head. She was an attractive woman, he thought, without any of the coquettishness that some women use to attract attention to themselves. She was natural and

166

straightforward. Over the past two weeks, he discovered that he very much enjoyed her company. When she failed to be available to take her meals at the same time that he did, he missed the companionship and light banter that they shared with each other. Even though they had spent a lot of time together, Glenn had to admit to himself that she knew a lot more about him than he knew about her. She was industrious and productive with her time; whenever she requested the services of a drilling crew for several days, she handled them with grace and expertise. By the time the men had finished the test holes they would have done anything for her. Faith was a great team player; and while she did not encourage familiarity, she was always approachable and the men felt at ease around her. It was a tribute to her professionalism.

"You look like you're hungry," Glenn was amused at the way she was eating.

"I am," she responded between bites. "I ate an apple and a piece of muenster cheese for lunch. I wanted to finish with the planar table while I had the helpers to run the rod for me. They've been great. Now, if we have a stretch of bad weather, I can take advantage of it and complete the maps and profile studies. Do you need the drafting table in the office for the next few days?"

"No. If you have your field stuff ready to be plotted, go ahead and use it for as long as you need. You must be ahead of schedule, aren't you?"

"Yes, by a couple of weeks," Faith replied happily.

"Have you had any trouble with the men?"

"Nothing that I can't handle," she answered, carefully sipping a cup of hot coffee. "In general, they've been the best I could ask for. Some drop hints here and there that they would like to know me better, but it hasn't gone any further. I want to thank you for helping with that. I don't know what the men have been told, but I've experienced more respect and assistance here than I have at any other job. I try to not dress suggestively or act in any way that would encourage intimacy, but sometimes it's a hard line to walk to keep the relationships on a positive level."

"You're a remarkable lady," he told her sincerely. "I'm glad you're on our team. Now, if you'll excuse me, I've got to go take a shower. Enjoy the rest of your meal. Goodnight, Faith."

"Goodnight, Glenn."

That evening was clear and cool enough so that the black flies and mosquitoes were scarce. When the moon was not out and the northern lights were not flashing through the sky, the nights in the northern latitudes were pitch black. Some lights from the cabins and tents lit up the compound, yet a few hundred feet away from the compound, it was so dark that a person could not see his hand in front of his face.

After finishing her supper, Faith picked up two letters in the mail pouch at the main office. She hurried back to her cabin to read the letter from her son, Tom. He was taking summer college courses at the University of Vermont at Burlington. Part of his summer was devoted to a forestry summer camp, an integral part of his requirements for the forestry bachelor of science degree. In his letter, Tom described in detail the team projects he would be working on, and Faith laughed at the way he described them. He was a good student. She missed him more than she imagined that she would. She had tried to be both father and mother to him, but over the years she had become painfully aware that it was impossible to play both roles.

The second letter Faith received was postmarked Montpelier, Vt., from a William "Bill" Savoy. She read his letter carefully two times and placed it in her pocket. It sent a shudder through her body. The words were hateful and mean and she felt threatened.

Montpelier, Vt.
June 29, 1969

My Dear Faith,

I've been trying to contact you for days and finally went to the University to speak to your son. He didn't have the address or location of your job so he gave me the address of Hastings Engineering in Philadelphia.

What are you trying to do, avoid me? I thought we had a better understanding than that. I spent some time on the phone to Hastings and got your approximate location in the wilds of Canada. What are you trying to prove, Faith? When I think of you in the forest like that surrounded by plenty of men I get angry. Is that what you want?

I'm anxious to see you again. Why can't we be better friends? You don't really know me yet and you won't give us a chance to get better acquainted.

I'll be waiting for you when you come home. If you don't come to me, then I'll come to you no matter how far away you are.

Your loving friend,
Bill Savoy

Later that night Faith took advantage of the insect-free evening and relaxed in a collapsible lounge chair set up in the rear of her cabin. It was private and she liked to lay back and study the stars. The solitude gave her a chance to review where she had been and where she was going. There was a need within her for some part of every day to be devoted to reflection. She was a very orderly and systematic person who did not easily tolerate abrupt changes in her work or personal life.

Faith knew that something had to be done about Savoy. The letter filled her with anxiety and outrage. The audacity of the man to seek out her son and pump him for information was more than she could stand. She had worked every day since she came to Trails End, and decided to take the next day off. She noticed the light on in Glenn's office and went to inform him of her decision. She knocked on the door.

"Come in, it's unlocked," Glenn called from the inner office.

"It's me, Faith. Sorry to bother you at this hour, but I saw your light. I'd like permission to take tomorrow off. I have some personal matters to settle. Maybe I'll take a hike on one of the trails nearby to see more of the countryside."

"That sounds like a good idea. Of course you should have time to yourself. You've been working too hard." Glenn motioned for her to take a seat in the center room of the cabin. "Is there anything I can do to help you?"

"No, thanks, I don't believe so."

Glenn thought for a moment and said, "Listen Faith, I've been thinking of getting away from this place for a few hours myself. I thought of taking the helicopter down to Lac St. Jean or Quebec. I've had something on my mind, too. What I'm trying to say is, how about the two of us playing hooky and spending the day away from here on one of the trails? I don't want to force myself upon you," Glenn said, afraid he might have pushed too far.

"No, not at all," answered Faith hesitantly. "My only concern is that you're my superior, and I don't want to be placed in a position where my job with your company is threatened or compromised. Do you understand what I'm trying to say?"

"Yes, I do, and I would probably have the same concern if I was in your shoes. When you get to know me better, you'll learn that I don't use my position to gain favors from people. I respect and admire you, and simply had in mind spending time with another engineer friend, that's all. Why don't you sleep on it if you wish, Faith."

"I didn't mean to make a big deal. I have a habit of speaking my mind and I meant nothing personal. A day off without any duties, playing hooky as you put it, may do both of us a lot of good. It sounds like fun, I'll see you early in the morning then. Goodnight, Glenn."

"Goodnight, Faith, I'll look forward to the morning." Glenn held the screen door open for her. "Do you want a light to find your way?"

"No, I'll be fine."

The next morning they met at the mess tent and ate a hearty breakfast. Glenn asked the chef on duty to make up a few sandwiches and a thermos of coffee to take with them on their outing. The maps of the area indicated that a Royal Canadian Mounted Police outpost was located at Fort Lewis, a Native American community on Lac Diamante about eight miles northwest of Trails End. Before they left, Glenn reported to the Trails End security detail about their hiking plan, promising them that they would not deviate from the established trails of the area. A well-worn pathway took them around to the north of Lac Diamante westerly toward Fort Lewis.

Faith was dressed in one of her coverall suits with a baseball cap and a light sweatshirt over the coveralls. Strapped to her back was a small lightweight pack containing extra socks, candy bars and personal items. Glenn wore a sturdy pair of work pants and shirt with an Army fatigue cap that Melvin had given to him. He also carried some extra items in a russet pack slung over his right shoulder and a World War II Army water canteen attached to his belt. They both wore comfortable sturdy shoes. Glenn warned Faith that he was not a marathon hiker because of his injury, but he would have no trouble maintaining a reasonable pace for as long as they walked.

"I didn't know that you wore a brace on your leg. Are you sure this is a wise course of action?" asked Faith, as they departed from the cleared portion of the compound.

"I'll be okay. It took me a number of years to learn to walk without a cane or crutches. I'm a little slower than most people, but I do have the stamina and capacity to walk all day long

171

provided I don't push too hard. If you don't mind, I'll break trail and set a pace I'm comfortable with, if you don't make fun of my being out of condition. I'll call for frequent rest stops," said Glenn, smiling at her.

"I'm glad, because I probably won't be able to keep up with you anyway. I'm not a young girl anymore," she answered in good spirits. "When I first arrived at Trails End I was terribly out of shape. The survey work has helped me tone up a lot, but I'm a far cry from what I used to be. Besides, this is supposed to be a day off, not a competition. We leave all that behind us, okay?"

"Okay," Glenn replied, pleased with her realistic attitude.

They started on the westerly trail, worn smooth from years of travel. Certain segments of the trail were blocked from the sun by towering spruce and balsam fir trees which arched overhead, creating what seemed like a tunnel through the forest. The darkness of the forest trail beneath the canopy of green branches had an unfriendly forbidding feel to it. Different sections along the trail were lined with smaller trees which allowed the sun to penetrate the crowns and illuminate the path for forest travelers. The trail was relatively flat with small undulations when it crossed through different watershed drainage patterns. Maps of the area did not indicate any large mountains, but there were a few ridges and valleys created by the glacier that ran approximately west to east.

The panoramas from these ridges were spectacular. Glenn and Faith stopped frequently to rest and enjoy the views. Their pace was leisurely and consistent. Both had passed the point where they got their "second wind," which made the effort to continue a little easier. The next ridge they encountered took place late in the morning, and they were hungry.

"If we eat our lunch this early," laughed Glenn, "we'll starve for the rest of the day."

"This is where candy bars come to the rescue." Faith triumphantly offered him a Hershey candy bar.

"They do satisfy a person's hunger. What do you do, buy them by the case?" he teased her.

"Not quite, but after years of being in the field, I've found that it's prudent to never be separated from your lunch or a good substitute," she smiled.

"You've had a lot of practical field experience, haven't you?" Glenn acknowledged seriously. "Thanks for the chocolate."

They located two spruce trees side by side and sat with their backs against them enjoying Faith's candy bars, and at the same time, admiring the distant panorama. The sky on the western horizon was beginning to get darker. The sun still shined brightly at their back, highlighting different terrain features in front of them to the north. In places, wildfire had burned large areas of land leaving behind blackened stubs of trees serving as silent sentinels to the intensity of the holocaust. Beneath the dead trees, acres upon acres of scorched earth were covered with bright red flowers.

"Those areas of red color must be the fireweed I've read about," noted Faith. "They're the first plants to grow on recently burned boreal forests. The litter build up from the spruce and balsam fir burns very hot once the fire starts. The litter contains a lot of oils and resins which are very combustible. Good forest management helps to keep that buildup to a minimum by clearcutting small patches of forest in patterns determined to reproduce themselves with a higher rate of spruce over balsam fir."

Glenn was impressed. "You sound like a forester to me. Have you been reading your son's textbooks?" he kidded her.

"I'm guilty of looking them over," she smiled. "It's such a wonderful field. I've loved the forests and the land all my life. I grew up on a small, one-family dairy farm, so you learn how to be a part of the land and to respect those who earn a living working it. Nobody knows the land better than those people closest to it. I want my son to be a part of the conservation movement that uses science, traditions, and common sense to solve problems. Many of the radical fringe environmentalists and special interest groups who claim to have the interests of the land at heart, distort facts to their advantage. All they're really after is the power to control and lock up the land which is a God-given gift for man to use wisely. If the environmental activists have their way, they'll reduce mankind to the same level as the cave dwellers who proceeded us, and that's wrong," she grinned. "Now it's me who's preaching!"

"You certainly have a passion for the subject," remarked Glenn, admiring the intensity of her feelings.

"Is it that obvious?"

"It is and I think it's wonderful. I envy your strong convictions for such a noble cause. You know, Faith, maybe we should rethink where we're going. Those clouds to our west don't look very friendly," Glenn said, looking at his watch. "It's now about eleven thirty in the morning. According to the map, we're within an hour from a cabin at the intersection of the trail and the Swift River. We're quite close to the Cree land noted on the map. The security people at the plant told me that the cabin was normally empty and available to travelers in need of shelter. What do you think?"

"Your logic sounds fine to me. Are you up to a faster sprint to the cabin? Tell me the truth, Glenn, because we can make a rough shelter in the forest if we start soon enough."

"I'm up to a sprint as you call it," Glenn answered with conviction. "So let's be on our way. Do you want to lead?"

"No, you set a pace that you're comfortable with. I'm not in as good shape as I thought, so don't try to impress me with more speed," Faith laughed, falling in behind him.

"You're a good sport, Faith," Glenn acknowledged.

They soon crossed the boundary of the Fort Lewis Cree Indians' reservation as Glenn had predicted. Three quarters of an hour later the trail ended at a fast moving river just as the heavens emptied heavy clouds of rain upon them. A large tree had fallen into the water reaching to within twenty feet of the far bank. In order to cross the raging water, they had to walk along the tree trunk as far as possible, then jump into the water close to the opposite bank. Glenn led the way across the swaying tree and jumped into the cold water. It was a shock to his system. The water was deeper than he had anticipated, reaching to his chest.

"The current is strong, Faith," he warned her. "First, throw your pack to me, then jump to my right." Faith did as he requested and leaped in the water feet first and waded to the rocky shore. Glenn helped her crawl up the embankment on her hands and knees. The wind was starting to pick up and the temperature was dropping rapidly. They were both thoroughly chilled and shivering.

"Come on Faith, we've got to keep moving. The cabin should be within a few feet of the river. Oh, I see it." said Glenn, pointing to the small log cabin, hanging onto his hat in the high winds. They quickly ran to its shelter. The door opened and they thankfully entered. Against the opposite wall from the entrance was a fireplace already prepared for a quick fire. Small twigs and branches had been placed in a small bunch with larger pieces built up around the outer edges and a few large pieces crossed over the top. All that was needed was a match to light the kindling wood.

"There must be some matches somewhere in here," said Faith checking the shelves.

"Voilà," cried Glenn. "I have a pipe lighter that will do the job just as well."

"Always prepared. You must have been a Boy Scout once," Faith laughed again.

Glenn held the lighter to the kindling and within seconds a warming fire was crackling on the hearth. It lit up the room showing a stack of dry firewood piled against the stone chimney. They carefully examined the interior of cabin. It was clean, functional and well-equipped for a wilderness cabin. A large table with several chairs was in the southeast corner beneath the only window. To the left of the door was a dry sink and shelves, and a bunk bed built against the northwest corner, between the wall and the fireplace.

"Look, Faith," Glenn called out. "There's something here on the wall by the table."

He pointed to a small bulletin board nailed to the wall. In the center of the board was a white sheet of paper with a typewritten message. The paper was yellowed and stained, but the typing was still visible:

Welcome to the center cabin!

You are the guests of a tribe of native Cree Indians from the outpost village of Fort Lewis on Lac Diamante. There is food in an earth cellar beneath the floor in front of the fireplace. You are welcome to whatever food or dry wood you may need. We ask that you respect the generosity of your hosts and leave the cabin as you found it so that the next forest traveler will also find a place to take refuge from the elements and partake of food if necessary.

I used this cabin during the winter of 1922 while working on a forest management plan for the Tribal Council at Fort Lewis. They have earned my respect and admiration. I had served in France with a young Army officer from the village, Lieutenant Joseph "Flying Eagle" Mann, who gave his life for freedom. His remains were among the "unknown." I ask in his memory that you use this cabin with respect and responsibility. That way it will always serve as a refuge for body and soul. Thank you.

Captain Mark Leroux, USMC
December 18, 1922

Glenn and Faith read the letter with interest.

"My God," Glenn turned to her in astonishment. "I know Mark Leroux!

Chapter Sixteen

"Who's Mark Leroux?" asked Faith.

"He's a member of the Medal of Honor Society. I met him at some of our gatherings. He was seriously wounded on Peleliu. What a coincidence! I can't believe it."

"The Medal of Honor Society," said Faith, forgetting about the soggy clothing. "You've earned a Medal of Honor? I didn't know."

"Not many people do. I don't make a habit of telling everybody. Besides, it was a long time ago and most people don't want to talk about the war," answered Glenn.

The fire burned brightly, filling the room with light and warmth. Heavy rain and howling winds continued outside. Gusts of wind shook the cabin as the storm intensified.

"If this doesn't let up shortly, we may have to stay here for the night," commented Glenn, watching for Faith's reaction.

"That looks like a possibility," she admitted, sitting in front of the fireplace taking off her shoes and socks.

Glenn searched the cabin for a candle or lantern and found both on a shelf near the bed frame. He lit them with his lighter. With the added light, Glenn noticed bedding and a mattress rolled into a tight package suspended from the ceiling by a rope on a pulley. The bedding was stored in mid air to discourage rodents from building nests in them. He untied the rope fastened to a peg near the window and slowly lowered it to the floor.

"There are several blankets in the roll," Glenn informed Faith. "There's also a provision for a blanket to be hung up around the bed for privacy. Why don't you take off those wet clothes behind a blanket and use one of the other blankets to wrap yourself in until the clothes are dry?"

"We should dry them." agreed Faith. "It's cold and raw outside. Using the blanket for a screen will be fine. Are there enough blankets for both of us? This is no time for false modesty. After all, we're both adults and we've got to do whatever is needed, that's all."

"You're right," he answered, relieved at her practical reaction to what might have been an embarrassing situation for both of them. He draped the largest blanket over the ropes strung around the bed and placed the mattress on the cedar sapling bed frame. They quickly removed their saturated clothing and wrapped themselves in a blanket while they arranged their clothing on chairs around the snapping fire. Glenn found an old jacket in the bedroll and tried it on for size. It was a little small, but he kept it on while he wrapped the blanket around his waist, fastening it with his belt. Afterwards, Glenn checked to see what might be available for food in the small earth cellar. He opened the trap door and jumped into the hole. He smiled at their good fortune, finding coffee, sugar, tea, and sea biscuits in individual metal containers which he placed on the cabin's floor. Further exploration with a candle yielded some cans of baked beans, peaches, and corned beef.

"We're in luck-there's plenty of food here," he said, climbing out of the cellar. "The Cree Tribal Council have done a good job stocking this isolated cabin for emergency use. When we get back to Trails End, my first priority will be to replenish what we've used and more. That's the woodsman's way."

Faith placed her remaining candy bars on the table while Glenn emptied his pack of sandwiches, a thermos of coffee, and packets of dried fruit and cookies.

"Are you ready for sandwiches and coffee?" asked Glenn.

"Yes, I've been hungry for the past few hours," Faith answered from behind the blanket. She was getting dressed with an extra pair of light slacks and sweatshirt from her backpack.

The cabin was now comfortably warm. Within a short time, they were sitting at the rustic half-log table eating sandwiches and drinking hot coffee.

"I never knew sandwiches could taste so good," she smiled, her hair slightly disheveled. "It's amazing that way up here in the middle of a vast unpopulated wilderness, you found that an acquaintance has preceded you to this cabin. What kind of a person is he, anyway?"

"I don't know Mark Leroux well. We've met at a few meetings of our Society in Virginia. He's a small man with sensitive dark eyes. I remember him as being a gentleman from the old school, and I, also, remember that his wife was with him. He was so proud of her. She's a beautiful full-blooded Cree Indian, probably from Fort Lewis. He's able to walk without crutches but his wounds from the war left him more limited than I've been. He'll be surprised to learn that we used the cabin," Glenn smiled. "Evidently he's a forester by profession. I never knew that."

"Today has been an adventure. I needed to get away for awhile. I've a problem in Vermont that's bothering me, and I'm at a loss as to how to handle it," confessed Faith, staring pensively into the burning embers.

"Sometimes it helps to share a problem with a friend," Glenn offered. "I promise you that whatever we talk about will never go any further. If I can help, I'd be glad to."

"It's not an easy subject to discuss," she hesitated. "More than anything, I'm afraid and ashamed that my son will needlessly become involved. There's a man I met named Bill Savoy. I've known him for several years. He's a pig and I avoid him at every opportunity. He was transferred to the same conservation district where I was working as an Agronomist.

180

He was always around me at the office and in the field. Twice he tried to force his affections upon me but I refused and had to beat him off. He threatened to go to my son with filthy lies if I ever reported him to the police, which I never did. I know now that was a mistake. I took the job with your company to move away from Vermont, hoping to be free of him. Yesterday I received this letter." She pulled the letter from her pack and passed it to Glenn.

Glenn had never seen Faith so emotional. He read the letter carefully, becoming more and more angered at the man's threats and audacity. "Did you leave a house in Vermont behind, Faith?" Glenn asked when he was through.

"Yes, my husband and I bought it when we were first married. When he was killed in action, the mortgage insurance paid off the balance of the money we owed on it. It's in Montpelier. Savoy used to spend hours spying on me through the windows with a powerful pair of binoculars. He's about driven me crazy." Faith wept holding her head in both hands. Glenn watched helplessly while she struggled to gain control.

"I'm not sure what can be done right now, Faith, but I can assure you that this man will be stopped from what he's doing to you and your son, or suffer the consequences. Creeps like that belong in jail or a mental hospital. If that's not possible, then they should be informed what it means if they persist in their ways... pain is a very persuasive tool when appropriately applied by a master." He spoke angrily.

"I don't want more trouble. My son should never have to be involved in such a thing. I've done all that I can to keep him from knowing anything about the disgusting situation."

"I was just thinking out loud, Faith," he assured her. "I'm glad you told me. I'll do everything in my power to help you so that you don't have to think about the creep again. Does he live in the same town as you?"

"No, he lives in Waterbury."

181

"That makes it easier. Let me think about it for awhile. Trust me, I won't do anything without speaking to you first. Do you object if I contact Bob Smart about this? He's a genius and I rely heavily upon his judgment, as you must already know."

"I don't mind Bob Smart, but I don't want anyone else in the company to know."

"I promise, the three of us will be the only ones and we'll never put anything in writing, so there'll never be a paper trail."

"I don't really want him to be harmed, I just want him to leave me and my son alone."

"You'll probably have to choose somewhere between those two wishes, Faith," Glenn coldly advised her. "We'll work something out. Let me help you carry the burden."

An hour later, Glenn threw more wood on the fire and rearranged some of their clothing to dry more evenly. He checked the shelves for utensils to make coffee and heat the canned food. He had an original Swiss Army knife in his pocket to open the cans.

"We need some water," said Glenn, sitting on the floor beside the fireplace. "I'm going to get dressed. My shoes are almost dry and the rest of the clothes are dry enough for me to wear. You might want to freshen up for the night and we need water for coffee. I haven't made coffee over an open fire since I was in the Army."

"Were you wounded when you won the Medal of Honor?" asked Faith curiously.

"Yes, but I came through better than most. The small brace on my leg and this scar on my neck are the only evidence of it. I survived. People like your husband were not so lucky, so I don't complain. I'm going out to get a pail of water. I'll be right back," he said, opening the door.

"Be careful," she cautioned. "The river bank can be tricky. Do you want me to come along and hold the lantern for you?"

"No, I'll be okay," insisted Glenn. Within seconds he was back. "I found where they dip for water. Now we can make a fresh batch of coffee if you trust my formula, or would you rather have tea? There are some tea bags in one of the tins."

"Coffee will be fine. I trust you're cooking," Faith smiled, combing her hair with a small pocket comb. "It's strange finding an empty cabin where we can come inside from the weather and make ourselves at home. These forest people really look out for others whenever they can. I like their customs and traditions."

The rain continued as the night descended upon them. They ate baked beans with sea biscuits and sipped Glenn's fresh boiled coffee. Afterwards, Glenn asked Faith for permission to light up his new corn cob pipe.

"I don't smoke often, but there's something about a pipe and the clean air of the forest that go together. I smoked a lot during the war, using more matches to keep the pipe going than I did tobacco."

Faith laughed softly. She was comfortable and felt secure in his presence. "I like the smell of a pipe. If it tastes as good as it smells, I can understand why it's such a popular habit."

"Do you mind if I discuss a personal situation I've been deliberating about? I'll share it with you if you'll give me your honest opinion how to handle it."

"I promise to do my best," responded Faith, rearranging her chair closer to the fireplace.

Glenn told her the story of his affair with Kathleen and his subsequent marriage to Jessica. He told her about Glenis and Melvin and their meeting at the Portsmouth Hospital, and reviewed the situation with Jim Farley. Then he carefully spelled out the findings of the investigator and the dilemma he was faced with. "What do you think I should do with the information we've got on Farley? I'm sure Kathleen is unaware of that part of his past."

"How do you know that?" asked Faith, listening intently.

"It would simply be out of character for her to contemplate marriage to someone capable of such an act. Perhaps we don't have all of the information and I've condemned him unfairly without a chance to defend himself."

"Perhaps that's where the solution to the problem lies," Faith suggested. "Maybe you should confront him with the information you now have and evaluate his response. If it confirms your suspicions, tell him to inform Kathleen because she has a right to know if her future husband is a liar or worse… a greedy crook."

Glenn considered her reply and liked it. It would be less traumatic for Kathleen if the information came from Jim Farley than from Glenn. He felt better already. "That sounds like a workable solution. Thanks for the suggestion. I'm glad we traded confidences with each other and I'm glad we're friends."

Faith didn't answer him and avoided his glances. She continued to stare into the dancing red flames, a worried look on her face!

"Do you mind if I ask you a personal question?" asked Glenn hesitantly.

"I never know how to answer that question," Faith quietly reflected.

"I'll ask it anyway. Are you seeing someone now or is there someone special in your life?"

"No. I'm not a young girl anymore, I'm forty-eight years old. I have a son and I need to work for a living," Faith answered in a firm low voice.

"You're not old, Faith," protested Glenn. "You're younger at heart than a lot of women decades younger. You sell yourself short. I didn't mean to pry into your private life. I apologize, I was out of line."

"Your question implies that a widow who has been alone all these years should have someone in their life. Well, if you want the truth, I just haven't found any person who measured up to my husband, and I don't want to settle for second best. It's that simple, really. Sure, I've dated a number of times and I turn down requests on a regular basis. I'm not what is commonly known as a 'swinger,' or a party girl," Faith answered directly. She was uncomfortable talking about her personal life.

"I'm glad that you chose my company to work for and I say that sincerely. I find you a generous caring human being, I'm proud to call a friend. I value friendships that are built on trust and respect, and you, dear lady, deserve a lot of credit for the way you've conducted your life. You've worked hard and been responsible for your son and yourself. You're an achiever, and I admire the doers of this world."

"You're going to give me a big head if you don't stop talking that way, Glenn," interrupted Faith, hoping to change the subject. "I don't know about you, but I'm tired. It's been an exhausting day, a fun one, but still tiring. The warmth from the fire is making me sleepy."

"I'll put some larger logs on the fire," said Glenn, looking the log pile over. "You take the bed, Faith. We'll leave the blanket in place as a privacy screen for you. That leaves two blankets for each of us, which should be plenty. I'll sleep on the floor between your bed and the door in case someone comes in unannounced. The door doesn't have a lock."

"How can you sleep on the hard floor?"

"I've slept in worst places for years in the war. Believe me, it's not a hardship. A person can sleep anywhere if they're tired enough. I'll get an extra pail of water so that you can freshen up in the morning. I hope you sleep well."

"Thank you, Glenn, goodnight. The first one to snore gets a shoe thrown at them," Faith chuckled, making up her bed.

The large logs burned for hours leaving a bed of glowing embers casting soft shadows over the interior of the small cabin. In the distance, wolves howled throughout the night as the rain continued unabated. Glenn watched the fire for a long time before he turned in. He could hear Faith's regular breathing after she fell asleep. Finally, the fire worked its relaxing magic on him. He closed his eyes and slept soundly.

The storm passed during the early hours of the morning. Dawn arrived with a bright sun slowly lifting above the eastern horizon. Glenn awoke while the cabin was still dark and checked the time on his luminous wristwatch. It was six- thirty in the morning. A small concentration of red coals glowed from the fireplace hearth beneath a light dust of ash. He threw the blanket off and lit a small candle trying to be quiet and not disturb Faith. He selected a small handful of dry cedar shavings from the pile of wood and ignited it with the candle. Within seconds the aromatic shavings burst into flames sending a shadowy flicker of light into the cabin.

Glenn placed the soot-stained coffee percolator on the fireplace grill and swung it into the flames, then he emptied the balance of the water bucket into a cast iron kettle hanging on a rod beside the hearth. Moist clouds of mist rose from the Swift River as Glenn dashed outside to replenish the pail of water. Holding the pail beneath the surface until all of the air had been displaced, he turned around quickly and came face-to-face with a Mounted Policeman walking towards him.

"Hello," signaled the policeman, raising his hand. "Would you by chance be Mr. Glenn Hastings?"

"Yes, I am! You surprised me."

"I'm Constable Jenkins of the Royal Canadian Mounted Police detachment from Fort Lewis. We received a radio message from security at Trails End that you failed to return last night. They requested that we try to locate you and a Mrs. Faith Hamilton." Constable Jenkins was a young man in his mid-twenties. Tall and well proportioned with a light complexion, he was the embodiment of the proper English Bobby and the independent Canadian Mountie.

"Faith Hamilton is still sleeping in the cabin," Glenn informed him. "We were caught in the rain storm late in the day and decided to seek shelter in the center cabin indicated on our map."

"I thought I'd find you here," smiled the young policeman with satisfaction. "If you had not been here, we would have had to organize a full-blown search party, and that means a lot of work, so I'm relieved, Sir."

"I've already placed a pot of coffee on the crate, compliments of our hosts at Fort Lewis. Would you care to join us for a cup of coffee, Constable?"

"I would Mr. Hastings. It was damp and pitch black when I left the barracks this morning, so a hot coffee will taste good."

"This cabin has been a wonderful refuge from the elements for a lot of people over the years," Glenn remarked, walking towards the door. "It would have been a cold wet night to pass in the forest without some shelter."

"Yes, the Tribal Council maintains the tradition of the center cabin that was established way back in the twenties when Mark Leroux used it," said Constable Jenkins holding the cabin door open for Glenn.

"Is that you, Glenn?" asked Faith from behind the blanket curtain. "I heard voices."

"Yes, Faith, it's me. We have a guest this morning. Constable Jenkins walked out from Fort Lewis to make sure we're okay."

"I don't mean to intrude, Mrs. Hamilton. Mr. Hastings invited me in for coffee. Are you all right, Ma'am?"

"Oh, yes," she answered. "We were warm and dry and helped ourselves to some of the food in the cabin. The Tribal Council is to be congratulated for being so generous and hospitable." Faith self-consciously stepped out from behind the curtain combing her hair.

"If you want to freshen up, Faith, there's some warm water in the kettle. The coffee should be ready now. There's nothing like coffee percolating over an open fire," declared Glenn in good spirits.

Constable Jenkins placed several small packages on the small table. "I wasn't sure what was left in the cabin for food, so I brought along a couple of Mounted Police field rations, similar to your Army C-ration packs. They're not gourmet dining, but they sure taste good when you're hungry. These contain biscuits and marmalade, which go well with coffee."

"Thank you, Constable," said Faith. "I'll wash up quickly, Glenn, then I'll join you for coffee." She disappeared behind the blanket.

Constable Jenkins removed his cap and took a seat at the table while Glenn located cups and plates. "We received the radio message from the plant security detail early this morning. On my way through the village to the center cabin, I met Mr. Leroux on the path. I told him where I was going and mentioned your name. He seemed interested and said that he knows you, Mr. Hastings. He sends his regards and extends an invitation to pay him a visit at his cabin in Fort Lewis this summer."

"I remember him well," confirmed Glenn. "It would be a pleasure to see him again. How's he doing?"

"He's about the same except that his legs are not as strong as they once were. I've been stationed at Fort Lewis for the past eighteen months and I've noticed a considerable decline in his ability to get around. He comes up with his wife for the summer months each year. Sometimes he teaches at the school in the village. The north country people think a lot of him and his wife, Bright Cloud. She's a nurse who still works at the infirmary she established after graduating from nursing school during World War I."

"They sound like remarkable people," said Faith, coming from behind the blanket to pour herself a cup of coffee. She took a seat at the table beside Glenn. "I feel better now, but I'll certainly enjoy a shower when we get back to the plant site."

"Faith is a hydraulics engineer for the construction phase of the plant," Glenn told the Constable. "We had planned to hike on some of the trails and enjoy some of the scenery, but the rains interrupted our plans."

"It's nice to meet you, Mrs. Hamilton, despite the circumstances," said Constable Jenkins, opening one of the field packs for her. "Here, help yourself to these biscuits and marmalade."

"Thank you," she replied warmly. "You remind me of my son. He's about your age. Do you like your work as a policeman?"

"Yes Ma'am, very much so. I'm from the prairie section of Alberta and find the boreal forest region of Quebec fascinating. The forest people are about the same all over Canada but the French don't like the idea of an English-speaking person having a position of authority within Quebec Province."

"I've encountered that especially in the metropolitan areas," Glenn remarked. "The province was not pleased to learn that the majority ownership of the plant we're building will be in the hands of Irish investors."

"The village of Fort Lewis is growing now that there's more industrial development in northern Canada. You may be interested to hear about a fascinating tale associated with Mark Leroux, his wife Bright Cloud, and her twin brother. I've heard it from several different people, and it has a lingering effect on the village and portions of their tribal lands."

"That sounds interesting, Constable. I'd like to hear the story if you have time to share it with us," said Glenn.

"Yes, please continue, Constable," Faith requested. "I had a feeling about this place when we first encountered it during the rain storm."

"Well," commenced Constable Jenkins, taking a long swallow from his tin coffee cup. "Running Deer was a beloved leader and chief of the Fort Lewis Cree tribe. He fathered three children, his daughter, Bright Cloud and twin boys, Flying Eagle and Red Fox. From the very beginning, the boys were opposites in temperament and values. Red Fox was a constant trouble-maker. Flying Eagle, on the other hand, traveled to the United States to study engineering and went into the United States Army in 1918 when he graduated from college. He was shipped to France and became a platoon leader in Colonel Leroux's company. The two men became close friends. Flying Eagle was killed in a gas attack on their section of the front and shortly after, was obliterated in an artillery barrage. Portions of his body were buried in an unnamed cemetery in France.

"Previous to his death, Flying Eagle had saved Leroux's life by coming to his rescue when the Colonel was knocked unconscious. Colonel Leroux, a captain at the time, had recommended Flying Eagle for a medal. After the war, Captain Leroux was given the assignment of awarding the Distinguished Service Cross (posthumously) to Flying Eagle's family. He traveled to Fort Lewis to carry out his mission, and there met Bright Cloud, a young nurse who had recently founded the infirmary at Fort Lewis. She and Captain Leroux fell in love with each other. It's a love story that the people in the north still enjoy talking about.

"Captain Leroux accepted the responsibility of preparing a forest management plan for the tribal lands, staying at this cabin while doing the field work. One day in the middle of the winter, he encountered Bright Cloud on the trail leading to the village. She was following a snowshoe trail left by her brother, Red Fox and two others. It seemed they had kidnapped a nurse from the infirmary and were taking her north to a stranded whaling ship in Hudson Bay where they intended to sell her for the crew's pleasure."

"My God, what an evil person he must have been," cried Faith.

"He was a beast in every way. He sold illegal whiskey throughout the region and raided animal traps from his family and tribal brothers. He was a bad one right to the core." Constable Jenkins was enjoying the telling of the story, and Glenn and Faith were captivated. "Well, Bright Cloud and Captain Leroux followed their trail to a place where Red Fox and his cutthroat band took refuge in an abandoned cabin for the night. Early the next morning Bright Cloud and Captain Leroux devised a plan to surprise the kidnappers. The Captain stalked a lone outpost guard and knocked him out, then he stormed the cabin door armed with a pistol and took out one of the inhabitants. Red Fox recovered from the forced entry by the Captain and was swinging an axe at him when Bright Cloud, who had crawled to the door step, fired three shots from a Remington Auto-Loader Rifle, killing Red Fox instantly.

"Red Fox is buried near Lac Diamante. A cenotaph similar to the one outside this cabin was established by the tribe for Flying Eagle. The area between his cenotaph and the grave of Red Fox is well-known for its violent weather and unusual electrical storms. It's as if their spirits are still battling with each other. Both Bright Cloud and Colonel Leroux believe that Flying Eagle's spirit watches over this cabin and the village."

"What a beautiful story, Constable. I had a feeling of peace and security last night in this cabin," admitted Faith.

"You're right," Glenn added. "There's an element of grace and harmony to this place. I felt it too, Faith."

"There's another part of the story that is even more fascinating," continued the Constable. "The Tomb of the Unknown Soldier in Arlington National Cemetery was dedicated after World War I. The story claims that the unknown soldier buried beneath the white marble stone is Flying Eagle."

"This must be sacred ground to the villagers then," Faith reflected.

"You could call it that," concurred Constable Jenkins, pushing his chair back. "If you two will excuse me, I've got to

191

return to the barracks. It's been a pleasure meeting both of you. We'll radio plant security that you'll be checking in with them today. Have a pleasant trip back to the plant site. Oh, by the way, the cenotaph memorials I talked about are here between the cabin and the river also. They're three large spruce trees that have been pruned of all of their branches to the very top. It creates a cathedral-like spire reaching for the skies." Glenn and Faith accompanied him to the door.

"It's a remarkable achievement," said Glenn, bending his head backward to see the very top of the memorial. "I want to thank you for coming out to check on our safety. The saga of Flying Eagle is a haunting tale that I'll not soon forget. And please, tell Mark Leroux that I'll be in touch before the summer is out. Good luck on your tour of duty, young man."

"Thank you, Sir," answered the young Constable. "It was nice making your acquaintance, Mrs. Hamilton. Good-bye."

"Good-bye, Constable, take care of yourself," said Faith, watching him step lively towards the village of Fort Lewis. "You know, Glenn, I wasn't kidding when I said that I felt something special about this place. Those tree spires are truly magical."

"They certainly are," Glenn agreed. "I'm going to leave a short thank you note on a piece of white birch bark, then we'll head out."

"I'm almost sorry to leave," Faith remarked, pulling her small shoulder pack over her sweatshirt.

"I know what you mean. I'll always remember this trip," answered Glenn in a low voice. "It's given me a chance to get to know you better. It's been wonderful sharing feelings and doing things with you. I..." Glenn's voice faltered, and he held his arms out to Faith. She stepped into them. They held each other close for several seconds.

"Something is happening, Glenn," she whispered. "It's hard to describe, but I've felt it since the first time I met you.

Can it be real?" Faith's lustrous blue eyes searched Glenn's for some answer to the longing in her heart.

Glenn placed a finger on her cheek sweeping aside a strand of her blonde hair and kissed her warm lips.

Chapter Seventeen

The breeze filtering through the spruce and fir trees was laden with the fresh scent of a new dawn. Small cumulous clouds circled above the towering cenotaph as the sun rose out of the east. Glenn and Faith listened to their hearts and embraced their emotions. Faith did not question the feelings she had for Glenn. Every contact she had had with him reinforced her initial discovery. She had been drawn to him from the first time they met at Bob Smart's home. It was a sudden awakening for her and though it made her heart sing for joy, she was afraid that it might not be reciprocated. All she prayed for was a fair chance to earn his love.

Glenn, too, was struggling with conflicting emotions. His love for Kathleen had not evaporated into thin air, and she remained deep within his heart. At the same time, he could not deny the softness of Faith's lips or the thrill he felt holding her. He admired and trusted her, knowing that they were a sound basis for building a lasting relationship. There was a comforting warmth and understanding in her that made him feel good. Was this spontaneous moment a betrayal of his long-standing love for Kathleen, or was it an acceptance of his new-found feelings for Faith? The dilemma bothered him because he saw no way of resolving the quandary without hurting someone he cared for.

"Glenn, can this be real, or am I imagining it?" asked Faith, searching his eyes. The question came from her heart, and she was hoping that he felt the same way.

"It's been a long time since I've felt this way, Faith. I can't believe it's happening to us. Don't be afraid," Glenn whispered in her ear. "There was a reason we came to this cabin, and it has cast its spell upon us. Could it be Divine Intervention?"

She smiled at his words. "Two lonely people reaching out for love has to be part of a master plan. I'll never forget this lovely place," she answered in a wavering voice.

"Neither will I," he told her, kissing her again. "But, come, we've got to be heading back or they'll be sending out search parties for us. Are you prepared for the inevitable loose talk at the Trails End? In an isolated location, without many distractions, the men will make a big deal out of our excursion. I feel a little guilty that I placed you in that kind of a situation."

"I don't dare to analyze what has happened here. I don't want to take a chance that it'll fade away," exclaimed Faith, breathing heavily as she stood on her toes to kiss him one more time. "It was as much my idea as yours. I say let the tongues wag. I'll tell them that the trip was a lot of fun and let it go at that. If they choose to make it a sordid affair, then that's their problem, not ours. I'm not going to let the gossip mongers rob me of the pleasant memories this hike has created or the feelings it has unleashed."

"I admire your common sense approach."

"For years," Faith continued with determination, "I was satisfied to do my job and provide for Tom and myself. In all those years since Thomas was killed, I've never had feelings for anyone that came close to what I had with him. Now, in a short period of time, you've been able to accomplish what no one else could, and you did it by being yourself. I'm amazed and a little frightened by how quickly it's all developed. Is it too fast, Glenn?"

"You ask what can't be answered, Faith. Let's give it time and let it grow. Mutual respect and trust are a good beginning. I'm also surprised and thrilled to discover that it's possible to feel the way we do. I was completely unprepared for something like this to happen, but I cannot deny it. Surely both of us are entitled to happiness by the simple fact that it has been denied for so long. The shadows are fading and the years are passing quickly. Is it reckless for us to reach out for love and happiness when we hardly know each other? Probably, but if we fail to take the chance, we'll never know, will we?"

"No, we'll never know," Faith softly repeated, pleased at his words. She followed him along the trail with a new bounce to her steps. Constable Jenkins had advised them that a tree had been placed across the river a few feet north of the cabin. They were not anxious to get wet again and were relieved to cross the boiling Swift River without getting their shoes damp.

By the time Glenn and Faith reached their destination at the Trails End, the day had turned warm and they were sweating profusely, their water canteens long empty. A warm shower and a change into fresh clothing were going to be welcome. They entered the construction compound behind the mess tent. No one was visible as they stepped from the thick forest into the open.

"By the time we get cleaned up it will be too late to get much work done," Faith said sheepishly.

"Before I take a shower, I better head over to security and inform them of our return." Glenn hesitated a moment and asked, "Any regrets, Faith?"

"None," she answered firmly. "Do you think it would be easier to continue like we always did within the compound? It may eliminate awkward explanations, at least for awhile."

"I think that's a good idea. Well, I'll see you later. Thanks for a memorable trip."

"It's been a great respite," Faith replied, walking towards her cabin.

Glenn checked with security and picked up his mail. The letter on top of the stack was from Glenis. He quickly returned to the privacy of his quarters to read it.

June 26, 1969

Dear Father,

A short note to let you know that I have just been notified that Andy has been wounded. The Army was not specific about the severity of his wounds or his whereabouts, but they assured me that he would be transferred to the United States as soon as his condition warranted the transfer. I'm not sure what that means.

I've been almost out of my mind with worry, and I wish I could be with him wherever he is. I share the bad news with you and ask for your prayers. I cried all last night. The uncertainty is the hardest part to bear.

I hope this finds you well. I feel better now that I've shared my grief with you. You seem so far away in the wilds of Canada.

All my love,
Your daughter,
Glenis.

PS: I'm holding news of Andy from Melvin. I pray for his safety, too.

The letter touched Glenn. Within the short time he had welcomed his daughter into his world, he had also accepted the responsibilities that went with being her father. He knew what her young husband must be going through and he felt helpless, but his helplessness extended only to Andy. As for Glenis, there was something tangible that he could do. He could go to her and share the burden with her in person. It was his time to give now, and he had a strong desire to be where he was needed the most.

After showering and changing his clothes, Glenn explored the possibility of leaving early in the morning on the return trip of the helicopter to Quebec City. He reviewed the construction schedule briefly. His construction assistant was due on site soon, which would free him for as long as he needed. Under normal conditions he would have been reluctant to leave a project in progress, but his heart told him that the needs of his newly-found daughter were his highest priority.

The mess line was beginning to form when Glenn took his position at the end. He hadn't eaten since morning and was hungry. By the time he went through the line and took a seat at their regular location, he saw Faith entering the tent. She was talking amiably with some of the equipment operators that worked with her.

"Hello stranger," she announced cheerfully, placing her food tray on the table facing Glenn. She saw a different person than the one she had just spent the day with. "Are you all right?" Faith asked with concern.

"I just received a letter from my daughter. Her husband has been wounded in Vietnam. Of course she's upset about it and I was thinking of going to York to be with her for awhile. I don't really know what I can do, but..."

"You can show how much you care by just being present. There's nothing more important than sharing the grief of a loved one. Take it from one who knows. Go to her, Glenn. That's what dads are all about."

"We have an assistant resident engineer coming to Trails End within a few days. Maybe you can fill in for me if something comes up before he arrives," suggested Glenn.

"Of course, I'll do what I can. The foundations are pretty much committed now, so there shouldn't be too many changes that need to be assessed. Go and do what you have to do without worrying about the project. Your role as a father is more important right now than your position as resident engineer. If my son seriously needed me at home, I'd go in a heartbeat."

"Thanks for making it so easy," said Glenn, grasping her hand across the table.

"I'll miss you while you're gone. You're a very easy person to like, Glenn. I'm falling more in love with you every day," she admitted, in a hushed tone.

"I promise to not be any longer than is necessary. I'll remember these last two days with you as two of the happiest I've had in years. Feelings from the heart are not a monopoly of the very young. Mature adults can feel the same emotions, perhaps even more intensely."

"Thank you for telling me that."

They finished their meal and went to Glenn's office where they reviewed work that had taken place while they were absent and assessed what was scheduled for the next several days.

"If some technical issues are beyond my expertise, then I'll defer decisions until you or your assistant return," Faith assured him. "No decision is preferable to a bad one made with insufficient knowledge. Things will progress smoothly. Go and carry out your duties like the good father you are. I'll be thinking about you and wish you a safe trip. I'll pray for your daughter and her husband. My heart goes out to them in this hour of need."

"Good-bye, Faith," answered Glenn, embracing her for several seconds. "I'll miss you." Faith kissed him one more time before hurrying out the door.

Early the next morning the courier helicopter settled onto the helo pad at the Trails End. As soon as it touched the ground, Glenn ran from his cabin and boarded it. The first rays were lighting up the eastern horizon as the helicopter pilot set a course due south at an altitude close to the tops of the forest trees. It was five-thirty. By noontime, Glenn was aboard a commercial flight from Quebec City to Portland, Maine.

Glenn rented an automobile in Portland and called ahead to check if Glenis was at home or the hospital. The phone rang several times. Glenn was ready to hang up when an out-of-breath voice answered.

199

"Hello?"

"Hello, is this Glenis?" asked Glenn, trying to block out the airport noises beside the terminal.

"No this is her mother."

"Kathleen, this is Glenn. Is Glenis all right?"

"I can hardly hear you, Glenn. Yes Glenis is okay. She'll be home shortly," Kathleen spoke loudly.

"As soon as I got her letter, I came as quickly as I could. I'm in Portland now, and will be there within an hour."

"We'll be expecting you. Thanks for calling." Kathleen carefully hung up the phone and turned to Jim Farley.

"What did he want, Kathleen?" asked Jim, sitting at the kitchen table. He was not in a happy mood. He and Kathleen had been trying to settle some differences of opinions on their plans for the future when the phone rang. He had a tendency to dominate a conversation and was frequently rebuffed by the independent-minded Kathleen. "Right when you and I should be spending more time together, something always seems to get in the way. This guy Glenn has a habit of interfering when he's not wanted."

"How can you say that, Jim? He's responding to a letter Glenis wrote to him about Andy. He doesn't know that Andy has been placed in a hospital in California. His concern is for Glenis, who just happens to be his daughter. Be careful Jim, your jealousy is showing and it's not pretty."

"It's like you to defend him," he accused hatefully.

"Please, Jim, I'm tired of arguing. Why don't we discuss this later when we've had a chance to think about things with a clearer head?"

"Are you that anxious to get rid of me now that he's coming?"

Kathleen glared at him. "If you want the truth, yes. The last time you met him you were rude and pompous. He was a guest in this house and I don't want a repeat performance. So please, let's stop this needless bickering."

"I don't like bickering either, Katherine. I love you so much it's difficult to think of this guy as having been your lover."

"The past is over and I make no apologies for it," Kathleen sighed, and warned, "Can't you see that this is going nowhere?"

"I thought we had a date this afternoon, as soon as Glenis arrives to take care of Ernest."

"We did, but…"

"Okay, then it's still on. I'll wait on the porch out of your hair until she comes, and then we can leave."

"Fine, if that's the way you want it, Jim," exclaimed an exhausted Kathleen.

James Farley sat impatiently on the porch reading the paper. Kathleen and her mother remained in the house. Little Ernest curiously entered the porch and climbed into his Radio Flyer cart. Like most four-year-old boys, he was filled with curiosity. He eyed Farley uncertainly as he pushed the cart around the porch and soon lost interest when Farley paid no attention to him. When Ernest's grandmother called him from the house, he quickly ran inside. James had just finished reading the paper when a strange car pulled into the driveway. Jim recognized Glenn still dressed in his field clothes.

"How do you do, Glenn," greeted James, standing over the porch railing to shake his hand.

"Nice to see you again, Jim. Is Glenis here?" Glenn asked, climbing the steps to the porch.

"Not yet. Her mother and grandmother are inside the house."

"Hello, it's me, Glenn," he announced, knocking on the door frame.

"Come in, Glenn," Kathleen called in a strained voice. "Glenis will be glad to see you. It's been a terrible time since we received notification of his condition."

"Kathleen, how's Andy?" Glenn asked, stepping into the sitting room where he noticed her mother. "Hello, Mrs. Cohen. I hope you'll excuse my field work clothes. I left northern Canada in a hurry with the clothes on my back and a shaving kit. I just wanted to see Glenis."

"You're always welcome in this home, Glenn Hastings, regardless of what you're wearing. Poor Andy, he's not doing very well. Kathleen can bring you up to date. I'll entertain little Ernest upstairs so you two can talk without interruptions."

"Hi there, young man," said Glenn, picking up Ernest. "Do you remember me?"

"Yes, you have a brace on your leg," answered Ernest frankly.

"Well, I guess it's true. I've come to see you and your mother and I want your grandmother to tell me all about your dad, so I'll visit with you later." Glenn placed him down on the floor.

"Why don't you come into the kitchen, Glenn. Thanks, Mom," Kathleen called to her mother.

"I hope I'm not interrupting anything," apologized Glenn, noting that Jim Farley still sat alone on the porch.

"This place has been in turmoil since we first found out about Andy. He was wounded by a land mine."

"God, no, not a mine," Glenn winced, remembering the horrible condition they had left some of his men.

Kathleen was distressed. "Yes, they say he may lose his legs. He's been transferred to the Presidio in San Francisco. Glenis has been worried sick about everything. I'm so concerned for her. I'm glad you came; she needs you now, Glenn."

"That's why I came as fast as I could. Tell me truthfully, Kathleen. Would she go to San Francisco if she had the chance?" Glenn asked, thinking about what could be done.

"The trip out would not be too bad, but she cannot afford to pay for a hotel very long…"

"Please, Kathleen. The last thing any of you should be thinking about at this time is money. I'll take care of that. I've got a plan in mind. Do you think she would be able to leave work on a few hours notice if I made arrangements for her and Ernest to fly to California?"

"Oh, I'm sure she would."

"Then it's settled," answered Glenn with a determined look on his face. "May I use your phone? It won't take long. I'm going to call my office and have them make reservations for the trip." Taking a small notebook from his pocket, he jotted down a list of things he wanted his office to take care of and then placed the call. His secretary answered.

"Hello, Pat, this is Glenn. Is Bob in the office? Would you put him on please? Pat, keep your line open because I've got a to-do list for you. Hi, Bob. I've got some things for you to do for me. First, I want a suite of two private rooms at a reputable hotel as close to the Presidio Army Hospital as possible for an undetermined period of time. Second, I want a first class reservation, for tomorrow if possible, on a flight from Portland, Maine to San Francisco for myself, my daughter Glenis, and my four-year-old grandson, Ernest. I also want a rental car with an automatic transmission available for us at the San Francisco airport. Now repeat those requests back to me, please. If you're still on the line Pat, you can start making the arrangements. This has a high priority over your regular work. Thanks a lot for your help."

Bob Smart repeated Glenn's requests and asked with concern, "What's happening, Glenn? This must be in regards to your daughter's husband."

"Yes, Bob. Unfortunately, we don't have many particulars right now."

"I understand. We'll make these arrangements for you and the reservations will be waiting for you at the flight desk in Portland. Good luck and keep us informed. Incidentally, how is Faith working out on the job site?"

"Faith is doing great work. We've become close friends. As a matter of fact, I left her in charge of the project until our assistant resident engineer, Ed Block, shows up. What's the status on his situation?" Glenn asked.

"He should be on his way to the site tomorrow. He's already left the office with some of the new plans and figures. Have a good trip, Glenn. Give our best to your daughter and her husband."

"I will, Bob, thanks for everything. Oh, wait a minute, one more thing. Would you please wire me five thousand dollars in cash in care of me at the York Village Bank? I'm almost out of pocket money."

"Consider it done, Glenn. Wait a minute, Pat just passed me a note. You have a TWA flight out of Portland, Maine for tomorrow at 9:00 a.m."

"Thanks again, old friend, and thank Pat for being so efficient."

Kathleen listened to every word. "You're certainly decisive. Glenis will be excited to hear about the plan. I know that she wants to be near Andy more than anything else in the world."

"It's the least I can do to make up for lost time," Glenn replied, checking to see if Jim Farley was still on the porch. "Kathleen, would you excuse me for a minute? I have something I'd like to discuss with Jim out on the porch."

"Yes, of course. Would you like a cup of coffee and something to eat?" Kathleen asked with some surprise. "I have a piece of apple pie left over from last night."

"That would be great, Kathleen, thank you." He walked out to the porch and pulled up a chair close to Jim and sat down.

"What can I do for you, Glenn?"

"Well, Jim, I have some information I want to discuss with you. It's a rather private matter, so I suggest that we keep our voices down so as to not be overheard by the rest of the household."

"What are you talking about?" Jim asked brusquely.

"I'm in possession of certain information pertaining to a residential development in New York State. Apparently, an engineer forged signatures on water purity tests in order to obtain occupancy permits, thereby endangering the lives and health of the children and adults who moved into the structures."

"You son-of-a-bitch," Jim whispered viciously.

"Hold it, you haven't heard me out yet, Jim. I don't mean to cause you any grief. My only request is that you inform Kathleen of that illegal and irresponsible act, or else I'll tell her and back it up with the facts we've collected. I'll give you the option of picking the time and place for your disclosure, but it should be soon. The choice is yours. Now, I'm going into the kitchen to have a piece of pie and a cup of coffee. Are you going to join me?"

Jim Farley's face was white with rage, and his eyes burned with hatred. He looked as if he had just been hit in the stomach and couldn't breathe. All he could say was: "You lousy son-of-a-bitch!"

Chapter Eighteen

Kathleen had set a place at the table for Glenn and Jim. Glenn came into the kitchen alone and sat down. He was quiet as he watched Kathleen cut a piece of apple pie for him at the counter. He felt dirty and regretted what he had done. It was a rotten thing to accuse Jim without giving him a chance to defend himself.

"Is Jim coming in?" Kathleen asked.

"I'm not going to stay, Kathleen," Jim announced, standing in the kitchen door. "I'll call you later tonight. We can take a rain check on this afternoon. I'll see you around, Glenn. I hope everything works out for Andy. Good-bye, Kathleen."

"You don't have to run off, Jim. Why don't you wait until Glenis comes?" urged Kathleen, puzzled at the strained look on his face and his sudden change of mind. Jim left with a wave of his hand. Kathleen poured coffee for her and Glenn and sat down across the table from him. "What happened between you two? Jim was upset about something."

"Nothing important," Glenn lied, unhappy with himself. He had acted hastily and was ashamed of his actions.

Kathleen sighed wearily. "He's been in a bad mood all day. We had an argument just before you came. Oh, I see Glenis coming up the road," she said, jumping up from her seat to greet her at the door.

"Whose car is that, Mom?" asked Glenis, running up the porch steps.

"You'll be surprised," answered Kathleen, pointing to Glenn behind her. Glenis screamed at the sight of him and immediately ran into his out-stretched arms.

She rested her head against his chest like a small child. "I was hoping you would come."

"How could I stay away at a time like this, young lady?" he said softly.

"Would you like something to eat, Glenis?" asked Kathleen.

"I'd love some coffee if you have any left, Mom. I passed Jim down the road, and he seemed preoccupied."

"Your father has some things to tell you that should make you feel better," said Kathleen intentionally remaining silent about Jim.

Glenn saw exhaustion on his beloved daughter's face. "Sit down and rest, Glenis," he said in a calm voice. "After talking to your mother, I made plans for you, me and Ernest to fly to San Francisco to see Andy. There isn't any medicine in the world that will help him like the sight of you and his son."

"I've been wracking my brain trying to plan a trip, and here you've already arranged it. I can't believe it, Father, thank you," she left her seat to embrace him.

"We leave for Portland first thing in the morning. Do you have a pretty dress that Andy will recognize on you?"

"Yes, I've got the red dress I wore the night he left."

"That will be perfect," continued Glenn, fortified by her enthusiasm. "Seeing you in a red dress will do wonders for a man in his position. Sometime this afternoon I've got to pick up something at the small bank in town, and I'll need someone to identify me. If you don't mind, Glenis, I'd like to open an account for you and Andy and deposit three thousand dollars cash in it."

"But, Father, I can't take your money like that!" she protested.

"Hush, child. Let me do this. It's only money, which means very little to me. This is no time to be bothered or worried about the expense of this or that. Right now the only thing you should have on your mind is your husband. I have one goal in mind, and that is to put a smile back on your face for Andy. Let me share in your joy. That means more to me than you know."

"You're very generous, Glenn," remarked Kathleen, noting the look of contentment on his face.

"I'll get things ready for Ernest and myself this afternoon. Why don't you go to the bank with him, Mother?"

"I could do that, if you want," she volunteered.

"It won't take long, Kathleen. I have another suggestion to make. How about all of us, including your grandmother, go out for a nice dinner to celebrate the reunion of Glenis and Andy? You look tired, Kathleen, and you won't have to worry about cooking a meal for the gang. Maybe a change of routine will do all of us some good."

"That sounds like fun, Mother. Grandmother likes to get out once in awhile even though she says your cooking is as good as some of the better restaurants," Glenis noted, energized by the plans underway.

"Okay, why not?" smiled Kathleen. "I'll go to the bank with you, Glenn, and get ready for tonight afterwards."

"After we get some money at the bank, I'll get a room at the Inn for the night," he mentioned.

"You're welcome to stay at the house," said Kathleen.

"I appreciate that, but I think it's for the best that I stay at the inn," said Glenn firmly. "Tonight we can celebrate our being together as a family, and tomorrow you'll be able to hold your husband in your arms. We have much to be thankful for."

"I love you, Father," cried Glenis, hugging him briefly before running upstairs to find Ernest.

"You've transformed her, Glenn," said Kathleen, pleased to see Glenis's spirits so high. "I'm ready to go to the bank any time you are."

"The money should be there by now. When Bob Smart tells me to consider it done, it usually means that it's being processed," Glenn laughed, walking out to the car with Kathleen. He opened the door for her. "Are we going to cause a stir at the bank for you?"

"That subject has been talked to death. I don't even think about it anymore. The bank manager, Margaret Foss, was a student of mine. She's a nice person and definitely not a gossip."

The small bank had two tellers. Glenn asked for Margaret Foss, and they were escorted into an office behind the counter.

"Hello, Miss Cohen. How's Glenis doing?" The bank manager greeted Kathleen. "Please have a seat."

"She's doing better now that her father has become a part of her life. Margaret, meet Glenn Hastings. Glenn, this is Margaret Foss. I remember her when she was a rambunctious youngster who always had a wonderful smile on her face."

"I'm glad to meet you, Mr. Hastings," said Margaret Foss, silently evaluating him.

"It's a pleasure, Ms. Foss. Do you have a transfer of funds for me?" asked Glenn, reaching into his pocket for an identification card.

"We do have your transfer, Mr. Hastings."

"Wonderful. Now, I'd like to deposit three thousand dollars in a checking account for Glenis and Andrew Richards. I'll take the rest in cash of whatever mix of denominations is convenient for you. I probably don't have to mention it, but I'd like your guarantee of confidentiality regarding this transfer and transaction by the bank and its staff."

"You have our guarantee, Mr. Hastings," answered Margaret Foss in a professional manner. "Your request is understandable. Miss Cohen and her family are some of the most respected people in our community. I cried when I was promoted to a higher grade out of her classroom."

"You're making me blush, Margaret."

"Well, it's true nevertheless. I'll be right back with the checking account paper work for Glenis and Andy and the cash for you, Mr. Hastings. Be patient; it may take a few minutes to prepare."

"Take your time, Ms. Foss," Glenn told her.

Once they were alone Kathleen watched Glenn. He seemed to be more relaxed and in command of himself than the last time she had seen him. The dark green work suit reminded her of the olive drab Army uniform he'd worn long ago. He still had that positive air of invincibility and determination, and he was still a handsome man, she thought.

"Modern technologies are terrific, aren't they?" Glenn remarked. "I make a phone call to Pennsylvania and within an hour or so, money is available on demand four hundred miles away."

"You don't have to do this, Glenn," said Kathleen.

"I've already told you how I feel about any money I have. If our daughter and her family are in need of anything, I'll consider it a privilege to help where I can." Glenn waved off her protest. He found it hard to believe that, after all the years that had passed, he was sitting beside Kathleen. "They love you in this town, don't they, Kathleen?"

"I've been well treated in York," she replied modestly.

A moment later, Margaret Foss returned with the money and a checkbook. "I hope you're satisfied with the denominations of cash, Mr. Hastings. It was a pleasure to meet you. Good luck. Good-bye, Miss Cohen, give my love to Glenis and tell her that we're all rooting for Andy."

"I will, Margaret, thank you."

"Thank you, Ms. Foss."

On their way back to the house, Glenn told Kathleen that he needed to buy some clothes for the trip. "I'll pick you up later for dinner. What time do you suggest, Kathleen?"

"Can you make it back by five-thirty? That will get us to a restaurant by six and give us plenty of time to enjoy the evening. I think Mother will like the idea."

"That's great. You pick the restaurant. Would you give this checkbook to Glenis and tell her to bring it in the morning?" Glenn requested.

"That's generous of you, Glenn," she replied.

He passed the book to her and came around the car to open her door. He did it automatically, and Kathleen remembered how he had done the same thing twenty-seven years before. "I'll see you by five-thirty. Tell your Mother not to snack or spoil her appetite," he laughed. Kathleen smiled and waved good-bye as she climbed the porch stairs.

Glenn reserved a room at the inn and made a quick trip into Portsmouth, where he purchased a suitcase and some suitable leisure clothing for the trip to California. He returned to the Inn to shower and shave. He felt good being able to do something positive for Glenis, recalling how much it would have meant to him if he could have seen Kathleen in the hospital when he was at his worst. Foolish pride had gotten in his way. He had insisted on maintaining his silence throughout the entire agonizing ordeal. He was determined to never let his pride do that to him again.

Glenn dressed in a pair of dark green gabardine slacks with a light green shirt and a black tie. He was satisfied with the dark green sport coat he had selected. Usually his tastes ran to browns but today the tint of green looked good for a change. At five-thirty sharp, he pulled into the Cohen's yard and climbed the porch steps. Mrs. Cohen and Ernest were sitting on the porch.

"You're certainly prompt, Glenn," remarked Mrs. Cohen. "I warned the girls to not be tardy. Dinner out will be a nice change of routine, thank you for suggesting it."

"You're welcome. Where do you think we should go to eat? I'm getting hungry."

"I've always liked Warren's in Kittery."

"I remember it, by the river. Kathleen and I went there once."

"Well, we're only two minutes late," confessed Glenis in an expansive mood, stepping out on the porch with her mother.

"Seeing how nice you all look, I'd say it was worth the wait," answered Glenn, winking at his daughter. Kathleen smiled without comment. "May I take your arm, Mrs. Cohen?"

"Anytime, young man. My legs aren't as steady as they once were, but I don't complain." Kathleen's mother linked her arm through his.

"Since you have the privilege of age would you like to ride up front or in the back?"

"I like to see where I'm going so I'll ride in front with you."

"It looks like Ernest is the lucky guy to sit between two of the loveliest girls in town," Glenn happily observed.

Warren's Restaurant was a familiar landmark on the Maine side of the Piscataqua River. It was decorated with seaside paraphernalia much the way it was when Glenn and Kathleen were there in 1942. The place had been filled with servicemen of all branches back then, and the clientele was noisier and sometimes boisterous, reflective of the war-time anxieties of the people. Tonight, the restaurant was much more subdued and elegant, thought Glenn.

The evening was festive, despite the serious overtones that remained unspoken. Ernest was his usual quiet self, eating a full platter of scallops and shrimp without spilling a drop on his clean clothes. He was a serious child with good manners, which probably could be attributed to his growing up in a household with three adult females. They concluded the evening with dessert and coffee, lingering at the table, enjoying the fellowship.

Glenn watched Glenis with pride. She was radiantly beautiful in the red dress she had described to him, her hair falling loose and full around her shoulders much the way her mother had done years ago, and continued today. Kathleen wore a light-blue dress with white trim and lace around her throat. It was amazing to Glenn how mother and daughter resembled each other. Glenis lacked the confidence and poise of her mother and was more excitable and out-going. Kathleen still had that remarkable quality of benign grace that had attracted Glenn to her the very first time they had met. He was a happy man with members of a family around him, enjoying every minute of the evening.

On the ride back to York Village, Glenn showed the passengers where he had the accident with his Studebaker. They were quiet and reflective; the unexpected events of the day had exhausted them all. Ernest fell asleep in his mother's arms before they had gone a mile down the road. Glenn pulled the rental car into the driveway and brought it gently to a stop so as to not awaken Ernest.

"I think we're all ready to call it a night," Glenn remarked as he opened the doors on the passenger side of the car and helped Mrs. Cohen up the porch steps. She turned to Glenn, "Thank you for a lovely evening," patting him on his arm.

"It was my pleasure, Mrs. Cohen," he replied, turning to Glenis who was still holding the sleeping Ernest. "Here, let me help you with him, Glenis."

"You can place him on the couch in the living room," she said in a whisper. Glenn had missed being able to hold the twins as they started to get older. It felt good to hold his grandson. He carefully placed little Ernest on the couch with a pillow under his head and quietly followed Glenis out of the room. Her fatigue was beginning to show.

"You rest well," he requested, hugging her reassuringly. "I'll be back to pick you up at seven in the morning. That will give us plenty of time to get to Portland and board the flight. So, I'll see you then."

"I can hardly wait, I probably won't sleep a wink."

"Give it a try," he said. "Good night." Glenis disappeared in the house leaving Glenn and Kathleen alone on the porch.

"I'll see to it that Glenis and Ernie are ready when you come tomorrow," she promised. "I enjoyed the evening, Glenn. I remembered the booth we sat in the last time we were at the restaurant, did you?"

"Yes, it was in the corner next to the one we had tonight," Glenn answered. "It was a pleasant evening tonight. Thanks for sharing it with me, Kathleen."

"Good night, Glenn," Kathleen whispered back, avoiding his eyes and stepping inside to the living room.

The night passed quickly for Glenn. He had asked the desk clerk to give him a wake-up call in the morning in case he overslept. It was a good thing he did, because the ringing phone woke him from a sound sleep. He quickly dressed and prepared himself for the trip, taking a light breakfast of coffee and a blueberry muffin in the inn's dining room. He pulled into Kathleen's yard one minute before seven o'clock.

Two suitcases were placed at the top of the steps. Glenn reached for them as Philip came out from the house. "Good morning, Glenn," said Philip, extending his hand.

"Good morning, Philip, you're up early. It's nice to see you again."

"Glenis and Ernie will be right out. Glenis is the happiest I've seen her in a long time. Thanks for helping to make that possible. It's like a dream-come-true to her. She's a good girl and we love her dearly. I'm glad that her dad stands as tall as he does."

"I appreciate that, Philip. How could a dad do otherwise?"

Glenis stepped out on the porch holding Ernest's hand. Mrs. Cohen and Kathleen followed silently behind them.

"Are you ready to fly on a big airplane?" asked Glenn, reaching out to hold him at the head of the stairs.

"Can I sit by the window?" his grandson asked.

"You certainly can. Kiss everybody good-bye and we'll be on our way to see your Daddy. You look radiant this morning, Glenis."

"I'm so excited that I can hardly stand it. Good-bye Mom and Grandmother and you too, Uncle Phil. I'll keep in touch."

"Good-bye to all of you," said Glenn, placing the suitcases in the trunk of the car and opening the front door for Glenis and Ernest. He waved to the three people on the porch and started to get behind the wheel of the car when his eyes met Kathleen's. Her eyes were wet with suppressed tears. Without thinking, he ran quickly to the top of the stairs and embraced her. "I'll take good care of her, Kathleen. Let me handle some of the responsibility for a change."

"All right, good-bye, Glenn. You know what's happening again don't you?" she asked in a whisper.

"I think I do," he admitted quietly. "So long for now," he kissed her trembling lips and ran back to the car, announcing in a loud voice, "California here we come!"

Philip placed a supporting arm around Kathleen's shoulders. "Things will work out, Sis. You're so wrapped up in Andy's injuries and Glenis that you don't have any time or energy left for yourself. Now is your chance to think about what you want for once. Glenn's right, let him share the responsibility. So far, it looks as if he's doing just fine."

"Phil and Glenn are right," Mrs. Cohen joined in. "Glenis and her family are in good hands. I worry about you more than I let on, my dearest daughter. Happiness has been a stranger to you for such a long time. I've understood and admired your loyalty to the past, but becoming a prisoner of the past is not healthy. What's the matter with Jim lately? You two argue more than ever these days. Don't deny it, I see a lot of things that would surprise you."

Kathleen's tears flowed freely now that Glenn's car had left the driveway. "I don't know what I'd do without your support, Mother and Phil. I've tried to not be a martyr in bringing up Glenis. Right now, I'm emotionally drained and tired. The terrible news about Andy has increased my concern for him and Glenis. I just don't handle chaos or conflict as well as I used to. I feel relieved that Glenn has stepped in to help." Tears ran down her face. "Jim has been difficult lately, and I don't know why."

Her mother held her in her arms and spoke softly, "I can't help you with the conflict that's raging in your heart. But I can see how your commitment to Jim and your love for Glenn are tearing you apart, and my heart aches for you."

Kathleen wept softly, "And now I'm afraid I've lost both of them," she cried, tearing herself away from her mother and running to her bedroom.

Chapter Nineteen

The large four-engine Constellation aircraft sat at the terminal while passengers boarded. Glenn stopped at the concession stand to pick up some reading materials before the three of them took their assigned seats on the plane. Ernest took his promised position by the window; Glenn sat on the outside next to the aisle. When the aircraft crew started its takeoff procedures, Ernest was all eyes and hung tightly to his mother's arm. He was thrilled when the plane became airborne and the ground seemed to drop away from the aircraft. Once the plane reached altitude, he relaxed and sat back in the seat.

"This is my first airplane ride, too," said Glenis. "It takes a little getting used to, doesn't it?"

"It takes awhile, but it's still safer than driving," claimed Glenn, positioning his seat for maximum comfort. "As soon as we get to San Francisco we'll drop our suitcases at the hotel and freshen up before heading to the hospital."

"I still can't believe that I'll be seeing Andy so soon," Glenis exclaimed happily. "What do I do if he's wounded so badly that it shows on my face? That would hurt him a lot, and he would know how I feel about his injuries."

"That's something you'll have to be strong about, Glenis. Whatever you do, don't let the severity of his wounds frighten you. Be honest in assessing their magnitude with him because he knows more than you do about them and their impact on the rest of his life. What he wants with all his heart and soul is for you to love and support him regardless of his condition, and if possible, for you to be a part of his fight to overcome the problems he'll have to face. Handling them alone is a frightening possibility."

"Is that what you had to do, Father?"

"Yes, until I met my wife, Jessica. She helped me a lot. You and Andy will be just fine. Just follow your instincts."

"Mother told me the same thing," confided Glenis, reflecting on the relationship she has with her mother. "The fact that you're going to California with me pleases her."

"I saw that in her, too. Your mother is a wonderful person. She's made a lot of sacrifices for you, and she deserves credit for being the strong person that she is."

"Tell me, Father, and I'm really not trying to meddle in your private affairs, do you have someone special in your life now? You seem to be more relaxed and comfortable than the first time we met. Mother noticed the difference too, and she said she heard you mention a Faith. Who's Faith?"

"She's an engineer with the company," Glenn answered frankly. "We recently hired her. She lost her husband in Korea in 1950 and has a son in college. She went to Canada with me on our latest project. We've become close friends and I enjoy being with her."

"I'm not prying. I just want to know all that I can about you. When I was a little girl I used to dream that you would come and marry Mother. I carried that same dream into young adulthood, too. When I first met you I thought that the possibility of the two of you getting together was small at best, but I have to admit, I still hope in my heart that it might come about."

Glenn understood and sighed. "I've already told you how I was searching for what your mother and I had long ago. It was a romantic dream that defied reality. She has Jim now. They've made a commitment to each other, and your mother takes commitments very seriously. I'll always cherish the moments we had together, but life goes on and things change. I was having trouble catching up with the changes, but I'm working on it. Faith has helped me a lot."

"I'm glad for anything that makes you happy. I want Mom's happiness too, but, to be honest, I'm having second thoughts about Jim. Mother hasn't said anything, yet, but I have this feeling that all is not well between them."

"Because of me?"

"Yes, although you're not all of it. I can't figure him out and I don't mean to be judgmental. If Mom knew that I harbored these reservations, she would be crushed. Uncle Phil feels the same way I do about Jim."

Glenn listened to his daughter's comments about Jim Farley and the knot in his stomach grew tighter. "Glenis, you're an adult with a family of your own to worry about, and I certainly don't want to add to your burdens, but would you mind if I shared a problem with you that's been bothering me since I spoke to Jim yesterday afternoon?"

"Of course I don't mind. Please, Father, what is it?" she asked eagerly, noting the worried look on his face.

"You must promise to never tell your mother unless I release you from that promise."

"You have my word."

Glenn told her about his suspicions of Jim Farley based on the information he had collected. Then he recited almost word for word what had taken place between him and Jim.

"Wow! That's a bombshell. Now I understand why he was so mad when I passed him on the road. He hardly acknowledged me. This is really going to hurt Mother. What if Jim doesn't tell her and they continue with their wedding plans?"

"I don't know. I wish I could retract my actions," Glenn shook his head helplessly. "It was stupid of me to confront him like that. I was so smug when I told him and was actually glad to shock him. He had been his normal sarcastic self to me and I thought he deserved it. In retrospect, it was terribly insensitive of me. I'll never tell your mother without double-checking all the facts. I'm afraid I've been too hasty."

"Mother will be furious if it turns out Jim is guilty of the deceit. I met him early in their relationship and have been around him ever since. If your information is correct, then it ties in with the few doubts I've entertained about him. He's a slick talker and sometimes he even has mother eating out of his hand, which is out of character for her. Obviously he's the dominant figure in the relationship."

"I'm afraid I've unleashed a monster," Glenn regretfully conceded. "I've even thought of apologizing to him. That may be too late now. I swear to you that it was not jealousy on my part that started this witch hunt. It was my intuition working overtime and concern for your mother's welfare."

"I believe you," said Glenis, grasping his hand. "Don't worry about it. If it ever becomes an issue, it could help clear the air and give them a chance for a fresh start."

"You could be right, young lady."

A rental car and reservations for a hotel were waiting for them at the San Francisco Airport flight operations desk. Glenn took Glenis to the large street map at the terminal building to orient her with the airport, their hotel, and the hospital.

From the airport, they drove to the Hotel Mayfair on the outskirts of the University of San Francisco campus. The Hotel Mayfair was an old brownstone building reeking of regal Victorian tradition. It was here that Glenis and Ernest saw their first palm tree. It was a happy milestone in her life. They were escorted to their reserved suite, where they dropped off their suitcases. Ernest had been wide-eyed and alert for much of the trip, and he had not uttered a whimper or a protest. Glenn was proud of his little grandson.

"We're only four miles from the Presidio," Glenn informed Glenis. "We can pick up Route 101 which will take us to the main gate of the base. It'll probably take about twenty minutes if traffic isn't too heavy. Are you comfortable driving in traffic?"

"I don't mind it. I'm going to slip into my red dress," Glenis announced eagerly. "Would you look after Ernest for a few minutes?"

"Sure, he can watch me shave."

Fifteen minutes later, they were on their way to the Presidio. Glenn asked Glenis to drive so that she could develop a familiarity with the route. They showed identification at the gate and were told to follow the signs to the hospital, a large brick building. The grounds of the base were impeccably maintained. It was a beautiful facility, one of the gems of all the U.S. military installations. By the time Glenis pulled the car into a parking space in front of the hospital, she was so nervous her hands were shaking. Glenn placed a calming hand over her trembling fingers, offering her silent support. He then removed his Medal of Honor from its case, and placed the sash around his neck. It was the traditional method of wearing the nation's highest honor for valor.

"I don't wear it often, but in places like this I do. I want the men to know that I'm one of their brothers in that special fraternity of warriors. This medal represents my rites of passage."

"It's a beautiful medal," Glenis said. "I've never seen one before. Oh, I'm so nervous, I'd better take your arm."

"That will be my pleasure. Come on, Ernest, take Gramp's hand and we'll go to see your daddy."

The information desk gave them Andy's room number. They took the elevator to the fifth floor. The moment they stepped out of the elevator they were overwhelmed by the smell of disinfectant. Ernest wrinkled his nose.

"We're here to see Lieutenant Andrew Richards," Glenis told the attendant at the nurse's station. "I'm his wife."

The Army nurse at the desk checked her register and pointed to a room diagonally across from the station. "Your husband has been promoted to captain, Mrs. Richards. He'll be happy to see you. He might be sleeping, but don't worry about that. He's very alert and you're just what he needs." The nurse looked at Glenn and Ernest. "And you are?"

"I'm Glenis's father and this is their son, Ernest."

"That's fine." The nurse noticed the Medal of Honor and gave him a salute. "It's a privilege to have you here, Sir. You may go into his room and stay as long as you want."

Glenis took Ernest's hand and pushed the partially closed door open. She saw her husband's head laying on the pillow as if he was sleeping. Traction wires and weights were positioned in several places around his bed. They were a shocking sight. Her eyes were riveted by the drawn lines on Andy's face. She rushed to his bedside and gathered him into her arms, tears of joy flowed freely. Andrew was shocked, and it took a few seconds for the reality of his wife's presence to register. His eyes softened and he too was blinded with tears. She was like an apparition from heaven.

Glenn examined the medical equipment surrounding Andy's bed while Andy and Glenis vented their grief and shared a private interlude. The ordeal ahead of them became easier at that moment, for the load was evenly distributed between the two of them. Glenn held little Ernest by the hand so that he would not touch any of the wire braces or plastic tubes within his reach. Glenn noticed the severe burn injuries on Andy's neck and arms. His left hand remained under the blanket, instead of using it to embrace his wife. Both of Andy's legs were in traction—a positive sign, that Andy would have future use of one or both of them.

Glenis pulled free of Andy's embrace and looked at him for the first time.

"They got me pretty good, Honey," Andy smiled woefully. "You've got to be brave. I might never walk again. I don't have any feeling in one of my legs and the other has only ten percent response... Then, you haven't seen this," Andy pulled his left arm out from under the covers and held it for her to see. It was completely covered with blood-stained bandages. Before she could say anything, Andy began to weep uncontrollably. He was hyperventilating and trying unsuccessfully to tell Glenis something as she did her best to calm him down.

Glenn stepped out to the nurse's desk. "Nurse, he's becoming overwrought, can you help him?"

"I'll get Dr. Hancock, Sir," she said, running down the corridor. Seconds later, she went directly to Andy's room with a doctor on her heels.

"Andrew, this is Dr. Hancock. Do you hear me?" There was very little response. Andy continued to make convulsive sobbing sounds as if he could not catch his breath. Dr. Hancock instantly injected a sedative. Within seconds Andy's body began to relax, and his breathing returned to normal. Glenis watched what was taking place with concern, yet she was in complete control of her emotions and professionally in favor of what was being done to her husband.

The doctor turned to Glenis. "You must be Captain Richards' wife. I'm glad you could come to be with Andy. He's been severely wounded, but it could have been much worse. He's going to be resting for a while, so why don't you come into the lounge area where we can talk in private."

"Thank you, doctor. I have a lot of questions, and I hope you have some answers," Glenis replied, still distraught. "By the way, this is my father, Glenn Hastings and Andy's and my son, Ernest."

"I'm honored to meet you, Sir," Dr. Hancock greeted Glenn deferentially. "Where did you earn the Medal of Honor?"

"In Normandy, during the breakout period in the hedgerows. May I be present while you bring my daughter up-to-date on Andy's condition?"

"Yes, Sir, follow me." They entered a waiting room beside the nurse's station furnished with comfortable chairs. The doctor closed the door behind them and directed them to sit down and relax. Glenn sat on a sofa beside Glenis facing Dr. Hancock. Ernest sat beside his mother.

"Just how extensive are his injuries?" asked Glenis firmly.

"We haven't had your husband long enough to completely evaluate him," Dr. Hancock spoke forthrightly. "My interpretation of what I've seen so far is that he may lose his left hand."

Glenis winced at the news and grasped Glenn's arm tightly. Blood drained from her face leaving her weak and light headed.

"Nothing is certain and I'm giving you the worst case scenario. I firmly believe in truthfulness when we're dealing with these men's lives. Andy has massive burns all over his body. Retention of his left leg is still in question. His right leg has some response to stimuli, which is promising. Blood is circulating in both legs and we've been able to stop the infections. He's being metered pain-killing medication and seems to be physically as comfortable as a person can be under the circumstances. His emotional condition will improve now that you are with him."

"I'd like you to know, Glenis," Glenn interrupted. "That at one time I was a candidate for amputation of both legs. It took a long time for my legs to mend themselves and I had to learn how to walk again. It took me five years to accomplish it. I mention this to inform you that medical science does not have all the answers, and to be encouraged by that fact."

"You're correct, Mr. Hastings," Dr. Hancock affirmed. "You're a determined man, and I salute you. Miracles do happen, especially when it's accompanied by a good dose of determination."

"I've been told a few times that it's cussedness," said Glenn, eliciting a smile from Glenis.

224

"I've covered all we know about Andy as far as medical science is concerned. He's been surly and bitter and very disruptive. That's one of the reasons I'm glad you're here. Right now he needs you, Mrs. Richards, more than he needs me to get better. It could take up to a year to predict what his physical state will ultimately be. I realize how his outburst may be upsetting to you, but it was encouraging to me as a measure of progress. It means that he's coming to grips with his potential limitations and that's a harsh fact for anyone to swallow. You're welcome to be with him anytime and as long as you desire, without exception. That goes for little Ernest here, also. He can play a vital role in offering his father a new lease on life and a reinforcement of his resolve to return to a useful one as close to normal as his injuries allow."

"Thank you, Dr. Hancock, you've made me feel better," said Glenis. "Now I know what I'm faced with."

"Your husband can talk, feed himself, shave, and play some games with his fellow patients. He could be a lot worse. I don't say that to minimize the gravity of his injuries, but to remind you to view them in the context of injuries that were potentially possible. You'll be an important part of his recovery and the speed in which it takes place, but you'll have to be strong at times."

"I'm a registered nurse, and I plan to take good care of my number one priority, my husband," Glenis told him.

"Mrs. Richards, I may try to put you on our nursing staff," Dr. Hancock smiled at her. "Now, do you have any further questions? Andrew should be able to talk soon. He's an intelligent and industrious young man. The idleness of his days are one of the things he finds most difficult to cope with. I'm sure you'll be able to channel those characteristic traits into meaningful projects."

"Thank you, Dr. Hancock," said Glenn. "Come, Glenis, let's see how Andy is doing now."

225

A nurse was monitoring the medication being metered through plastic tubes in Andy's arm when they returned to the room. He was half-sitting, his head supported by a pillow. His eyes were still closed.

They clustered around Andy's bed watching him periodically become alert, only to close his eyes and surrender again to the sedatives. Glenis pulled a chair beside Andy's bed so that she could see him and he could see her when he opened his eyes.

"I'm going to take a walk around the floor with Ernie," Glenn announced. "Do you think it's wise for him to see the injuries some of the men have?"

"I don't see how it can hurt him," Glenis replied. "Maybe when he's older he'll be able to reflect on the sacrifices of soldiers like his father. I'm going to help Andy get well. We've got a whole life ahead of us and we're going to share it if I have to brow beat him to do it." Glenis displayed the devotion and self-control Glenn knew she possessed.

"I know you will," said Glenn, kissing the top of her head. "He's a lucky man to have you for a wife." She squeezed his hand before he left. Glenn knew the minute he saw that smile and the resolution in her eyes that the trip was going to accomplish positive things for her and Andy.

Glenn and Ernest slowly walked around the floor, visiting several different wards. They saw men with every imaginable injury, and yet, in the midst of such pain and misery, Glenn sensed a tangible air of optimism. The men talked and chatted with him and Ernie as if they were old friends. Glenn shook more hands in an hour than he had for years, and it made him feel good. These were his kind of people; he respected them. They had given everything they had and asked for very little in return. Their camaraderie, the constant barrage of jokes and running commentary helped make each day tolerable. No one was allowed to stand alone. They rallied around the weakest man or the most seriously wounded and virtually willed him to recuperate. Glenn never saw the same kind of compassion and sharing in the outside world that he had always found in the wards full of soldiers with broken bodies and injuries defying description. The challenges these men faced were enough to humble the strongest person, and fill him with thanksgiving that the nation had men like these with the courage to place their fragile bodies between their country and its enemies.

Later that evening, Glenn, Glenis, and Ernest returned to the hotel and ate dinner in the dining room. They were exhausted, and it was all Ernest could do to finish his chicken soup and toast, after which they took him up to their suite and placed him on a bed in his mother's room.

After Ernest had settled for the night, Glenn and Glenis relaxed in the sitting room. "It's been a big day for you, Glenis, and I know that you're tired. Before you turn in though, I'd like to discuss a few alternatives with you. It's not necessary for me to be with you once you get settled into the routine you'll be following. I'm going to check on the possibility of a hospitality room at the base headquarters. It might not be available, but we can try."

"That would be a lot easier." Glenis was pleased at his consideration.

"Also, I'd like to check out what it would take to transfer Andy somewhere on the East coast, closer to your home. Maybe a Veteran's Administration Hospital will be able to care for him once he moves to the therapy stage. Would you object to that?"

"Not if it could give him the same quality of care that he would receive in an Army hospital."

"I'll work on these things tomorrow," he promised. "Now you get to sleep, my dear daughter. I'm weary tonight, too."

"Goodnight, Father," said Glenis, giving him a hug and kiss. "We really made a difference in Andy's life today, didn't we?"

"We sure did," Glenn smiled. "He's a fine young man. With your help, I think he's going to surprise everybody how well he recovers and adapts to his limitations. Good night, Glenis."

* * *

That same night, on the opposite side of the country, Kathleen tossed and turned in her bed and lay awake for hours. She had spent most of the day with Jim, who had showed up soon after Glenn and Glenis left for Portland. Jim had tried to call her when the family was out to dinner at Warren's Restaurant, and he was furious that Kathleen had not let him know about their outing. It had been a day filled with arguments and accusations that completely drained her. Her life seemed to become more complicated and chaotic with each passing day.

She also worried about Andy and how Glenis would react to his injuries. There was no call from them. Kathleen prayed for direction in her life, and she prayed for her family and Glenn and Jim. Something was different about Jim these days, and it angered her. He was becoming more and more possessive and critical of everything she did. Phil told her that he had noticed that tendency from the beginning, and perhaps he was correct. In a peculiar sadistic way Jim tried to blame her for whatever was bothering him at any particular time. Their attitudes toward each other had changed. Maintaining the relationship was becoming a full-time job and Kathleen was questioning if she was up to the task. She agonized over the situation throughout the night and was unable to come up with a satisfactory answer.

The next morning Kathleen was still in bed when her mother called to her that coffee was ready. It was almost nine-thirty. "Are you all right?"

"I'm awake, Mother. It was a long night. I'll be down in…"

The ringing phone interrupted them. Her mother answered it, and Kathleen hurriedly threw a bathrobe on and ran downstairs to see who it was. As she had expected, it was Glenis. Her mother asked about the flight and how Andy was, and then she passed the phone to Kathleen.

"Hello, Glenis, how's Andy?"

"Hi Mom, I knew you'd be worried if I didn't call this morning," Glenis's voice sounded strong and reassuring. "He's been hurt bad, Mom, but we're going to work with him and make him as whole as we can. At least he's alive. He's even laughing and joking like he used to do. When we left the hospital last night Ernie was so precious. Father lifted him up on the bed beside Andy. Ernie laid his head down and looked directly into Andy's eyes and smiled at him; Andy cried like a baby. He really needed to know that we're with him and we're going to be a part of his recovery. I'm going to stay here for a while. Father is going to check into the possibility of moving Andy closer to the New England area. My, he's been a tower of strength. Nothing seems to stop him when he wants something."

Kathleen smiled at her description of Glenn. "It's a trait he's always had."

"He's coming back to New England after he's sure I'm settled into a routine here. The hotel rooms are gorgeous and close to the hospital. I'm actually driving in California traffic. Oh, yes, I've seen my first palm tree. That was exciting."

"You sound great, Glenis. I'm so glad to hear you talking this way. Give our love to Andy. He's always in our prayers. Thank you for calling, dear. Please, take care of yourself. We love you."

"Love you and Grandmother, too."

Kathleen hung up the phone relieved to hear Glenis in such good spirits. "She sounds very positive and motivated, doesn't she, Mother?"

"I was encouraged at how strong she sounded," agreed Mrs. Cohen. "I'm not surprised. She comes by that determination and strong will naturally from you and Glenn."

"Mother!" Kathleen blushed.

Later in the day Kathleen was returning from grocery shopping when the phone rang. She expected to hear Jim's voice. "Hello?"

"Hello, this is Faith Hamilton. I'm calling to see if Glenn Hastings is there, or if you know where I can reach him. Are you Kathleen Cohen?"

"Yes, I'm Kathleen. He left yesterday with his daughter for California. We heard from her this morning. They're at the Mayfair Hotel in San Francisco. You should be able to reach Glenn there."

There was a pause on the line. "I've written the hotel down and will try it. Why don't I also leave you my number here in case you hear from them? Would you ask him to call directly? We have a newly constructed phone line to our plant site. A few things of a technical nature have come up that I'm not able to make a decision about, and his assistant resident engineer has not shown up on the job yet. I'm sorry to bother you with my problem. He told me where he was going. I hope your son-in-law is doing well."

"Thank you, Faith, I'll be glad to pass on your telephone number to him."

"That's fine. Actually it's his office number: 1 212 654 2886. If you speak to him, tell him that the problems are not serious enough for him to cut short his visit with his daughter. I just need to pick his brain on a few matters."

"I understand," said Kathleen, surprised at Faith's candor and sincerity.

"Your daughter must be proud of him. He's been a wonderful father to his boys. Well, I have to run. It was nice talking with you, Kathleen. Thanks."

"Thank you for calling, Faith." Kathleen placed the phone on the receiver and revisited every word of their conversation. Glenn had shared a lot of his past with her. Kathleen didn't know what to think about it, but her reaction to Faith was favorable. Her down-to-earth quality radiated integrity. Kathleen was pleased with the assessment and intimidated by it at the same time. The reality was that Glenn and Faith had something going besides a professional relationship!

* * *

In northern Canada, Faith hung up the phone and reflected on her impression of Kathleen. Her reaction to Kathleen's quiet unassuming manner was surprising. Kathleen had that precise always-in-control way of talking, like most school teachers, but there was warmth and honesty there, too.

Faith followed her pragmatic instincts without delay, and called the Mayfair Hotel.

"Hello, Glenn, this is Faith."

"Hi, Faith, it's nice to hear your voice. You sound a long way off. How are things going?"

"They'll be better now that I can talk with you." Faith discussed the situation she was faced with at the plant site. Glenn made several suggestions and recommendations. Faith understood his instructions, taking notes on their solutions. She gave Glenn the new number for the office and told him that she had called Kathleen.

"When did you call York?" asked Glenn.

"Just a few minutes ago before I called you," Faith answered honestly. "She gave me the name of your hotel. She seems very nice."

"Do you recall the stuff we talked about regarding her fiancé? Well, I did as you suggested. It sounded like a sound plan. Jim got very angry and called me a few names. I feel guilty about it now. I know it sparked some bad feelings between them even before I left, and I was wondering if maybe he had

231

mentioned it to her. I have a hunch I've overstepped the bounds of decency."

"It's done, Glenn," she exclaimed forcefully. "You acted in good faith. If we follow our hearts, we can't go too wrong." She paused a moment and continued, "I have something to tell you about my great admirer in Vermont. I called Tom this morning as soon as we got the direct phone line hooked up. He told me that Bill Savoy has been arrested on a breaking and entering charge and attempted rape on a woman in Montpelier. Tom mentioned that the article in the newspaper quoted an attorney predicting that he'll get five to ten years in prison. Whoopee, one of my worries has been removed. Now you won't have to look him up and apply some pain as you called it," Faith was laughing as she spoke.

"Faith, you never cease to amaze me," answered Glenn, laughing with her. "I'm not certain when I'll be back, but it's not necessary for me to baby-sit Glenis. I'll call to let you know when. If you have any more problems you want to share with me, just call, you know the number, good-bye, Faith, I miss you."

"I miss you too, Glenn."

Glenn spent the day alone in the hotel room with Ernie trying to locate a Veterans Administration Hospital close to York that could care for Andy. He tried calling Kathleen's number, but there was no answer.

* * *

The atmosphere at the Cohen residence, when Glenn tried to call, was far from serene. Kathleen had taken her Mother to Phil's house for a visit and returned home looking forward to a quiet day catching up on some of her reading and studying for the summer course in education that she was taking. The lack of sleep the night before had left her tense and weary and more intolerant of things she would normally have paid no attention to. Life was becoming too complicated!

Jim Farley drove fast into the driveway, bringing his car to a sudden stop in a cloud of dust. Kathleen remained in her seat at the kitchen table with her educational materials spread out in front of her when Jim pounded on the door. She hollered for him to come in.

He entered the kitchen slamming the door behind him. "I thought I should drop by to pass on a little information to you about your great Glenn Hastings," he shouted.

"What are you talking about, Jim?" Kathleen demanded sharply. She knew by the vindictive tone of his voice that this was going to be a showdown.

"Well, the other day when we were sitting out there on the porch, he told me that he had some damaging information about me, and threatened to tell you if I didn't tell you first. Well, you can tell your soldier boy to go to hell. The things he accused me of are not true and never were true," screamed Jim. His intimidating stance frightened her.

"What were the accusations?" demanded Kathleen, standing to confront Jim face to face.

"None of your business. Ever since he came into your life this spring, you've changed. He was the one who got you pregnant and you never forgot it," Jim viciously accused.

Kathleen was furious at the accusation and reacted with a slap across his face. "Don't you ever put words or thoughts into my mouth or interpret my behavior with your filthy tongue. What in the world has passed between you and Glenn that was so bad that we've deteriorated to this?"

"If you really want to know, Hastings said he had information that I violated an Engineer Society code of ethics. It was nothing. All he wanted to do was make trouble between us. Even before he spoke to me about the incident, I had decided that I wasn't going to play second fiddle to anyone. It's finished, Kathleen, and I'm relieved he brought it to a head. We were riding a dead horse, and it's time to bail out and go our separate ways."

The phone rang several times while they were arguing but Kathleen ignored it. If it was her mother on the line she did not want her to be subjected to their confrontation.

"You do what you want, James," she cried. "I'm not going to stand in your way or beg you to change your mind. Can you swear that his account of your transgression is false? You know I'll find out what he told you one way or another."

"The son-of-a bitch is lying. What he wanted to do was break us up. You had your chance to send him down the road, but you couldn't do that."

"He's Glenis's father..." Kathleen protested.

"Well, isn't her name Cohen?" Jim shot back. "I don't see her wearing his name!"

"Get out," demanded Kathleen, turning her back on him.

Farley left, slamming the porch door, breaking one of the hinges, and kicking up loose gravel as he spun his tires out of the driveway. Never in her life had anyone talked to her as Jim just had. The accusations were bad enough, but the crude and vile way he took delight in reaching out to hurt and insult her left Kathleen feeling empty and hysterical. She sat for a long time at the kitchen table, staring into empty space, her body so tense she began shaking all over. The phone rang again. She answered it expecting Jim to be on the other end.

"Hello," said Kathleen, trying to sound natural.

"Hi, this is Glenn."

"You're just the person I want to talk to," cried Kathleen, anxious to learn the facts. "Jim just left here. He claimed that you accused him falsely of some terrible things. All I want to know from you is the truth. Were your accusations true?"

"As far as I know they were accurate. The information came from the chairman of an ethics committee," defended Glenn, hearing an overwrought Kathleen he did not know.

"Why didn't you discuss them with him without your ultimatum involving me?" Kathleen demanded pointedly.

"It was my intention to have him discuss it with you if he thought it appropriate. I wish now that I had remained silent. I've felt bad about it ever since."

"Did you give any thought to how it would affect our future plans?" asked Kathleen in a loud trembling voice.

"I knew it would have a bearing on your relationship with Jim. If the allegations were true and he failed to inform you of them, then it would reveal a flaw in his character that would have repercussions for you in the future. I only wanted..." Glenn was at a loss for words.

"You played God, Glenn Hastings, and it's blown up in your face. I don't like things done behind my back, and I'll thank you to stop interfering in my life." Filled with anger and helplessness, Kathleen hung up the phone with a bang. A cry of despair began in her heart and burst from her lips. She gasped for breath, and was sick to her stomach. Her world was falling apart and there was nothing she could do about it.

Chapter Twenty

Glenn was stunned at Kathleen's outrage and anger. She was a different person on the phone, but she was right. He had played God. He wondered what to tell Glenis and decided that it would be for the best to keep it to himself. Glenis had enough on her mind now. He had been successful in obtaining a transfer for Andy to the Togus Veteran's Administration Hospital, with the most modern therapy facilities in the State of Maine. The hospital was considered one of the best in the nation.

It had taken several days of negotiating and cajoling on Glenn's part for the Army to agree to the move. Andy's doctors insisted on keeping him at the Presidio for at least one month in order to fully evaluate his medical fitness and potential for further therapy. Glenis agreed with that course of action. She called home every other day to inform the family of Andy's progress and events relating to his eventual transfer.

After a week in San Francisco, Glenn told Glenis that he was going to return to the job site in Canada. He intended to stop in Philadelphia to review how everything was going at the home office. He discussed the possibility of taking Ernest back to York. At times the little boy was a distraction, and required frequent care which, on occasion, disrupted his mother's focus. After careful consideration, she agreed to the idea. It would not be long before she would be coming home to York and Andy could see Ernie on a regular basis.

Glenn had not spoken to Kathleen since she had hung up on him, but Glenis had talked with her and nothing was mentioned about the incident. Glenis had checked with her mother about Ernest coming home ahead of her. Kathleen approved of the move, so that Glenis could concentrate on her recuperating husband. Kathleen did tell Glenis that she had been sick, but if she was unable to care for Ernest, Phil's wife, Rose, would be glad to take over. Ernest played often with his cousins, so he would be comfortable staying there, if necessary.

On the day before his departure, Glenn made the rounds of the hospital wards one last time to say good-bye. He and Andy had become good friends during the past week, spending a lot of time talking Army talk and playing cribbage. Andy beat him every time. On the last day they played a game, Glenn had smuggled a bottle of champagne into the ward and they all drank a toast in paper cups to a new tomorrow. Andy was improving more every day. Glenis would remain at the hotel for the duration of her stay. Rooms at the base were unavailable. Glenn made sure that she had adequate funds for anything she might need.

Glenn and Ernest left San Francisco and stayed one night at Glenn's apartment in Philadelphia. That night he called Kathleen to inform her that he would be in York at about noon the next day. She sounded weak and tired over the phone.

"Are you all right, Kathleen?" asked Glenn, worried about her.

"I'll be well enough to take Ernie," Kathleen answered soberly.

"I'll see you at noontime then."

The next day, they arrived at the Portland Airport where Glenn rented an automobile. Little Ernie was glad to be going home to his grandmother and great grandmother. Glenn fastened him securely in the rental car.

"In a short time we'll see Grandmother Cohen," Glenn told him. Ernest had become more and more restless from the confined quarters at the hospital, the hotel room, and on the airplane. He needed a chance to run and play. It was past noon when they pulled into the Cohen driveway. The first thing

Ernie did was jump out of the car and run to play with his Radio Flyer cart.

Mrs. Cohen heard them climb the steps and came out to greet them. "My, my I believe you've grown since we last saw you," she said happily. "How was the plane ride?"

"Okay," Ernie replied, distracted by his Radio Flyer cart on the porch.

"He's got a lot of pent-up energy clamoring to be unleashed," Glenn laughed, carrying a suitcase and a canvas bag to the porch. "How have you been, Mrs. Cohen?"

"I've been as chipper as ever," she answered. "But Kathleen has been under the weather a lot lately. She's sleeping upstairs. I'm not going to wake her, she needs rest. I'll watch Ernest for a while."

"I'm sorry to hear that," Glenn answered, disappointed that he was not able to see Kathleen. "Has she seen a doctor?"

"She went to one a few days ago. She's exhausted," said Mrs. Cohen with a sigh. "She's always caring for someone else and neglects herself. I'm not surprised that it has caught up with her."

Glenn was concerned. "How serious is it, Mrs. Cohen? I thought she sounded tired when I talked to her yesterday."

"She insists that she'll be fine, and I haven't been able to make her do anything different from what she's doing right now."

"I have a plane to catch and can't stay too long," Glenn told her. "I was hoping to see Kathleen before I left for Canada. Tell her I wish her well. Glenis sent a few souvenirs and things for you and her mother in the canvas carrying bag. Ernest's things are in the suitcase. Good-bye, Mrs. Cohen. So long, Ernie, it's been great being with you, now be a big boy and take care of the ladies of the house. Tell Kathleen that I..."

"I'll tell her that you're concerned about her welfare."

"Please do."

Glenn started the car and waved to Ernie and Mrs. Cohen on the porch. He checked the windows on that side of the house for any sign of Kathleen. Finding none, he turned the car around and headed for Portland with serious misgivings. The trip to Canada went swiftly. The further he traveled north, the more he was bothered by the unsettled affair he was leaving behind. He should have insisted on seeing Kathleen. Now he continued to agonize over the role he had played in her emotional collapse. He planned to write a letter to her as soon as he got settled into the cabin.

When Glenn climbed out of the helicopter at Trails End, he was met by an exuberant Faith running towards him.

"Welcome back, stranger!" she said loudly, so as to be heard above the sound of the helicopter's rotors. "I've missed you more than you know."

"Hi, Faith, it's good to see you, too. You're looking good. This Canadian air seems to agree with you."

"I've been busy and we've accomplished a lot since you've been gone. You're going to be surprised. Your assistant, Ed Block, has been on the job almost night and day."

"I knew I left it in good hands."

"I did what I could, but it was Ed who has really made it take off," said Faith, minimizing her efforts. She saw a changed Glenn before her. He was obviously worrying about something. "Is everything all right with your son-in-law?"

"Yes, he's doing fine. Glenis is staying with him until he transfers to the East coast in a month or so."

Together they walked to the office where Ed Block, a short wiry young man with an oval face and crewcut, met them. He was a recent college graduate filled with ambition. They went over the progress that had been made since Glenn's absence. Much had taken place. Glenn grew distracted and caught Faith looking at him. He smiled at her. She looked away with a worried expression on her face. Shortly afterwards, Ed Block finished reviewing the situation and excused himself, leaving Faith and Glenn alone.

"Something is wrong, Glenn!" Faith stated with alarm, as soon as Ed left the cabin. "You look as if you didn't really want to be here."

"That's not true, Faith," protested Glenn. He saw what was in her heart, and had a nauseating feeling in his stomach that he had betrayed her. The last thing he wanted to do was to hurt her. "I'm glad to see you, Faith. It's just been an unusual trip," he said trying to reassure her.

Faith was troubled. "Before you left, Glenn, I was under the impression that we had shared something special together. I was honest about my feelings for you. I thought it was reciprocated, maybe I was wrong to do that. The morning that I watched your helicopter lift off a couple of weeks ago I had the strangest sensation that things were going to be different when you returned. Now, I discover that my premonitions have become reality. I'm not blaming you, but we shouldn't deceive ourselves. We owe each other the truth, even though it may hurt."

"How can I explain it, Faith?" asked Glenn, sitting down at the table, thankful for her candor and sincerity. "Yes, you deserve the truth. Before I left here, I honestly believed that I was falling in love with you. It wasn't hard, you know. You're a wonderful person that any man could love. The trip we took to the center cabin generated sincere feelings that were real and I was pleased to entertain them. Do you remember what I told you about Jim Farley?"

"Yes, we talked about how it could be handled for the best of all concerned."

"Well, I handled it very badly and am responsible for an ugly rupture with Kathleen. She's been sick since it happened. When I left York this noon her mother did not let me in to speak to her…"

In that moment, Faith understood that Glenn's heart was still with Kathleen. "I see. Do you think that I would be wasting my time if I continued to hope for something more than what has already developed between us?"

"Faith, that's a hurtful question."

"I was thinking that the next good weekend you and I could return to the cabin with a replenishment of food supplies," Faith shared her plans with him.

"I'd forgotten about that," exclaimed Glenn, recognizing the disappointment Faith was feeling. "Yes, we could do it if you want."

Faith sighed. "The time we spent there is one of my fondest memories in years. If you don't mind, this time I'd prefer to make the trip alone. Things have changed, you've changed. My feelings just grew stronger…" Faith stood up and stared out the window trying to define the emotions running through her.

"I'm so sorry, Faith. Please forgive me," cried Glenn, aware of the difficulty of his request. "Believe me, I'd give anything to wipe out your sorrow. You've done nothing but give of yourself, and you deserve better. I was true to my feelings at the cabin. But Kathleen…"

Faith silently turned her back on Glenn and left the office. Tears had formed in the corner of her blue eyes. She quickly brushed them away, hoping that Glenn had not seen them. Her premonition had come true, her dreams were not to be, but that did not lessen the pain of rejection. Returning to her cabin, Faith sat in the dark for hours, not bothering to eat. Everything and nothing passed through her mind until, finally, a plan of action developed that would allow her to salvage some of her hurt pride and dignity. She called Kathleen Cohen, even though it was late in the evening. Mrs. Cohen answered.

"Hello, is Kathleen Cohen at home?"

"Who's calling?"

"This is Faith Hamilton. I'm calling from Canada. I want to speak to Kathleen about something very important to both of us."

"Just a minute, she's right here," responded Mrs. Cohen, handing the phone to Kathleen.

"Faith?" Kathleen asked apprehensively.

"Yes, it's me. I apologize for the late hour, but I'm at a crossroads and need to find out from you which way to turn."

"I don't understand," replied an unsteady Kathleen, accepting a chair offered by her mother.

"Glenn just returned to the plant site and he's terribly upset about you. I know about the things he discussed with Jim Farley. I can verify their truthfulness, Kathleen. You must know that I love him."

"I've had that feeling," Kathleen slowly admitted.

"Well, Glenn has the idea that he has violated whatever you and he had together when he declared his feelings for me. I honestly believe that his affection toward me is genuine, yet, it has not displaced his love for you. Glenn is a more fragile human being than you think. He's at the threshold of tolerance and needs something more than he now has in his life. He needs love."

Kathleen started to cry openly on the phone. "Why are you telling me this, Faith? You know what's in my heart."

"That's the main reason I'm calling you, Kathleen. No, I don't know what's in your heart, and neither does Glenn. Do you love him or don't you?" demanded Faith in a loud, tremulous voice.

"Yes, I love him," Kathleen wept softly.

"That's what I wanted to hear from you. You two belong together. Time is running out, Kathleen. Seize this moment, it may not present itself to you again."

"He's been in my heart for twenty-five years, Faith. I don't know what to say."

"If I were in your shoes I would never let him get away from me. I know he loves you and I believe he loves me a little. If you two don't make this thing happen, then I promise to pursue him and do anything it takes to claim him, but that would not be fair unless you outright reject him."

"I could never do that."

"The pain of rejection will be easier to handle if I have the assurance that he'll be happy with you, Kathleen. It's all up to you."

"You're quite a person, Faith."

"Treat him right, Kathleen. He's a wonderful man, worthy of any sacrifice. Shower him with love."

There was a moment of silence on Kathleen's end. Then she said, "Thank you for having this conversation with me, Faith. I admire your unselfishness. Even though we both love the same man, do you suppose it would ever be possible for us to be friends? I'd like to have a person like you as a friend."

"I'd like that too, Kathleen. Glenn told me that you were ill. I hope you feel better soon."

"This call has been the medicine I've needed for a long, long time. Thank you for having the courage to call me. May God be with you, Faith."

"Good night, Kathleen, rest well."

Early the next morning, Faith pounded on Glenn's cabin door and entered his bedroom without being invited.

"What's going on, Faith?" asked Glenn, still groggy from a sound sleep.

"I had a long talk with Kathleen last night, and I've come to talk to you as a friend, probably the best friend you'll ever have, so listen carefully. You've got an hour to catch the helicopter out of here. Get dressed and be on it. Kathleen is waiting for you in York. If you don't go to her now when she really needs you, you'll hate yourself for the rest of your life. Do you love her?"

"Yes."

"Then what are you waiting for? Catch that helicopter and go to her. This may be your last chance for happiness. Listen to your heart, Glenn, nothing is standing in your way now."

Glenn was speechless. "I'm sorry, Faith. Believe me, I never meant to hurt you."

"I know that, so prove to me that my instincts were right. Ed and I have this project under control. Go, before anything happens that you'll regret."

By the time the helicopter could be heard in the distance Glenn was ready with a packed suitcase. Faith watched and waved to him from her cabin door. He waved back and threw her a kiss as he boarded the aircraft.

At the Cohen residence, Ernest was still sleeping when his grandmother tiptoed down the stairs to make coffee for breakfast. Mrs. Cohen had preceded Kathleen and was sitting at the table eating a piece of toast and drinking coffee.

"Good morning, Mom."

"You look as if you had a good night's sleep, Kathleen."

"I slept well for the first time in days," she answered, pouring herself a cup of coffee and taking a seat beside her mother. "I'm going to see if your hairdresser will be able to take me this morning."

"That sounds like a good idea," agreed Mrs. Cohen, relieved to see her daughter looking and acting like her old self. "I'll take Ernie with me to Phil's; he's coming to get me for the day while Rose goes shopping."

"Thanks, Mom. What would I ever do without you? I'll call for an appointment."

"Tell her to make room for you or else I'll take my business somewhere else," Mrs. Cohen smiled.

Later in the morning, Kathleen went to the hairdresser and did some grocery shopping before returning to the house. There was a new spring in her step. The world suddenly looked much brighter. The man she had fallen in love with twenty-five years ago still loved her! It was a miracle and she wasn't going to wait any longer. She planned to call Glenn today after working hours.

That afternoon Kathleen spent some quiet time rereading several of the letters she had saved from Glenn when he was overseas. He was much younger then, yet in many ways he had the same way of expressing himself. She didn't hear the automobile turn into the driveway, so the knock at the door startled her.

"Come in," she called from the kitchen replacing the letters in the shoe boxes she used for storage.

"Anyone at home?" Glenn announced himself. Kathleen heard that familiar voice and ran into his arms. "I had to come, Kathleen. I love you. I never stopped loving you. Life has no meaning without you. Forgive me if I hurt you with the way I handled that stuff about Jim."

She held a finger to his lips and then kissed him warmly. "Just never say good-bye to me again. For the past few weeks, every time you told me good-bye you walked away with my heart. Promise to never say it again."

"I promise if you'll marry me."

"Yes, yes I will, I've always been yours," she cried, wiping tears from her face. "Is it really true that after all those years we can be together as one? God has been listening to my prayers. I was watching you from my bedroom window upstairs when you dropped off Ernie. I almost ran after you. My world collapsed when I saw you drive away. If you must go again, take me with you."

"We've earned the right to a future together. I have a suggestion. Would you take me down to the fish shack and heat up a kettle for tea? I'd like to toast our future with a special cup from your dad to me."

"I love you, Glenn Hastings," she said, kissing him again. "Phil will be down there. He can be the first to congratulate us."

Phil saw the car turn into the driveway of the wharf recognizing Glenn and Kathleen. "Hello, Glenn. What a nice surprise, welcome," he said, examining them closely. "I see a smile and color in my sister's cheeks I haven't seen in ages."

"We have some good news to celebrate, Phil," Kathleen said. "You tell him, Glenn."

A beaming Glenn announced, "We want you to be the first to know that your sister and I are getting married, and we would like to make a toast that our passage on the road of life will be blessed with love and fulfillment."

"It'll be a pleasure," cried Phil, hugging his sister and Glenn before he ran to the shack to turn on the gas tea kettle. "It won't take long, I used it earlier this morning. I was afraid I'd never have the chance to salute you with our family ceremony and tradition. Welcome to the family."

The sun cast its last rays of the day across the small fishing wharf reflecting its orange and red hues upon the moving water of the river. The western skies were ablaze with a red horizon. Generations of sailors have considered it a good omen for fair sailing tomorrow. A soft summer breeze swept the fresh ocean scent across the river as Kathleen, Glenn, and Phil raised their autographed cups, and gave thanks for that which had been, and beseeched God's blessings on the journey they were about to undertake together.

Postscript

That same evening, four hundred miles due north in the Canadian forest wilderness, the heavens were alive with stars glittering like diamonds. The cobalt-blue voids were highlighted by a symphony of color from the aurora borealis as it curled and rolled in the evening sky. On the distant horizon, a shooting star left an explosive trail of fire and smoke in its wake, and the north wind howled across the barren landscape announcing its promise of colder nights and a waning of warm summer days. The wind swirled around Faith's cabin, intensifying her feeling of isolation and detachment from the real world. She lay on her small bed, staring at the ceiling, feeling alone, forsaken, and insignificant. She silently wept, sharing her grief with the infinite uncaring wilderness that surrounded her. Her thoughts were with Glenn and Kathleen. She knew they rightfully belonged together, but it did not ease the pain of what could have been... might have been...

The End

Other Historical Romance Novels
BY
Clifton LaBree

A Song for Lisa   A Historical Romance

This is the story of a young American woman captured by the Japanese in the Philippines, 1941. Like most prisoners, she was brutalized and sadistically treated with a cruel disregard for human life. Three years later, Lisa and her companions had reached the low point of starvation and abuse .....

Lake of Three Sorrows   A Historical Romance

A warm spiritually uplifting story of courage, commitment, and sacrifice. This is the story of Dale Cooper, a battle-weary American soldier who served in two world wars.

Flickering Flame *(Colonial Series Book One)*

A historical novel, about the Cullen family who settled in Portsmouth, New Hampshire, and their participation in events prior to the French and Indian War. Freedom and opportunity were on the march, but it extracted a heavy price. Frontier settlers were ruthlessly killed and butchered by rampaging Indians lead by French officers and Jesuit priests who frequently incited them to greater levels of inhumanity...

Raising the Torch *(Colonial Series Book Two)*

A continuation of the saga from Flickering Flame, Colonial Series book one, of the Cullen family in Colonial Portsmouth. This is a moving story of love and sacrifice when a small colony had the audacity to fight for independence from their motherland...

NON-Fiction Books

By

Clifton LaBree

NEW HAMPSHIRE'S GENERAL JOHN STARK,

LIVE FREE OR DIE: DEATH IS NOT THE GREATEST OF EVILS   Publisher - Fading Shadows Imprint

A fresh look at one of America's staunchest defenders of liberty and freedom. John Stark was a courageous New Hampshire citizen-soldier who fought in both, the French and Indian War, and the Revolutionary War. His pursuit of leadership excellence on the battlefield distinguished him as one of the most successful combat commanders of the war, and one of the least appreciated.

His selflessness, modest life style, and devotion to the cause of freedom are an inspiration that time has not diminished. He remains today the embodiment of the frugal, independent, and cantankerous New Hampshire Yankee.

GENTLE WARRIOR, GENERAL OLIVER PRINCE SMITH, USMC.

Published by - Kent State University Press. Kent, Ohio, 2001

The Story of one of the United States, Marine Corps best General Officer. His flawless performance in Korea is a story that needed to be told.

www.ingramcontent.com/pod-product-compliance
Lightning Source LLC
Chambersburg PA
CBHW072217170626
46813CB00003B/974